THE PHOTOGRAPHER'S TRUTH

What Reviewers Say About
Ralph Josiah Bardsley's Debut Novel, *Brothers*

"A stunning success… This is a novel you don't want to see end."
—*American Library Association*

"In the realm of understated family drama, this book rushes to the front of the pack."—*Convergence Book Reviews*

"Bardsley's writing style is flawless and elegant."—*Inked Rainbow Reviews*

Visit us at www.boldstrokesbooks.com

By the Author

Brothers

The Photographer's Truth

THE PHOTOGRAPHER'S TRUTH

by

Ralph Josiah Bardsley

2016

THE PHOTOGRAPHER'S TRUTH

ISBN 13: 978-1-62639-637-1

THIS TRADE PAPERBACK ORIGINAL IS PUBLISHED BY
BOLD STROKES BOOKS, INC.
P.O. BOX 249
VALLEY FALLS, NY 12185

FIRST EDITION: JULY 2016

CREDITS

EDITOR: JERRY L. WHEELER
PRODUCTION DESIGN: SUSAN RAMUNDO
COVER DESIGN BY MELODY POND
COVER PHOTO: GABOR BESZEDA, PHOTOGRAPHER; ELLIOTT MORIN, MODEL

Acknowledgments

Thank you:

Dana, for your constant love and support in this process. Thank you, Ma and Dad, for everything. Thank you, Mike, for the long drives across the desert when we discussed large parts of this book. Thanks, Erin, Eliza, and Helen, for letting him take that trip with me. Thank you, Erin Bush, for taking the first read of this. Thank you, Tanya Ricci, Mary Squires, and Kate Bardsley, for your help in the editing process. Thanks to Elliott Morin and Gabor Beszeda for the cover. Thanks, Racepointers, for your support and enthusiasm.

Thank you, Radclyffe, Sandy, Ruth, Cindy, Jerry, and the whole crew at Bold Strokes Books, for being amazing to work with.

Dedication

For my father, who taught me never to waste a day.

PART ONE:
WELL ENOUGH IS ALONE

The word photography is taken from the combination of two Greek words—Phos, meaning light, and Graphé, meaning a drawing. Together, the word literally means a drawing of light. The origin of the modern word is often disputed, but Wikipedia credits Sir John Herschel, an Englishman, with formally introducing the word to the public during a lecture to the Royal Society in London, on March 14, 1839.

CHAPTER ONE—CHROME AND CODING

The first time I saw a Mapplethorpe print, I was twenty years old. It was my junior year in college, and I had gone with my roommate to New York City on spring break.

I spent my college years in the middle of Vermont, a few hours north of New York by car. I attended a small private college, just a cluster of cozy brick buildings tucked into a valley away from all the big cities of the world and covered by a blanket of thick, soft, rolling snow for most of the time I was there.

I can't say what made me choose that school in particular. I had never seen it, except in brochures and pamphlets, before I stepped off a bus at the age of eighteen in the little town that lay just beyond the boundaries of the campus. I arrived with a backpack and a single duffle bag that held enough clothes for a week, a set of notebooks, and a few toiletries.

I only wanted two things out of college at that point—to study engineering and to get as far away from my native California as possible. Growing up among the perfectly manicured lawns of Menlo Park on the San Francisco Peninsula had left me with a wild urge to get out and break away. I wanted college to be more than the long sleepy days of fading sun, the endless freeways, and the dry expanses of the Northern California coast that seemed to swallow you in one giant gulp. At eighteen, that world seemed like a fantasy I wanted desperately to grow out of. California was like a bike with training wheels, and I wanted to get out on my own. I didn't figure at the time I'd spend my college years in a Currier and Ives painting, but I had no way of knowing what it would turn out to be like.

My parents, who were probably a lot smarter than I ever gave them credit for, agreed to let me go to Vermont only after I had made it abundantly clear I wouldn't be attending any of the schools they'd presented. Their suggestions included the majority of the California State University System, all schools infinitely closer and infinitely more affordable than the one I ended up picking. They insisted there was a lot to see in California, and I could surely find whatever I was looking for without crossing the country. But I wanted to be different. I knew there was more to the world, and I wanted to see it, taste it, touch it, be part of it. When I was accepted to the tiny engineering program at a small Vermont school nestled in the Green Mountains, I jumped at the chance without a second thought about anything. Including the snow.

The snow in Vermont starts in the first weeks of October or sometimes even in late September. At school, the first few dustings of white always brought a sense of romance with them, setting the campus into a deep Robert Frost spell. We would bundle up in our winter jackets or sit around the cafeteria with hot cups of coffee, studying and looking out the windows at the magic of stars floating silently to earth. By the time Christmas break rolled around, the snow sat along the edges of the streets and campus walkways in waist-high piles. Everybody's feet were a little soggy and a little cold, but still we all trundled through the days, living out the stolid ethos of the Vermont Winter.

For those four years, the only break I got from the Vermont winters was the couple of weeks at Christmas when I went home to California. The cool rains and cutting winds of the Northern California winter had once seemed a bit of a hardship, but after my first December in Vermont, I couldn't wait to get back to the relative warmth of the San Francisco Bay. The place I had longed to escape from had suddenly not seemed so bad, at least not in the middle of winter.

But the real impatience didn't start to set in until we were all back after January break. Winter dragged on and on, keeping us in its clutches, forcing us to withdraw into the early evenings and dark nights. Our campus, and, indeed, the entire state of Vermont, was still covered by several feet of snow in late March when Spring Break finally arrived. The surrounding country, a carpet of spruce and maple and oak covered hills, rolled on forever, separating us from civilization and giving us the insulation we needed to develop our minds and train for whatever the real world was going to throw at us after four years of study.

I remember a sense of suspended reality from those days, as if the world were being held at a distance and everything that happened at that tiny campus was shielded in rooms of oak paneling and faded oriental rugs like a set of dollhouses in a child's playroom.

I first met Vince very briefly, early in my freshman year at school. We were in the same incoming class. During freshman orientation, we were grouped together in an ice-breaker where we introduced ourselves and told everyone something special about ourselves, a truly terrifying experience for a group of self-conscious eighteen year olds.

Vince was a short and rather stocky guy with broad swimmer's shoulders and just a little bit of a belly, the vestiges of a formerly athletic physique. He was stout, but not pudgy, and he had dirty brown hair and light brown eyes that glistened even in the dark. He had a way of staring at things as if he was taking them apart in his head. His ancestry was some sort of eastern European, which gave his skin a light olive tone even in the darkest Vermont winters. We spoke a little bit at orientation and then only occasionally after that when we would meet in hallways or sidewalks crossing the campus. He was one of a handful of art students at the college. When I did see him, he was usually heading somewhere in paint-stained jeans and a dark sweatshirt, carrying a toolbox full of paints or a blank canvas. If we had been at a bigger school, I probably wouldn't have remembered him at all.

We were assigned to the same dorm room our third year. As juniors, we should have each had a single room, but the college's housing was stretched to capacity that year and we were grouped together. I arrived at school that August to find Vince already sitting on the bed closest to the window with his back propped up against the wall and a giant black duffle bag on the foot of the bed.

"Cigarette?" he said, holding out an opened package of Camels as a peace offering.

"No thanks," I replied, my tone barely civil. I had been through two years of roommates, and as a Junior, I felt entitled to a single room. I had been looking forward to a little privacy, and instead here I had to live with an art student.

At first I detested him. I hated his smoking and the fact that he was studying something as useless as painting. But really, I just hated having to live with someone. I tried to keep my attitude to myself. If I didn't succeed, Vince was good about pretending no animosity existed between us.

But to my surprise, Vince ended up being a good roommate. He wasn't messy, he never had anyone over, he pitched in for things like cleaning supplies and paper towels, and he never stole anything. Compared to the nightmare roommates I'd found myself with for my freshman and sophomore years, Vince was a pretty good deal. After a few weeks of carefully maneuvering around each other, we actually started to become friends.

Vince was exactly the type of person I never would have met on my own. Well, let me rephrase that. I may have met someone like Vince, but I never would have been friends with him. Of course, I was so shy in those days, I had a hard time gravitating toward anyone. The small group of friends I did have consisted of fellow engineering students I'd met through course work or study groups. While I did see them outside of the college's single Sciences Building for meals and the occasional beer, I wasn't much of a social butterfly. There were the weekly dorm room parties, where everyone who lived on campus seemed to coagulate. They usually popped up on Thursday or Friday nights. I participated in those get-togethers, though I never stayed long. People did a lot of drinking, and I had no desire to be around when things got messy.

Slowly, I began to realize that Vince and I had some similarities. He wasn't exactly a calculator-carrying member of the engineering crowd, but we had almost the same hours. While I spent all day at my equations and proofs, he spent all day at the Art Studios building on our campus, where he supposedly painted. I say supposedly because I never really saw anything of his, and he rarely, if ever, talked about his own artwork. During the crunch time around midterms and finals, neither one of us showed our face except for meals in the dining hall and again at night.

Any stranger would be forgiven for looking at the two of us and seeing only caricatures. We were the two loners, Vince with his ripped, stained jeans and constant cigarette smoking, and me with my graphing calculator and multiple pens in my shirt pocket. But neither one of us were really loners. We were just at an awkward stage somewhere between childhood and adulthood.

Vince was a much better conversationalist than I was once you got to know him. He could talk to anyone about anything, and he liked to listen to people. As the ice between us began to thaw, we started to connect and our quick conversations about schedules and cleaning duties evolved into bigger discussions about life. By the middle of the fall semester, we often spent long nights talking about things that college students talk about: religion, the government, what we were going to do with our lives so that we wouldn't end up trapped like our parents in an ordinary world that we couldn't or wouldn't want to escape from.

These conversations always took place in front of our open dorm room window in the middle of the Vermont winter. Smoking hadn't been outlawed in the dorms yet, so Vince would lean out into the cold Vermont air to exhale. I would sit on the edge of the desk next to him, trying not to shiver. I'd listen to him talk about Miró's painting, or he would listen to me talk about Moore's Law. Needless to say, our room stank like the ass-end of an ashtray.

Shortly after Thanksgiving of that year, I learned Vince had a secret he'd been living with for some time. It wasn't a bad secret, and I don't think he would have hidden it if I or anyone else asked him about it. He just had to catch the rest of us up, and that required the right timing. Unfortunately for Vince, the timing didn't work so well with everyone in his life.

We had almost a week off of school at Thanksgiving, the Wednesday before through the Monday following the holiday. It was a lot of time off, but not everyone could get home over the break, so the campus stayed open. I could not afford the flight back to San Francisco, so I ended up spending Thanksgiving in the dorms. But Vince only lived across the border in New Hampshire, about fifty miles away. He'd spent the week before the break complaining about having to go home, but I didn't ask why.

I knew something had gone very badly at home when he returned to the dorm the Friday after Thanksgiving, almost a full four days before classes started up again. He had a black eye and a semi-circle of bruises on his neck. His face was swollen and red, and it didn't take a genius to see he'd been crying on the drive back.

"Hey," he said, walking into the room and throwing his duffle bag on the foot of his bed before landing beside it in an exhausted harrumph.

"Hey," I said, looking up from the engineering textbook I'd been struggling to get through. But he didn't say anything more. He just sat there, mute. I knew I should probably do something, but I didn't know exactly what, so Vince stared at the wall and I stared at him. Finally after a few minutes, I closed the book and sat up on my bed facing him, just a couple of feet separating us. Our dorm room seemed to close in around us, and I reached out and touched his chin, gently moving his head to one side to get a better view of the bruising around his eye. "You need some ice for that," I said. "Do you want me to go down to the cafeteria and get some?"

Vince waited for a few seconds, eventually nodding in a slow, drowsy, mechanical way, without speaking. I grabbed my keys and campus ID card off the desk and silently walked out of the room, closing the door behind me. Halfway to the cafeteria, I cursed myself for not thinking to take my coat. The November wind bit viciously at my skin through the thin sweatshirt I had on, but I didn't go back for the coat. When I returned with the ice ten minutes later, my hands were blue and my nose was running. Vince was still in the same spot as when I'd left.

"Here," I said, handing him the plastic bag full of ice. "Lean back and put this on your face.

He stared at the bag of ice for a few seconds before reaching out slowly to take it from me. "Thanks," he croaked. He took the bag of ice from me, scooted up to his pillow gingerly and slowly leaned back.

I went back to my engineering book and let him be for the better part of the next hour. The occasional shift of the melting ice on Vince's face and the rustle of my page turning were the only sounds in the room as I waited and gave him space. When he finally sat up and set the bag of melted ice gently on the floor beside his bed, I looked over at him. "Must have been some fight," I said, sitting up and swinging my legs over the edge of my bed to face him again.

"It wasn't a fight."

"Oh." I nodded, unsure of what to say.

"My dad."

I caught my breath. I wasn't sure I had heard him correctly. "Your dad?"

He nodded.

Something started to ring in my ears as I imagined Vince's father slamming a fist into the side of his face. A sick feeling grew in my stomach. I thought about my own dad and all the disagreements we'd had, especially during my high school years. I'm sure I'd made him as angry as anybody ever had, but he'd never once laid a hand on me. The thought made my skin shiver.

"You're surprised." Vince read the look on my face. He shook his head slowly, the blackish blue of his bruised eye glossy against the grey November afternoon light. "It's okay. I was surprised, too. It was the first time he ever hit me." After a few seconds, he added, "it's the first time anybody's ever hit me."

"Oh," was all I could manage.

"You might as well know what started it," he said.

"If you don't want to talk about it, it's okay," I said.

Vince shook his head. "I told him I'm gay."

"Okay," I said. Somewhere off in the distance, I could hear people shouting. It sounded vaguely like the guys from the maintenance staff, their garbled voices too far away to make out. "What happened then?" I asked.

"What do you mean?" Vince stared at me vacantly. "I told him." His hands flopped loosely on his lap. "Then he hit me and tried to strangle me. It was so strange. It wasn't even him. He blanked out." Vince laughed, a short, almost choking sound coming from his chest. "I don't think he meant to do it. He just shot up from the table when I told him. Everyone was screaming, and my mom was hitting him and then he stopped. He seemed to come to, and he started to apologize."

"What did you do then?" I asked.

"I left. I couldn't think of anything else to do. That was this morning. I left and came here."

I nodded.

Vince returned my nod and left to go to the men's room down the hall. When he got back to the room, he stood for a moment at the end of his bed before finally deciding to lay down. "I'm going to sleep for a little while," he said.

"Okay." I picked up my engineering book. "Do you want me to go to the library and give you some space?"

"No," he shook his head slightly against the pillow. "But don't bother to wake me up for dinner. I just want to sleep."

"You didn't take anything did you?"

"No," he smiled. "I didn't take anything. I just want to sleep."

I nodded and let him drift off. He slept for the rest of that day and into the night. When I got up from reading to go to supper, I quietly checked his breathing and found it to be normal, so I didn't worry about him. When he rose the next morning, he looked at himself in the mirror and gently touched the puffy bruises around his eye. By this time, the color was starting to change, turning from dark blue-ish black to shades of deep red and even a little yellow around the lids of his eye. Neither one of us ever spoke about Vince's father again.

Vince was the first gay man I had ever met. I know what that sounds like now. I'm sure I'd met gay people, but none who had ever been openly gay. We live in a very different world today. That was the mid 1990s, and Bill Clinton had just cemented "don't ask, don't tell" into our national consciousness as an acceptable way of thinking of and classifying those whom we had previously branded deviants or perverts.

I thought of myself as a liberal in those days; indeed I voted for Clinton in his second term. At the time, I thought "don't ask, don't tell" was a satisfactory compromise. What business is it of the government's who did what in their private lives? That tells you all you need to know about where I came from and what my perspective on the world was at that point. It never occurred to me that everyone should have equal rights in regard to whom they love or that "don't ask" was just a slightly more compassionate way of telling people they couldn't be themselves in public.

I didn't stop to recognize it was actually a mandate for people to be silent about their very nature. And more importantly, it never occurred to me that a silent population could never have equal rights. But I'm getting ahead of myself, or I'm going off on a tangent. Either way, it doesn't really matter to this story, except that after the day Vince arrived back in the dorm with a black eye, he became the first openly gay person I'd ever met.

"Did I freak you out the other day?" he asked about a week after Thanksgiving. "About the whole gay thing?"

We were sitting at the two small desks in the room, facing away from one another. Final exams were coming up in a couple of weeks, and we were both heads down in our respective studies.

"The gay thing?" I said after a few seconds. "I don't know. I wasn't freaked about it. I'm cool with it."

"Okay." He was quiet for a while. "We're still friends?"

"Dude." I turned around to face him, my oak chair scraping loudly against the wooden floor as I did. He was still looking down at whatever book was in front of him on the desk. "Of course we're still friends. What the hell? I don't care who you do it with."

He faced me after a few seconds, a flood of relief in his eyes. "Cool," he said. Then after a few seconds longer. "No one, um, no one really knows here. So, I think maybe if you wouldn't say anything…"

"Oh, so you're not out?" I asked.

"No," he shook his head. "It's enough being an artist. Everyone expects you to be a fag." He looked as if he were staring back over a very long road. "I've learned not to wear it on my sleeve."

"Don't worry. It's your business. I won't say a word about it."

"I suppose you know a lot of, you know, gay people." He paused. "I mean coming from San Francisco and all?"

I shook my head before I could even stop to think. "Not really. I mean, we see them in the city all the time. But I don't know anyone who's gay. You're the first I've ever met."

"Oh." He looked a little surprised.

I didn't know exactly what to say next, so I asked, "do you have a boyfriend or anything?"

"No." He shook his head and got up from the desk, pacing back and forth for a second before sitting down on the bed.

"Oh."

"There's not exactly a lot to pick from at this school," he said. "But it's all right. I don't need to have a boyfriend right now. I'm not here for that."

I nodded. But I couldn't think of anything to say, and the conversation stalled. Vince shifted and tapped one foot on the floor as he sat on the end of his bed. I could tell he was uneasy, and I wanted to say it was a lot to take in, but I was okay with it. He didn't need to worry about me. I was still his friend. I wanted to say I admired him for not being afraid to break the rules, to go against the grain of what everyone expected him to be.

But I didn't know how to say any of that, so I sat at my desk, half facing him and letting the quietness of the room drown both of us. Finally, when I couldn't take the tapping of his foot any longer I said, "You know it's okay with me if you want to bring somebody back to the room. Just, you know, let me know somehow—a note or something. I'm totally cool giving you your privacy."

He nodded and smirked. "A sock on the door type of thing?"

"What?"

"Like in the movies," he said. "They always leave a sock on the door, and the roommate can't go in the room."

"Oh yeah." I smiled.

"Well, don't worry about it," he said. "I don't think that will happen any time soon, but thanks for that. Really." He let out a full on laugh. "How sad is that? I never ever even thought of the possibility of a hook up here."

The conversation pretty much died after that, and we each focused on our own studies. I felt as if I had somehow reached one of those milestones along the way to adulthood. Here was someone who was vastly different from my suburban California roots. There were still things I didn't ask and Vince didn't tell me about. I'm still not sure how or if he resolved things with his parents. I don't know where he went for Christmas break that year, but I almost didn't want to know.

I felt bad I couldn't offer my own parents' home for him to go to, but they wouldn't have understood why someone who lived fifty miles from the college wouldn't go home for the holiday. They would have been curious, and their questions would have been so uncomfortable that the whole thing would have just been miserable for everyone. But wherever he went, he made it back to school after the break with no black eyes or visible bruises.

Later that year, we went to New York for Spring Break. It was a last minute decision. Neither one of us had many friends at school, and the few I did have were headed to Cancun or Florida or somewhere that required a flight, which I could not afford. My parents and I had recently had the harrowing discussion about the next year's tuition and they'd been firm with me about money. We weren't exactly flush with cash in those days, and a plane ticket anywhere before summer break was not going to happen.

It was my first trip to New York City. For Vince, it was a return to a place he knew well. We decided to leave the night after our last class. He drove, and we split the gas money. We found a gritty room in the Hotel 17, a rundown place that looked a lot like a vestige of the 1950s in a state of glamorous decay. The hotel had been the setting for a Woody Allen film and several photo shoots for magazines, including Vogue. Madonna had supposedly lived there before she became famous, and all of the guidebooks we'd looked at said it was an adventure. The place had a single bathroom at the end of each hall and our room was wallpapered with faded green and gold paper that looked to me like something out of an Old West bordello.

We arrived just around midnight, and found the hotel had given us a single queen-sized bed rather than the two twin beds we had requested. When we protested, the clerk at the dingy reception desk behind a pane of bulletproof glass just shook his head and told us it was the only room they had left. We grimaced but didn't think too much of it. We were both exhausted, so we went up to the room and fell asleep almost immediately.

Sometime around three that morning, I woke up to a scream down at the end of our hall. I'm not sure what or who it was, but it brought me up out of a dead slumber. As soon as I was awake, all I could hear were the noises of the city: the traffic outside on the street, a garbage truck at the end of the block, a couple arguing down on the sidewalk outside the hotel. All of it was so much louder than the cool Vermont nights. I rolled over, stole a pillow from Vince's side of the bed, and squeezed it down over my head to try and drown out the noise.

Vince and I spent the next day walking through the West Village, taking in the gritty excitement of the city. Even after all these years, I still remember the smells and sights and sounds of the city that day. Voices clashed all around me, a hundred different languages yelling all at the same time, the rush of traffic in wave after wave of horns and sirens, and jackhammers and constructions sites and the street musicians—the sounds of millions of people all crowded into the same few blocks. It was exciting and frightening and electric all at once, and it was such a drastic contrast to our snowy little Vermont college or my suburban California home. We walked on and on, past brick stoops and graffiti-covered walls. The clear glass buildings of midtown seemed to stretch up into the horizon for miles.

Vince was an expert at New York, and he knew his way around the neighborhoods, the bars, the shops, and the clubs. We largely ignored the major tourist attractions and headed to the trendier Bohemian parts of town. We spent the day searching for bootleg CDs in hard-to-find indie record stores and looking through

THE PHOTOGRAPHER'S TRUTH

bookshops that resembled small warehouses instead of the clean, neatly arranged shops of my California home.

New York today is a very different place than it was back then. Today, in this new century, the city has a carefulness about it. While it's not exactly a quiet city, I often feel more on guard about the energy of the place whenever I go back now. That wasn't the case back then, on my first trip there with Vince. There had been no September 11th in those days and there was a sense of invincibility.

Vince was a patient tour guide with me. As an engineering geek, most of my life had been spent in physics and math books. My childhood had been full of science fairs and Erector Sets and computer camps. I hadn't had the exposure to all the culture that Vince had. So he helped me out, guiding me through the Village with little hints on what books were absolutely necessary to purchase and what CDs were really worth buying and which ones would be out of fashion in the next few weeks.

That evening was warm for spring in New York, and we had wandered quite a way from our hotel. We decided we would be frugal and find something for dinner to bring back to the hotel. We were vigorously discussing the merits of a small Italian deli that looked like someplace we could afford, when Vince stopped and pointed eagerly at a shop window across the street. He realized it was a photography gallery he had read about, and he wanted to take a look since we were there. I was getting hungry, but that day wasn't a day for rushing things and so I nodded in agreement.

I wasn't a photography buff. Besides using my parents' camera on a few vacations, I knew almost nothing about taking or, for that matter, looking at photographs. But I wasn't going to say any of that. Vince already knew I was a cave man when it came to art appreciation. So I kept quiet and followed him. I strolled the length of the shotgun gallery while he went his own way. I stared blankly at the walls of cheap painted sheetrock, listening to the creaky wooden floors underneath my feet, letting my friend take his time on each photograph.

I didn't see the Mapplethorpe print until I got to the back of the shop. Even then, it may have been the six-digit price tag that got my attention first, I can't honestly say anymore. The picture was titled *Couple Dancing*, a black and white print of two men holding each other close. Both men were naked except for ornate golden crowns on their heads—at least, in my mind they were golden. The picture struck me with its gaunt elegance, one man shorter than the other, leaning into his partner's shoulder, eyes closed, a serene expression on his face. The picture had such beauty, such symmetry. Neither one of the men was looking at the camera, but Mapplethorpe had somehow captured the power of the moment without the need for a direct interaction with his subjects.

I must have been staring at the photo for a very long time, because at last I felt Vince behind me.

"It's a beautiful print," Vince whispered.

I nodded, not knowing what exactly to say. Something about that picture struck a chord in me. I felt like I had never really witnessed passion and loneliness before that moment. The powerful black and white images, the ghost of hope in the men's faces, the way Mapplethorpe captured a split second in time and used it to illustrate love and lust and loneliness and comfort all at once—it was a revelation to me.

"What do you like so much about it?" Vince asked me as we stood in the shop together, the silence of the room nearly drowning us, forcing us to whisper instead of speak.

"I'm not sure. I think all the emotion and the sense of impending loss," I said.

Vince swallowed silently. "That's Mapplethorpe for you, especially around 1984."

Vince's shoulder touched mine. Instead of moving away, I kept still and absorbed the feeling of him next to me. Something changed between us in those moments, giving me a new sense of closeness with him. I can't say how long we stared at the photo, but at some point I began to focus on Vince instead of the picture. His shoulder was warm next to mine, and I could feel his skin on my skin where our arms touched at the elbow. I could feel my breathing speed up and a thin dampness of perspiration all down my back.

Finally I stepped away from him, unable to maintain the closeness. I moved closer to the photo. "I just don't get it though. They're both men, and there's this deep intimacy."

"And?" Vince stood where he was.

"Well," I waited for a few seconds, unsure of exactly what I wanted to say next, and a little worried I might offend Vince. "Honestly, I'm a little surprised it doesn't make me uncomfortable."

"It's okay," Vince laughed. "It just means you're not a bigot."

I laughed with him. "I guess."

"Besides," Vince continued, "the thing I like about Mapplethorpe is he shows intimacy on a continuum, and that's really what I think it's all about for us, at the heart of it."

"What do you mean?"

"I mean Mapplethorpe shows men and women, men and men, women and women. He shows you the truth of human nature, not some Western ideal of what love should be. I mean, really, when it comes down to it, you're bound to fall in love with who you fall in love with. We're all somewhere along this great big spectrum, and when we meet someone we truly love, it shouldn't matter what sex they are."

I kept my eyes focused on the picture, suddenly feeling very vulnerable.

Vince shook his head. "Come on. Unless you're going to shell out a hundred grand for that picture, I don't think any of it really matters. Let's go get dinner."

We stuck to our budget that night and headed back to the Hotel 17 with a six-pack of Bud Light and a couple of deli subs from the Italian place we'd been looking at earlier. Vince took one look at them and assured me they were unlike anything I would have ever tasted in California. We sat up late that night going through the compact discs and the books that we had bought during the day. Vince had brought his portable CD player and a set of tiny little travel speakers, so we lay on the bed, listening to the noisy live-recordings of Nirvana and Pearl Jam in low fidelity while we ate our subs and worked our way through the six pack.

The bed was crowded with chips and Saran Wrap and CD covers, and we lay on our elbows facing each other over an obviously Xeroxed copy of liner notes to Pearl Jam's *Ten*, trying to read along as we listened to the songs.

"It's not bad for a bootleg," Vince said, setting down his half-eaten sub delicately on the bed and adjusting one of the speakers that sat between us. The fuzzy quality of the cd improved a little, but his elbow slipped and he shoved the CD player into my chest, causing it to skip violently. When Vince went to grab the player, he grazed my chest with his hand, resting it for a moment just above my heart.

"Sorry," he said quietly, moving his hand away. The CD player had stopped altogether for a few seconds, and the room was quiet for a heartbeat before my ears adjusted, and the sounds of the city night bubbled up through the window casement. Our eyes met, and the energy of the room shifted. I often look back at those few seconds and ask myself exactly what changed. I don't know if I'll ever understand what happened, why it was any different at that moment than it had been looking at his face the thousands of other times I'd seen him. But something was definitely not the same.

Something in the darkness, some trick of the shaded light from the single ancient hotel lamp and its dirty yellow haze. Something had upset the balance between us. I felt my skin tingling where he had touched me. A heat emanated from his hand and spread like the feeling of warm water across my chest and down into my stomach.

We lay still for few seconds. Vince started to pull his hand back, but he stopped. He must have known what I was feeling. I must have had some look in my eyes I hadn't known was there. When he looked up at me, I leaned down and kissed him.

When the music started again, Eddie Vedder's raspy voice startled me, and I jerked my head back a little too quickly. He backed away too, but our eyes remained locked on one another, and he leaned over and we kissed again, more deeply this time. Thinking back over that night, I search for clues to how I felt. I look for inklings of guilt or some sense of foreboding as we lay there on that dingy hotel bed, knocking CD cases and bags of chips to the floor, discovering each other's bodies. But I had none. There was no sense of doom or shame, not until the next morning.

The dawn seeped through the window in streaky grey streams of light that next morning. I lay awake with Vince curled up naked beside me, snoring quietly. The heavy hotel blanket lay bunched up at the end of the bed, and only the threadbare sheet covered his body. He was beautiful, cords of muscles, remnants of the athlete he had been in high school, rippled through his broad shoulders and thick arms. His olive skin glistened with the slight sheen of sweat, and his brown hair had an almost chocolate luster in the grey light of the morning. But as I looked at him, I began to feel a dawning sense I had done something deeply wrong. I had somehow committed myself to some agreement I could not let myself fulfill.

I sat up as quietly as I could and swung my legs over the side of the bed to the floor. But before I could get up, I heard him roll over. I felt his hand on my back.

"I'm sorry," he said.

I shook my head and looked back at him, his golden-brown eyes still deep with sleepiness, pillow lines etching a star under the corner of his left eye.

I shook my head. "It's not your fault," I said.

I headed to the bathroom and brushed my teeth, getting ready to somehow face the day ahead. The night between us was over, and as we looked at each other that morning, I could feel the gulf grow between us. All I could think of was that Mapplethorpe photo we had seen the evening before. But now it didn't seem beautiful at all to me. Instead, it haunted me. It made me feel as if something was hanging right above me, just out of my reach, ready to cloud over my entire future.

We quickly made excuses that morning and went about the rest of the day. What had happened really had been an accident, and I had been just as much to blame as him. In fact I didn't blame him at all, really.

In the days following that night, Vince did what any good friend at that stage in life is supposed to do—he avoided all awkward conversations. The next evening, he took a pillow and volunteered to sleep on the floor. I should have argued. Something inside of me wanted to argue deeply, but I didn't. The morning after that, I was extremely thankful for his kindness.

It enabled us to enjoy the rest of our trip without the weight overhead of a deep discussion I might regret or come to view as some sort of soft coercion after a period of time. After that first night, we abandoned our sense of thrift and spent the week heading out to bars and dance clubs, sleeping late and slumming it in greasy spoon diners for breakfast and lunch, and finally returning to school in Vermont with almost no money left for the rest of the semester.

I read somewhere that Mapplethorpe once said, "I am obsessed with beauty. I want everything to be perfect, and of course it isn't. And that's a tough place to be because you're never satisfied." Mapplethorpe did more than simply put a mirror up in front of people at exactly the right time, he constructed what he captured. He created a truth that he wanted to see.

As for Vince, I didn't see him much after that year. Although we vowed to stay in touch, we both had single rooms our senior year, and we were both so absorbed in our own studies, we didn't have much time left over for socializing. We're Facebook friends now, and we'll occasionally message each other or like one another's photos. But I doubt I will ever see him in person again, let alone have another night full of smoky conversations about the meaning of life with him.

The lasting impression of that week, the first thing I still remember about it after all these years, isn't sleeping with Vince. It's the Mapplethorpe print in that little gallery. That photo made me realize what a thin line we walk between being lost and really alive. That was the dance, that was what the title "Couple Dancing" meant to me. The dance was the combination of beauty, confusion, and chaos that makes life interesting. But you could see from the faces of the subjects in the picture, having one element out of balance can drive us slowly and completely mad, even in the arms of someone we love. Oddly enough, life is the most beautiful, the most fulfilling when we're the closest to that line between lost and alive.

❖

I should introduce myself. My name is Ian Baines, and even though the Mapplethorpe picture in that steamy little gallery in New York City made an impression on me, I soon forced myself to forget it after I left the city and school. I went back to my native California with my engineering degree. In the end, whatever I had been searching for in the world, I didn't find in Vermont. Or if I did find it, I didn't recognize it. I'd had enough of the winters and the smothering blankets of snow that covered everything for half the year. Today, I am a software engineer.

Yes, you read that correctly. I am a software engineer. Let's just get that out in the open. I write computer code for a living, or at least I manage people who write code.

I know, I know. If you're like most people, you won't react to that with any sense of awe or wonder. You won't say, "A software engineer—oooh, I wonder what his nights are like," unless maybe you're a software engineer, too. But I love what I do.

Maybe you've heard people talk about the joys of making things with their hands, creating something out of nothing. The joy I find in my job is similar. I create things out of nothing. Only I do it with my mind and a keyboard. I have worked by myself, I have worked with giant corporations, and I have worked at sexy new start-ups. They are all very different, but the one thing that all of those experiences have in common is that I get to build something.

There is a bridge between the world of machines and the world we live in and see every day—the complicated world of relationships, of color and irrational sequence. That bridge has different names— software, code, programming language. Call it what you want, but know it's the connective tissue between our physical and digital worlds. To some, software is simply a set of directions that tells a piece of machinery how to interpret and react to the physical world. But to those of us who understand it, code is an approach to life. It is a way of thinking about and interpreting the world, emphasizing the minimum of complication.

Good code is not complicated. It exemplifies simplicity, reliability, and the potential to evolve. It must take the most complex of functions and instructions and convey them in the simplest string of letters and numbers possible. Bill Gates once said "measuring programming progress by lines of code is like measuring aircraft building progress by weight." That quote brings a sense of proportion to things. The more complex or weighty the software code, the more exposed to error it becomes. It is not Robert Mapplethorpe, but in some ways software engineering is also a reflection of our lives. It directly correlates to the way we live with and interact with the technology that shapes us.

For a long time after college, my life existed in binary. Black or white. On or off. It was either one thing or it was not. No grey areas. No blur. I had created a life built on simplicity. For me, simplicity was elegance. I never thought back to that night in the Hotel 17 with Vince, and it never occurred to me that my need for the certainty of a black and white world might somehow be connected to it.

After college, I moved back to California and didn't leave my Silicon Valley again for many, many years. Oh, I took work trips and vacations, but I made California my home. And, before you ask, yes, I began to slowly grow into the stereotype that you probably think a software engineer is. I'm about six feet tall with straw blond hair. I'm skinny and pale, and I wear a lot of old tee shirts, worn out jeans and flip-flops to work. Unlike some of my colleagues, I draw the line at sandals and socks. I don't particularly like black tee shirts either. I prefer something with a little bit of color. My particular favorites are old airline tee shirts. When I met my wife at a bar in Palo Alto, she told me the old airline tee shirts made me a hipster, not a geek. I laughed at her comment, but I loved the way she had seen me as something different than everybody else had.

My wife's name is Ellie, Ellen actually, but she goes by Ellie. It has been seventeen years since that night in the bar, and I still wear old airline tee shirts whenever I can. We have been married for sixteen years, and we have two boys. Robin is fifteen, and his little brother Gareth, Gary as he likes to be called now, is two years younger.

Ellie is a contract attorney. She mostly works with big technology companies too, only she helps them understand the nuts and bolts of all the legal documents they sign. We do very different things, but we move in the same circle of people in and around Silicon Valley. When we got married, we decided we'd had enough of the Valley's sterile office parks and cookie cutter developments full of semi-detached town houses and never-used patios. We moved up to "the city," to San Francisco.

Our first house was a tiny cottage on the side of Telegraph Hill, nestled into the woods along the Filbert Steps. The two of us barely had space to turn around in the living room, but we managed to get our foot in the door of the San Francisco housing market—no easy job in the early 2000s. When we had the boys, we traded up and moved into a bigger, but still modest by West Coast standards, house in Pacific Heights. With the extra space and multi-million dollar debt came good schools, a safe neighborhood, and an incredible view of the Marina, the Golden Gate Bridge, and the San Francisco Bay.

San Francisco is a city that sparkles. Literally, the sidewalks are paved with glitter in them. It is either some freak citywide accident of cement mixtures or some intentional reminder that you are in Oz. I'll never know. At various times during my life here, I've suspected different truths.

The city stretches out over a series of steep hills and rocky outcroppings. And something is always in bloom, every time of year. Where the streets and sidewalks end, you will find a lush mix of trees and flowers clinging to the edges of the hills. The neighborhoods: the Haight, the Pan Handle, the Castro overlap like a patchwork, lazily cascading over each other in an easy flow of lumber and cement, rolling down from the top of Twin Peaks to the Financial District and on to the water. The Financial District is the outlier in San Francisco. Its skyscrapers and broad sidewalks don't seem to fit with the rest of the city, at least not to me.

It's also always just a little cold in San Francisco. I forget that from time to time now, since I've been gone for a while, and the chill of the city has left my bones. The summers are cool and damp, and the winters soaking wet except in the occasional drought year. It's never frigid; it's just always chilly. I wonder if the Native Americans who lived there first had a special word that encapsulates that feeling of always being on the edge of cold. Not quite real cold, but something sharp and chromatic that stiffens your fingers and makes you feel like there's steel in your veins.

Things moved forward in my life along the tracks you would expect for someone like me. I focused on work, and like any good engineer I measured my life in concretely defined, almost binary ways. I got a steady stream of promotions. I moved from one job to the next when the right opportunity came along, frequently enough to make me look exciting on paper without being flaky. I measured milestones along my boys' lives—first steps, the last days of diapers, kindergarten and first grade.

Ellie and I were relatively happy, I guess. We had grown comfortable in life, in that race to achieve happiness and financial security. At least, I think it appeared that way to the outside world. But looking back, something inside of me was asleep. I didn't truly realize it, and I think part of Ellie was as well. A distance grew between us and manifested itself in little arguments, missed dates, and minor irritations. Little by little, these began to add up across our life together. We watched as our efforts to stay close or get closer only drove us apart little by little, and we were powerless to stop it.

CHAPTER TWO—THE BELIEVER

I didn't know you'd already made them dinner." Her voice was soft and full of sadness as I entered the bedroom and closed the door quietly behind me. The lights were off, and my eyes hadn't adjusted to the darkness, but it didn't matter. She was somewhere across the room, either sitting in the overstuffed reading chair she sometimes fell asleep in or already lying in the bed. I wouldn't have looked at her then, even if I could have seen her.

"It was supposed to be our night out together."

"I know," she said. "And I'm sorry, but I had to finish some stuff up at the office, and I thought I should get home to feed them. I didn't know you'd already done that."

"Would you have changed your mind?" I knew my voice had an edge, but I couldn't help it. I started to unbutton my shirt.

"You smell like beer."

I laughed, a little resigned. "Don't change the subject, Ellie. You wouldn't have changed your mind. You didn't want to meet me out, did you? You could have just said so."

"Of course I wanted to meet you out, Ianto." I smiled at the use of my nickname. Ianto, the nickname for Ian, was what my parents had called me. Ellie had picked up the name from them after the first time she met them. She had a way of saying the syllables gently, cradling the soft Welsh word in her mouth, even in the most heated conversations. My mother had liked that about her from the beginning. It had given her confidence that Ellie was the right one for me.

"It was supposed to be our date night, of course I wanted to see you," she continued with a sigh. "I'm sorry Ianto, I really am."

I finished unbuttoning my shirt and let it drop to the ground. "I know," I said. "I wanted to see you, too. I sat there for a long time, waiting."

"Let's try again tomorrow," she said. "I'll leave work early, and we can have a date night anywhere you want in the city."

"Sure," I said, unfastening my belt and letting my jeans drop in a pile on the floor next to my shirt. Earlier that evening, I had sat at an outdoor table in a small café in the San Francisco Marina, just a few blocks down from the Pacific Heights neighborhood where we lived. I was supposed to meet Ellie for a drink after work as part of our "date night." We had decided to set aside one night a week for ourselves as a couple, to try and focus on our relationship. It's not that anything was bad in the relationship. She worked long hours and so did I. I traveled a lot for work, and we had two teenage boys in school and on sports teams.

But she never showed up. She forgot, and an hour after we were supposed to meet, she texted me to apologize and let me know she was heading home to get something to eat for the kids. I had already made the kids dinner and left it on the counter for Robin, our fifteen year old, to heat up in the microwave when he and his little brother got home from practice. But I didn't bother to tell her that.

I didn't really feel like going home, so I stayed until everyone else in the café was gone. The air was cold and damp, and the mist in the wind seemed to hold still without falling or stopping. I used to love the Marina, but I didn't see the same mystical or magical place I did when we first moved to the city. The mute crowds walked by, staring through floor-length windows behind where I sat waiting. But they didn't make a sound, not a single quiet noise, as their eyes passed briefly over me, a lone man sitting by himself in front of a beer.

"You know," she said, "maybe the date nights aren't the right thing. Maybe we need to think about something else."

"Like what?" My eyes had adjusted to the darkness, and I could see she was sitting up in bed against the headboard, her legs tucked up beneath her.

"I don't know, we hardly ever, you know," she smiled.

I peeled back the covers on my side of the bed and lay down, pulling them up to my shoulders, the linens fresh and cool against my skin.

"Maybe we need more than just talking." She un-tucked her legs, rolling over to lay her head on my chest. "Maybe it's a different kind of quality time that we need to spend together." She drew a single finger down my sternum, stopping just above my belly button.

"You couldn't find the time to meet me out for a drink, Ellie." I rolled over on my side. "Let's just go to sleep, okay?"

The next day when I woke up, Ellie was already downstairs getting Gary and Robin ready for school. I could hear the rumbling preparations for their school day, books and lunches packed into backpacks, pocket money secured, directions for after school events reiterated and clarified.

I rolled out of bed and stumbled to the closet, scooping up my clothes from the night before and dumping them into the hamper before pulling on a fresh pair of jeans and an ancient Eastern Airlines tee shirt. It was an original from thirty years ago, something I'd picked up on one of my trips to the Crossroads consignment shop up on Market Street. It was one of my favorite shirts and it always managed to elicit stares and comments. Sometimes that made me feel good and other times, it just made me feel old.

The age-softened cotton fabric fell loosely about my lanky frame, and I glanced at myself in the mirror to see a head of messy blond hair, and brown eyes peering out from a face full of freckles. My frame made me look younger than my forty-three years. I pressed my hand along my rib cage, smoothing over a crease in the front of the tee shirt, then headed to the bathroom to brush my teeth.

"Good morning," I said, entering the kitchen and sitting down at one of the bar stools along the back of the center island. Robin and Gary were finishing up pieces of peanut-buttered toast and slurping down the last of their orange juice.

"Morning, Dad," they yelped in unison.

"Good morning," Ellie said. She was already dressed in an elegant pantsuit, her long dark hair pulled back into a twist, giving her a decidedly severe look.

"You look nice. Trial today?" I asked.

She smiled, leaned in and kissed me on the head, staying there for just a second longer than usual. I knew, in that unspoken way that long-time couples know things, that she was sorry about last night. I was too, and I wanted her to know it. I put my hand on the back of her leg.

"Ew, gross, Mom, Dad, knock it off." It was Robin.

CHAPTER THREE—A NEW SENSE OF FASHION

Airline tee shirts aside, I was by no stretch a fashion junkie. I had enough trouble dressing myself on a good day. But oddly enough, fashion would change my life. No, worn-out airline tee shirts did not suddenly catapult me to the runways of New York and Milan. Something altogether more exciting than that happened: a new project at work came my way. At the time, I was working for a start-up company called Nova Vocé with my friend, Andrea. Andrea and I had worked together for a long time at different jobs.

When she started Nova Vocé a few years back, she approached me about being a part of the company. A temporary bout of insanity tempted me to take a shot at it, and I left the security and cushy perks of the big company job I'd been at. But late nights were already my thing, so I didn't mind the extra work that came along with a start up.

It started with the click of my boss's shoes on the polished concrete floor behind me one night. The Nova Vocé studios, as we liked to call them, were part of an old warehouse in the South of Market, or SOMA, district in San Francisco. It was a cavernous place filled with two long rows of contiguous work stations. Dozens of coffee cups and kale chip bags littered the table tops, spread out around giant monitors and every configuration of keyboard, joystick, mouse, and gaming console you could imagine.

There were no offices, only a couple of conference rooms. All of us worked together along the two long narrow strips of desk space. A row of giant windows that baked us all before noon looked out over Folsom Street. This time of night, the place was almost empty.

"Happy work anniversary," she said as she approached my work space. I glanced down at the clock in the corner of my computer screen. It was ten thirty at night. She must have been back in the conference room for me not to have noticed her.

"Thanks." I turned around to look at her. "You're here late."

Until the last few months, she'd been an extreme early bird, always in before six in the morning and out by around four or five. She was now in the seventh month of her first pregnancy, and her early mornings had gotten a little later, but she was almost always still in before me. I was seldom the first in our house to see the sun, and I never got to the office before ten-thirty. She smiled sideways, and something in the way she looked at me was just a little off. Her eyes were glassy. It could have been fatigue, but her smile betrayed an excitement she could barely contain.

"Yes, I am." She sat down in the empty chair next to me, pushing it backwards and spinning in it. The roller-wheels made a hollow scraping sound as the chair half slid, half rolled a few feet across the concrete. "Ask me why."

I laughed at her. I knew her well enough to know that she almost never got this excited over anything except work. "A new project?"

"Bingo. You're good." She rolled back towards me. "How'd you guess?"

"Seriously? You're practically beaming. Three months ago, I would have said it was the budding maternity, but given how much you complain about having to pee all the time, I'm assuming it's not that. It could only be a new project. What is it this time? On site support for an integration project with Walmart?"

She let out an elaborate guffaw, slapping her knee for even more effect. "Walmart? Please, that's peanuts. Try again."

"Come, on Andrea, we could be here all night. Just tell me."

"What do you know about Môti?"

"The clothes company?" I shook my head. I'd seen the label on some of Ellie's more expensive dresses. "They're French or Italian, right?"

"'Clothes company?' Really, Ian? You're such a cave man. Môti is only one of the biggest designers in the world. They own five different brands, and Môti bags are every woman's dream."

"Ahh. Okay, right, handbags. How could I have missed that?"

She shrugged. "Like I said, you're a cave man. But," she drew in a long breath. "You're a cave man who is about to learn a lot more about fashion."

"Hmmmm." I bit my lower lip. "Tell me more."

"Well, you know how I put together that big proposal while you were in Singapore working on that banking project last month?"

I nodded, vaguely remembering she had asked me to look at something for her, but I didn't have the time to review it because I was in the middle of fixing about a million bugs in a foreign exchange software platform we had been implementing for the past six months. The project had initially been a big budget deal for us, but the amount of time and resources it had sucked out of our company meant that we'd make a small margin, if anything, on it.

"That proposal was for Môti," she said with a smile. "I had a call with their Paris office early this morning, and I've been finishing up the contract details all day. That's why I'm here so late." She drew in another deep breath, clasping her hands in front of her, setting them gently on her belly and leaning back into the chair. "They accepted our bid. It's a huge project," she almost squealed.

"That's awesome," I said, trying to match her enthusiasm, but also wondering how we were going to take on one more project with everything else we had going on. We were already short-staffed, and the two of us were flying all over the world working on projects like this one because we couldn't find enough of the right people to hire. The competition for talent in Silicon Valley was fierce. But sitting there, looking at how excited she was, I couldn't burst her bubble with a question about staffing. "What does the project entail?"

"They're calling it *Projet de Musée*. As I'm sure you know, given your expertise in fashion," she landed a faux punch on my shoulder, "Môti has one of the largest private historical collections of fashion in the world. They have just about every piece from almost every design collection they ever created, going back to 1910, when the label was founded. They kept it all, and whatever has gone missing over the years, they've searched out and bought."

"Wow," I nodded in rhythm with her enthusiasm. "That's a lot of clothes. Don't tell Ellie. I think she's in competition with them."

"Very funny, Ian. Anyway, their library or collection—whatever you want to call it—is a great big mess; just racks of clothes and piles of stuff crammed into an attic storehouse in their downtown Paris headquarters."

"Piles of stuff? You mean like dresses and handbags and, what do you call them, accessories?"

"Well, that and a lot of the original photos, video reels and magazine spreads that featured their collections."

"Really? They kept all that media? That's kind of cool. But what are they going to do with it? What's our project?"

"Well, I guess they want to create a museum."

"Wow," I whistled. "Like a real museum?"

"Yep, a real museum where people can come and see the history of Môti fashion."

"That sounds like a whole lot of work."

"It is," she nodded. "They bought a new building right next to their current headquarters, and they're gutting it. They're going to move everything over there, but they need all their assets—the clothes, the film, the purses and jewelry—to be tagged and cataloged in a database so they can track it all before they actually move it into the new museum."

Our eyes met. "Ah, so that's where we come in."

"Exactly." She gave me a giant smile.

"Oh, well… That makes a lot of sense, I guess." My phone buzzed, and I looked down to see a text from Ellie asking when I would be home. "Well," I picked up my mobile from the desk and cleared the screen, putting it in my pocket. "Congratulations. That sounds like an awesome project, even if you're probably going to be the only person there who knows what a computer is. When are you headed over to Paris?"

"About that." She put on her sweetest smile and rubbed her belly in exaggerated baby-on-board circles. "I don't think I'm exactly the best person for this job."

"Oh no." I shook my head.

She nodded.

"No, I'm already working on about fifteen things."

"We'll clear your schedule. I can take on the stuff here, Ian. I just can't travel anymore."

I stared at her.

"Please, Ian. This could really put us on the map. Working with a brand like Môti is huge. Everyone will know about us."

"Exactly how much travel?"

"Well," her face went blank. "It's a lot, actually."

"How much?"

"Three months, on site."

"Three months?" I shook my head. "No way, Ellie will kill me."

"You can come back on some weekends. She can visit you. Ian, come on, we need to do this."

"I'll think about it."

She frowned. "Ian, we really, really can't let this one go."

I sensed something in her voice. "What do you mean? We let projects go all the time. You know we're understaffed by about fifty percent. Why can't we let this one go?"

"Because I already signed the contract."

"Oh." I tried to hide the hurt in my voice. I was stunned. Nova Vocé was technically Andrea's company even though I had some ownership shares. She held the majority of everything. She had started the business, and she could do what she wanted. But she'd always consulted me, made me feel like a partner rather than an employee.

"I know it's the right thing to do." An apology crept into her tone, but she wasn't going to let up. "It will help us with recruiting, too." She was trying to smile, but I'd put her on the defensive, and

I could tell she was unhappy about it. "Everyone will want to work for the 'Môti guys'. Think about it Ian. That will be us."

I nodded. What use was arguing when the decision had already been made. "Yeah, I guess you're right." In the silence between us, I could hear a truck chug by and a homeless person scream on the street below. The night noises of San Francisco reminded me we were in a start-up in a warehouse in SOMA. "I'll talk to Ellie tomorrow."

Andrea smiled at me, her features suddenly drawn and tight, reminding me she understood the difficulty of balancing work and life as much as I did. "You'll make it work," she said, lifting herself gingerly out of the chair. I could tell she struggled to conceal the strain of getting up. "It's our most important client now, Ian. Do you know what it could mean for us? It needs to be our priority for the next three months. We need to get this right, and I need you for this."

"I understand." I nodded slowly and she smiled, and then wandered away down the row of desks toward the door, closing it softly behind her.

When she'd left the office I suddenly felt the lateness of the hour. The building was quiet except for the humming and buzzing of the machines and the crazy street sounds from outside closed in around me. Three months would be a long time, and this was not going to go over well at home.

CHAPTER FOUR—YOU ARE A HORRIBLE PARENT

I broke the news about Project Museé to my wife the next night. Admittedly, I could have chosen a better time.

"No." The word landed with a blunt thud in between us. I hadn't even gotten to the details of the project, except for one small one— that I would be gone for three months. For most of our marriage, Ellie had put up with long hours at the office and business trips away from home before, but nothing on this scale.

We were in the kitchen cleaning up after a tedious dinner during which Robin and Gary argued almost non-stop about everything from who got more peas to who had the better hoodie. We also found out Robin had conveniently forgotten to start a major homework assignment that was due in two days, and Gary had gotten detention for calling a girl in his math class a "snatch." Yes, I'm sure I could have waited for an easier time to discuss a three-month business trip with Ellie. But waiting any longer would have put me in dangerous territory if, or rather when, she asked me how long I had known about this project and why was I just telling her now?

"Jesus, Ianto. Three months?" Our kitchen was small, and we didn't have much room between us. Ellie leaned back against the sink, gripping the edge of the counter. I could see the tension in her body, the muscles of her arms flexed under the loose tee shirt, her knuckles white from the way she held her fingers. "You know where that leaves me, right? As a single parent again for twelve whole weeks."

"I know, Ellie, and I'm sorry. I really am, but there's nothing I can do about this. I can't say no."

"Of course you can. It's easy. You just say the word. It's not even a big word—one syllable, two little letters. You can do it, Ianto. Who is making you go? Andrea? I'm sure you can even find a way to make her feel good about it when you go back and tell her that your wife isn't going to stand for it."

"Ellie." I could feel the energy draining out of my body as I reached over and put my hand on her arm. "I can't say no to this. It's important to the company. It could be our big break." As I listened to myself, it all sounded like a replay of my conversation with Andrea the night before, except this time I wasn't the one protesting.

"Important, huh?" Her arms tensed even more and I drew my hand back. "Like the last project in Singapore was important, or that security software thing you did two years ago when we didn't see you for two weeks around Christmas?"

I looked down at the floor. I could only tell her so much. She didn't live in a world of start-ups, and she couldn't see the never-ending drive for something to finally put yourself on the map. When I looked back up at her, I could see her building a wall in front of me. I saw it in her eyes, and the furious tapping of her pinky finger on the counter. I shook my head, thinking that maybe it wasn't her who couldn't see things, maybe it was me. Perhaps it was some sort of depth perception problem in my head.

"What about the kids? Are you okay without seeing them at all for three months?" she asked.

"It's not like I won't see them at all. I'll be back every other weekend and I'll..."

"You'll be working on those weekends, you know that. You work on your weekends now."

"Don't do this to me." I focused on the bridge of her nose. I couldn't look at her in the eyes. "Don't make me feel like I'm a horrible parent for doing this."

"You're not a horrible parent. You're hardly a parent at all."

"Wow." I turned around. "Just, wow." I really couldn't look at her now. I couldn't let myself say I was just trying to do what it takes to succeed at my job.

"I'm sorry." She grabbed my arm gently and pulled me back toward her. "I'm sorry, that really wasn't fair."

"No." I looked directly at her now. "It wasn't fair, Ellie. I don't want to do this."

She was silent.

"I don't have a choice."

"I know, I know." She put her hand on my shoulder, and I pressed my face to her head and smelled the scent of her hair, the familiar note of her conditioner mixed with just the suggestion of sweat. I could feel the center of my chest tightening in angst, but I was too tired to talk about it anymore. We'd been through so many of these conversations, always taking it to a full pitch and watching it recede back into the more humane hum of a sixteen-year marriage.

"It won't be forever," I whispered into her neck.

"I know." She squeezed me tightly for a few seconds. "We'll figure it out, we always do." She released me after a moment. When I backed away, she looked at me, meeting my eyes directly. "When do you want to tell the kids?"

"I hadn't thought about timing," I said. I knew that was exactly the kind of thing that would send her off again. She was the one who thought of all the details in our relationship. If not for her, we'd probably still be living in an apartment building in Palo Alto and eating out every night. She'd planned out an investment strategy, the right schools for the kids, the right cars to buy. I would be lost without her, logistically at least.

"Well," she said, the restraint evident in her voice. We'd arrived at one of those delicate peaces neither one of us wanted to break. I could sense the annoyance just there beneath her skin, but she didn't give into it. "We should probably do it soon. Do you think they could come visit you when you're over there?"

I nodded. "I had thought of that. I don't see why not."

"Well, maybe we can highlight that as a positive?"

I nodded again. "Will you come and visit?" I asked.

"If you want me to," she said, her voice slow and deliberate. "But I'm not coming over with the boys. I'm not going to babysit while you continue to work. You have to take the time off and spend it with them there."

"Of course."

"Okay, then we'll make it happen. When do you have to leave?"

"The end of next week." I watched her eyes as they danced around the room. I could see the wheels in the back of her head going. She was making a series of calculations behind those eyes. I didn't even bother to try and think about what she was figuring out—plane routes, costs, what I would need to pack, the school schedules of the kids. She would work it all out, she always did. In the process, I would be left on the sidelines, feeling slightly ignored but completely relieved of this part of the duty.

CHAPTER FIVE—PRACTICE

"Why would you hit that kid?"
Robin kept his eyes down and didn't answer me. His white soccer shorts and teal blue shirt were marred with grass stains and dirt splotches from his shoulders to his legs. He still had his knee-length socks pulled up over his shin guards. In better times, I would have told him to take his cleats off the car seat. But the tears on his face cut right through me and gave him instant immunity to that minor sort of transgression. All I wanted to do was grab him up in a big hug and tell him everything was going to be all right. But he had pushed me away when I leaned over across the center console of our Range Rover to try and wrap an arm around him.

"Do you want to tell me what really happened?"

He shook his head no. His tear-streaked cheeks were almost dry, but not quite. He had started crying the second he got in the car. I knew there was more to the confrontation than the coach had told me. I was trying to piece it together, but so far I had been unsuccessful.

"Look, Robin," I reached over and tousled his hair. It was the safest form of affection I could think of, "I can't help you if you won't tell me what happened."

"Nothing happened." He turned towards the window and looked out vacantly.

"Something happened," I said. "You ended up in a fight. The coach called me at work to come get you, and when I got to the field, you were on the bench."

"I don't want to play soccer anymore," he said, still not looking at me.

I took a deep breath and swallowed the frustration I felt with my son. "Okay." My tone was measured, and I took care not to rush the words. I knew Robin wouldn't be persuaded by applying pressure. He had a stubborn streak in him that would send him in the exact opposite direction of any perceived coercion. "If you don't want to play next season, you don't have to."

"I don't want to play any more this season."

"Robin, do you want to tell the coach and the rest of the team that you're quitting?"

"I don't see why it matters. I hate everything about that team. I hate soccer. I'm no good at it, so I don't see why I have to do it."

"Okay, let's take things one step at a time. You want to quit soccer. Why don't you lay the groundwork with me? Tell me why and maybe we can work something out."

We pulled up to a stoplight along Broadway, and he stared out the window across the Bay towards Alcatraz. I could hear the rattle of his breathing as he struggled to keep himself from slipping back into another bout of tears. The light turned green, and I pulled forward slowly. Instead of going straight towards our house, I pulled up onto the side of the road into a loading zone of one of the giant sand-colored art deco apartment buildings that dot the hillside of Pacific Heights along Broadway. I unbuckled my seatbelt, leaned over the console, and wrapped my arms around him. He struggled a little bit at first, but then collapsed into my shoulder and I could feel him let go again into a giant heaving wave of tears.

"Hey, big guy," I whispered to him. "Whatever it is, it'll be okay."

"No, it won't."

"Shhh," I rocked him a little bit, tightening my grip around his shoulders.

"Dad, I cheated," he choked out the words in giant gulps. "On a test."

"In school?"

"Yeah, in Biology. And…" He gulped for air through another onslaught of tears. "And…Craig said that he saw me and that he was going to re-report me."

"He said that at practice today?" I asked.

"Yeah, he did. And I got scared and I punched him."

Of all the things that came to my mind at that moment, I knew none of them were the right ones to say, so I just stayed quietly holding him. Finally, after a few more minutes, he straightened up and pulled away just a little bit from me. "Is there a Kleenex in the glovebox?" He opened the latch without waiting for an answer and pulled out a couple of Starbucks napkins and blew his nose noisily into them.

Finally, after what seemed like an eternity, I cleared my throat. "Robin, what are you going to do about the test?"

He shook his head, as if refuting an inside dialogue that only he could hear. I looked over at him and met his eyes. "Are you going to tell Mom?" he asked.

I tried to stifle a laugh. "Robin, that's hardly the biggest issue here."

"You don't have to get yelled at by her," he retorted.

I wanted to tell him that yes, I did often get yelled at by his Mom, but I knew that would head the conversation in the wrong direction. "Robin, what are you going to do to make the situation right?"

"I don't know." He sighed heavily and looked out the passenger window again. The lower corner of the window had fogged up, and he drew a smiley face with his index finger.

"Do you want Craig to have that power over you?"

"Huh?" he asked, his head turned quickly towards me. "What do you mean?"

"Well." I put my hand on his shoulder. "As long as he knows you cheated, and he can tell on you, he's going to hold that over you. But you can fix that."

"Beat him up?" Robin said.

"Robin, you know that's not the answer."

"What, tell on myself?"

"Robin, if you admit you cheated, you might fail the test. You should fail it. What you did was not right. But then nobody else has that over you, and your reputation will be a lot better for it."

He looked away from me again. I looked down at the clock on the dashboard. It was four thirty. "Do you want to call the school now?"

"Can you do it?" he asked.

"Yes." I took a slow, steady breath. "I absolutely can." He seemed to relax a little bit. "But I shouldn't. You're fifteen years old, and you should really call your teacher or go in and talk to her before school tomorrow. I can go with you to have that conversation, but it should really be you who does it."

"Ugh, Dad. Why?"

"You tell me why."

He nodded silently. "Okay. Can we call her tonight?"

"Sure," I said. We sat for a few more minutes. He was deep in thought, probably scared out of his mind at the prospect of admitting to a teacher that he cheated.

"Why did you cheat?" I asked.

"I was stupid. I didn't know we were having a test. I forgot to study, and I panicked."

"You know, it's easier to live with yourself if you flunk a test than it is to live with yourself if you know you cheated."

"I know, Dad." He bit his lower lip. "Can we go now?"

I nodded. "Yeah, we can go now."

"Am I grounded?"

"No." I turned the car on and pulled back out onto Broadway in the direction of our house. "Not if you take care of this tonight, or at the latest, tomorrow."

We spent the rest of the ride home in silence. But as we pulled into the driveway, he turned to me and said "Thanks Dad" before collecting his backpack and heading into the house.

I smiled and sat there.

CHAPTER SIX—BREAKING THE NEWS

We decided to break the news of my stint in Paris to the boys the next night at dinner. Ellie would have usually been the person to announce major family news, but she insisted I talk that evening. I sat facing them that night, waiting and watching for just the right moment to tell them I would be gone for three months. They knew something was coming down. I could tell by the way Gary sat up straight the whole time at the table, stiff as a board. I felt a little sorry for him. I'm sure in the back of his mind, he was wondering if the rigidity around the table had something to do with his cheating on that test. Finally, when he couldn't take the suspense anymore he asked, "Why are you home so early tonight, Dad?"

I laughed. "Is it really that unusual?"

Robin and Gary looked at each other. In what can only be described as a sitcom-inspired moment, Robin stopped with a fork full of asparagus midway to his mouth, set it down and let out a deep sigh. "Are you two getting divorced?"

Ellie and I looked at each other across the table and stifled a mutual smile. I realized at that moment we made good parents. Even if our partnership was a little quirky sometimes, it was solid. "No, Robin, we're not getting divorced. I am going away for a little while for work, though."

"For work?" Gary eyed me suspiciously, pushing back his plate and folding his arms. "Just work?"

"Yes, Gary. Just for work." I looked at him and then at his brother. "I'm going to Paris for a work project. The bad news is I'll be gone for three months." I stopped and waited for a reaction. The seconds ticked away and nothing. The two of them sat staring at me. In the background, Ellie smiled, a tight-lipped smile that looked like I should be reading something from her face, but I was blank, completely missing whatever message she was trying to send. "I know that's a long time, but the good news is that I'll be back and forth for a few weekends, so we'll still get to see each other." Silence. Still no reaction from the boys, still the tight-lipped smile from my wife. "And more good news is that your Mom and I have talked, and we think it would be good for you guys to come over and visit me while I'm over there."

Explosion. Gary was up and out of his chair, throwing his arms up in a mock 'field goal' and mouthing the words "yes, yes, yes." Robin remained in his chair, but looked back and forth from me to Ellie, with his mouth agape in exaggerated disbelief.

It was hard to believe in that moment they were almost young men. Their features and expressions were so thoroughly like they had been when they were little kids; it took my breath away to see them in that light, and it saddened me just a little when I thought about all the time that had passed. Robin was fifteen and Gary was fourteen. I was amazed at the way they grew into fully formed human beings with their own personalities.

The day before I left was a Saturday. I sat on our deck watching the fog recede slowly back across the Bay towards the Golden Gate Bridge, deep hazy fingers reluctantly letting go of the edges of Marin and the San Francisco water front down below. Alcatraz and Angel Island glistened in their freedom, basking in the eastern sun. I rubbed my eyes, then I drew the blanket tighter around my shoulders and hugged my cup of coffee to my chest. In front of me, my laptop glowed blue with a magazine story about the future of work, which I had started to read a half an hour ago and gotten nowhere on.

I tried to take in the whole of the Bay and the city beneath me. I tried to memorize all the details I saw: the green lawns of Fort Mason, the orange glow of the bridge emerging through the last remnants of fog, the squat but graceful dome of the Palace of Fine Arts. My San Francisco, the city I'd grown to love and think of as my home over the past two decades. All of its grace and grubbiness combined to make it the only place I had ever felt at home.

The French door creaked open behind me, and Robin crept out, wrapped up in a cocoon of blankets and sheets from his bed. He closed the door softly as he tiptoed across the deck and sat down beside me, leaning into my shoulder and closing his eyes. His hair looked like a bird's nest, and he smelled like bed.

"Good morning, sleepy head." I smiled down at his closed eyes.

"Mmmmm," he grunted back at me, rubbing his head a little more on my shoulder. We sat together for a few minutes without saying a word, just taking in the cool San Francisco morning. I tried to stay in the moment, but I kept thinking about the future. I realized this was the last time I would see him for weeks. And the next time I was home would only be for a few days before I took off again. I looked around at the deck, the house. I thought for just a moment about what it took to maintain all of this, and how much of a risk it had been taking on a start up at this phase in my life. Somewhere in the back of my mind, I knew this all might evaporate if Nova Vocé didn't work out. I knew that Andrea was right to chase these type of big brand clients. But three months away? I felt a pang of guilt in the pit of my stomach.

"What time do you leave?" Robin's gravelly morning voice interrupted my stream of guilty thoughts. I was still surprised by the teenage voice he had acquired over the past twelve months. The high-pitched cartoon-like voice he'd had as a little boy was gone, and in its place was this slightly sporadic but mostly deeper tone of voice that sounded daily more like a man.

"Tomorrow night," I said. "Seven thirty."

"Are you excited?"

I shook my head. "Not really. Maybe a little nervous, but I'm really thinking about how much I'm going to miss you guys."

"Me too." He reached around and hugged me with two long gangly arms. I shrugged off the blanket and wrapped my arms around him. My heart was heavy as I thought about how much I would miss him and his brother. I could feel tears beginning to well up in my eyes, but I took a deep breath and kept it contained. Barely. Looking back on that morning, maybe I should have let the tears flow. What difference would it have made at the time? Maybe all the difference in the world. What was I teaching my oldest son by not crying when I knew I wouldn't see him again for weeks? The answer was probably, all the wrong things.

PART TWO: PARIS

There is an iconic photograph, taken by Cecil Beaton for Vogue in 1948. In it, eight models are draped in chiffon and taffeta ball gowns, images of perfection in early color. The use of light and shadows bring some of the women into the forefront and removes others into the background of the image. Beaton, a master of light, uses his camera like a weapon, erasing lives and creating others, forcing the viewer's eye into a corner, ensuring we see exactly what he wants us to see. The image brings home the energy and thrill of the post-war years. Everyone was about to change the world and set it on the trajectory of the New Century. The ball gowns were from Charles James. Not that it matters, but he was a prolific designer of the time.

CHAPTER SEVEN—IN FRENCH

The Môti headquarters building could have surfaced out of a Victor Hugo novel. Situated in the 8th Arrondissement right off of the Champs Elysees, Môti was in the heart of old Paris. You could spit and practically hit the Tuileries and the Louvre. The building itself was Second Empire. Looking at it from the outside, the structure divided itself into two sections, an ornate granite and marble façade topped by a slate grey mansard roof that took up the top quarter of the structure. Balconies ran the length of the building along every floor and brass railings looped gently across the front arching into fleur-de-lis, ending abruptly where the building snugly met its neighbors on either side. Môti took up the entire building, eight floors of iconic fashion design layered into the utmost in Parisian elegance.

Walking into the building that first day I found the interior as intimidating as the exterior. In the lobby, an enormous field of glossy white marble floors led to even glossier black marble walls. A deep mahogany and gilt desk from the Louis XIV period stood sentinel at the end of the room, and a giant crystal chandelier dominated the air above my head. But that was where the classical ended and the modern began.

All along the marble walls flat screen monitors flashed runway shows from around the world. It was Môti couture in action. A giant round carpet in the center of the room displayed the Môti logo, a giant red 'M' in Times New Roman font, with a smaller, white "ôti" in italics, layered over the front right corner of the 'M'. I didn't see any chairs or tables, and absolutely no furniture beyond the receptionist's desk. There wasn't even a receptionist behind the desk, just a man standing in front of it clicking away at a glowing mobile phone. He smiled when he saw me. As I came closer, he clicked the device off and slipped it into his pants pocket.

"You must be from Nova Vocé. I'm Alfonse." He stuck out his hand and we shook. "Welcome to Môti."

Alfonse. I recognized the name from several emails. He was the Historical Curator for Môti, and my contact for the project. I'm not sure what I expected him to be like. I think in the back of my mind, I pictured a bookish little man. The word curator made me think of dusty old museum staffers in tweed jackets and horn-rimmed glasses. The person waiting for me that day couldn't have been more different. He wore a black tank top ripped in three spots and held together with safety pins, and a pair of leather pants. His hair was blue and pink and blond, and he had a tiny diamond stud below his lower lip, just above his chin. He stared at me as we shook hands, looking from my head to my feet and then back up again. I could feel him taking in my outfit. I looked down at my button-down shirt, grey slacks, and grey sport jacket. I was sporting the complete Silicon Valley look, a stunning comparison to his safety pinned chic.

"Ian," I offered.

"How was your flight in?" He smiled. "Did you arrive last night?"

"Yes," I nodded. "The flight was fine, thanks. A little long, but uneventful, which is all you can really ask for on that kind of flight."

Alfonse and I hadn't ever spoken before, but I knew a little bit about his background from Andrea. She had handled the contract and the initial conversations around managing Projet de Musée. His job was to administer the collection and cataloging of Môti's fashions throughout the years, and help create the exhibits for the new Museum, which would presumably be finished some time in the coming months.

"Good, good..." His lips tightened into a polite smile. I could tell he was trying to decide between another bit of small talk or diving right into the details of the project and how we would work together. "So you are going to help us get our closets organized, huh?"

"That's the plan." I tried to warm up the conversation. "I understand you have an amazing historical collection."

"Yes, we do." His face softened a little, and he lost the cold stare. "So, how will this work, exactly? What are you going to do first? I'm not all that familiar with technology."

"The plan is to first go through everything you've got up there—clothes, hats, bags, and any other memorabilia that Môti has collected throughout the years and tag it with a tiny chip so we can easily track it. Then we organize it and get it ready for the museum. If everything is ready in the new building, you can move it right over."

"Yes, I see." Alfonse smiled. "And what, exactly, is your role?"

"I'm the project lead," I said. "I will be here most of the time, but a team will be helping me back at the office and occasionally you'll see more people from my company out here doing a lot of the ground work—tagging items, scanning photos into an electronic database, all of that. I will be overseeing the program and doing some of the actual coding, but mostly I'll be your contact managing the program and making sure it's on target."

"Okay," he said.

"And I understand you've chosen a couple of your own staff to help out on the project?"

Alfonse nodded. "Yes, you'll meet them later on today. Come on, I'll show you to the current library." I followed him up the stairs and down another marble hallway to a bank of elevators. "We have one of the largest historical collections of any of the Paris fashion houses," he said as we walked. "But it's not just the clothes and bags and hats that you mentioned. Môti started saving its own collections very early on. But soon after the First World War, we began saving more than the garments. The war changed everything about life in Europe, and at the time, we felt that fashion could help tell the story of that new world. And, fashion, as I'm sure you know, is more than what we wear. It's the combination of material elements and the cultural interpretation of those elements." The elevator arrived, and we stepped in. He pressed the button for the eighth floor and kept talking. "We started saving all of the photography and magazines and video footage of our clothing that we could—every fashion spread, every runway show, every celebrity Môti moment. If we can capture and collect it, we do."

"Wow." I let out a half whistle, half sigh. "That's a lot of archiving."

"Yes, well, it takes up most of the eighth floor." The elevator doors opened, and he gestured with an extended hand for me to go first. "Welcome to the library. This is where I think you'll be spending most of your time."

As I stepped out of the elevator, I smelled old clothes and paper. There was no floor lobby, no hallways, just a giant room with high wood beamed ceilings and chandeliers hanging every twenty feet or so. We were at the top of the building, essentially an ancient ballroom converted into a storage room. Row upon row of wooden shelves filled the space from the elevators clear out to the windows and all the way down to the end of the room, as far as I could see. The shelves housed boxes and hangers and piles of magazines. "Whoa." I stepped away from the elevator and walked a few feet down the first row of shelves.

"Yes, indeed. Whoa," Alfonse echoed my words without enthusiasm and continued to walk through the stacks of boxes towards the windows. "It's organized mostly by year and date. You can see at the end of each row is a card with some information on it about the year. But it's not all quite that easy. Oversized garments, hats and dresses with trains, are at the end of the room, over there. Photo archives are a mix. Some are scattered throughout the shelves, others are in the drawers back by the work stations."

"Work stations?" I asked, following him.

"Yes," he nodded. "As I mentioned, I've arranged for a couple of our IT staff to help you out, and I've set up desks and work stations for you over there," he pointed. "Under the chandelier closest to the window."

"Ah." I nodded for him to lead the way. "Thank you."

"So you are basically going to put all of this on a computer?" he asked as we made our way back through the rows of shelving.

I nodded.

"Good," he sighed. "Because we're still figuring out exactly what exhibits we want to open the museum with. This should help that process. You will make sure we have pictures and details of everything so we can easily search for specific things, right?"

"Yes," I nodded, relieved to finally hear a note of enthusiasm in his voice. "We're going to set up a storage system so you can easily find whatever you're looking for. The little tags we will put on each item are trackable, so you'll be able to physically locate everything up here in these stacks or in the new museum. Wherever stuff happens to be."

"Perfect," he said, the enthusiasm suddenly draining from his voice. "It sounds like you pretty much know exactly what needs to be done. You'll need to work independently of me for the most part. I'm happy to help with guidance, of course. But I'm very busy."

I nodded. "Don't worry, I understand. I may just need a little help from you in learning about this library."

"Good." he interrupted me. "Philippe and Roony can help you with that."

"Who?"

"The IT guys I mentioned. I'll introduce you later on today or tomorrow. They can help you with navigating this place."

"Okay. Then I'll just get started refining the project outline, and maybe we can sit down and go through it later this week?"

"Perfect." He clapped his hands and leaned back slightly. "Well, coffee is on the third floor if you want any. Otherwise, my office is on the seventh floor. I'll check back with you at the end of the day."

"Um, okay." But before I could add another word, he had turned and headed back towards the elevator.

I stood for a few minutes taking in the enormity of the project. Then sat down at the empty desk, pulled my laptop out of my bag and started trying to make sense of what I would do next.

The hours went by quickly that day as I split my time between revising my project plan and wandering through the place, exploring the stacks of clothing and ancient magazines that lined the grid of shelving. It was easy to see how someone could get lost up here. It didn't seem real. It was the kind of place you might dream about as a kid or maybe see in some fantasy movie castle.

I made notes of things as I wandered, marking down how the boxes and garments were already labeled, when I could figure it out. Patches of chaos sat alongside well-ordered parts. One shelf lined with neatly packed plastic boxes with clear white labels would suddenly give way to piles of half-opened cardboard boxes, broad ribbons of fabric strewn about the shelves and littering the floor, hinting at the half-told story of the rest of the box.

Before I realized, it was late afternoon and I looked up to see Alfonse standing over by one of the shelves of magazines, studying me. "Oh," I stepped back a little in surprise. "Hello."

He smiled when I noticed him. "I thought you might want to meet those two IT guys I promised you," he said.

I looked around at the stacks of clothing and thought it might be a good time for a break. "Okay. That sounds good."

"Follow me," he said, turning on his heel and walking back towards the elevator.

I followed him through some of the offices on the third floor to a small break room where a group of people stood around holding small cups of espresso and chatting noisily in French. Some of them were dressed like Alfonse, others in more traditional styles, but almost all of them exquisitely polished in whatever their chosen look was. I picked out the two tech guys immediately. They were the only ones in jeans and tee shirts.

Phillipe and Roony came over to introduce themselves. Roony was a giant of a man, well over six feet tall and stocky, with dark brown hair and large brown eyes that smiled out at the world on their own. Phillipe was much smaller in size and seemed to quietly shrink away from conversation. Something about them--maybe the way they seemed to walk in lock step, or the way their eyes seemed to move in tandem throughout the entire meeting—gave me the impression they had been a team for a long time.

"Phillipe, Roony, this is Ian," Alfonse's voice boomed, and he gestured broadly towards me as if he had just unveiled a statue. The conversation in the room went quiet, and I could feel everyone's eyes on me.

"It is nice to meet you." Roony was the first of the two to speak, a strong Parisian accent hardening his words. "We are looking forward to working with you."

"Nice to meet you, too," I said, reaching out and shaking his hand.

"Have they got you set up in the attic?" Phillipe asked, taking my hand in his after Roony had let go and shaking it vigorously.

I nodded. "Yep, I'm up there in all the dust and splendor." I looked over at Alfonse and laughed. He smiled, and I could tell he was unsure if I was joking or not.

"Tomorrow, we will join you up there," Roony said. "Alfonse is having maintenance move our desks up there, too."

I couldn't tell if he was happy with that or not. "Yes, he told me. That's great," I said. "There is so much to do I'm looking forward to the help."

All three of them smiled at me but said nothing.

❖

If the Môti offices were overwhelmingly glamorous, my apartment was the exact opposite. It was tucked into a side street off of the Boulevard Saint-Germain, which made it a fairly short walk to work. It was a fifth floor walk up with a tiny living room and a galley kitchen off to one side. A single bedroom and bathroom sat off the other side. The walls were all bare and white, and it was sparsely furnished with a bright red leather-vinyl couch, a plastic dining set, and two incredibly uncomfortable beige armchairs from IKEA. The one saving grace of the apartment was the small balcony off of the bedroom, looking down over a courtyard below and out across a cluttered skyline of Paris rooftops.

I didn't get to speak to Ellie and the boys until late that first evening. After a quick hello and a few questions about the flight, what Paris was like, and if I was already learning French, Robin asked for a car. He let me know he'd been thinking about it, and he would be very responsible if he had one. I told him his mother and I would talk about it. Gary was busy with summer baseball, and his team was doing pretty well. He talked in detail about practice and the game he'd had that weekend. But when I asked about what else he was doing, he didn't have too much to say. "Did you start any of your summer reading list yet?" I prompted him.

"Dad, it's only been a couple of days since you left. I can't be expected to have started that stuff. Come on, it's early in the summer."

I laughed. "Well, that's true right now. You've still got plenty of time. But you have to start soon, That's a pretty big list of books. What are you going to start with?"

"I don't know, Dad." His answer was enough for me to picture him on the other end of the phone, wriggling to get out of the conversation.

"Okay, well, just think about it. You want to get ahead for next year if you can."

"Uh-huh." There was a long pause. "Well, I gotta go Dad. I've got another practice soon. Here's Mom. Love you."

"Love you too, Gary."

"How are you doing over there?" I could tell by the way she spoke that the boys had left the room.

"Well, they should have started this work months ago. I knew it was going to be a pretty big project, but it seems like it's getting more and more impossible with every new thing I learn about it. I'll figure it out," I said.

Silence. This time not the silence of an impatient adolescent, but the silence of my wife. "You know…"

I waited for her to continue, but something seemed to hang in her voice.

"Know what?" I finally prompted her.

"You know, if this job is too much, just leave it. Nova Vocé is not going to fire you."

"Yes, they would if I left this project."

She took a deep breath. "Well, do whatever you want to do. But you can come home any time you want. If you feel like this isn't something that will be successful, then don't waste your time. Just come home, honey. We'll figure out something."

But I knew I couldn't go home now as much as I wanted to. As crazy as things felt here, I couldn't duck out and leave it. It would have been career suicide. "I love you."

"I love you too," she said.

"I've got to go now, Ellie. I'll call you tomorrow."

"Okay, honey. Try to get some sleep tonight. Turn off the ringer on your phone."

I laughed. "If only."

"They don't own you," she said. "I know it must feel like they do, but they don't."

"Night, Ellie." I said after a moment.

"Night."

I hung up the phone and lay down in bed. I tried to close my eyes but it was useless, I wouldn't be able to fall asleep for hours.

CHAPTER EIGHT—LEARNING

The hot and sticky summer marched gradually on. As it did, the Môti attic slowly, quietly became my life. My days were filled with trunks of Môti clothing, accessories, press clippings, and photos from the last century. As I sifted through the shelves of the attic, the boxes began to take on a life of their own, each a time capsule from a specific season, a specific period. I hadn't realized until those days in the attic how tightly fashion was tied to the world of current events.

The attic was a glimpse into what the world was like at different points in the past—what people dressed like, what they found beautiful, how they viewed life. As one of the first fashion houses of the 1900s, photos of Môti collections started to appear in *Vogue* and *Harper's Bazaar* as early as the late teens. Môti clothed the elite of post war Europe, showing up on everyone from wandering Russian aristocracy to jazz hall starlets and British expats.

The cuts were low and slinky in the early years but kept pace with the times, fascinating generation after generation. Most, if not all, of these looks had been glamorized in the popular newspapers and magazines in fashion spreads and editorials from the beginning of the last century until now. I occasionally found myself so absorbed in a particular box that I would look up and the clock would say midnight on it.

Not that the late hours bothered me. Even after a few weeks in Paris, I still had trouble sleeping, so I worked all the time. I often left the office late at night during those days on the project, only to wake up in the early hours of the morning, unable to sleep. Sometimes, in the middle of the night, I would just give up on sleep and roll out of bed, flip open my laptop and start going over whatever I hadn't finished the day before.

Gradually things started to pick up steam on the project. Andrea found and hired a few people in San Francisco and sent them over to work onsite. We also found some temp workers in Paris to help with the sorting and tagging. Their jobs were to parse through the materials in each box, labeling everything with tags that detailed the fabric, time period, style, and any other random elements we thought a museum curator or designer might want to search by. A lot of the tagging was up to our imagination. Alfonse and the rest of the Môti team were a nice enough group of people, but none of them had the time to sit with me and help sort through any of the photos.

Late one evening as I was leaving for the night, I passed a stack of cardboard boxes someone left on the floor by the elevator. Whoever had left them must have been planning on going through them the next morning. But I noticed that the date on the first box was July 15, 1967. My birthday. It's silly, I know. I wouldn't be able to actually remember anything from the year I was born. Still, my mind raced backwards, wondering what it must have felt like to be a full-fledged part of the world at that time. The Vietnam era, the civil rights struggles, the Cold War, cheap gasoline, President Nixon, the facts and anecdotes filled my head like I was searching for answers on a history test.

I picked it up and carried it back over to my desk. I popped the top off of the box and immediately the smell of dusty acetate and old polyester filled my nostrils as I lay the box top down on the table next to me and leaned over it to get a better look inside. Some of the boxes I had been through were neatly organized, with things folded and sometimes even sealed in plastic mothproof bags. This one was not. A pile of bright colored fabric was stuffed into the box, as much as it would hold. I reached in and pulled out the first dress, being as careful as possible not to damage the fabric.

The fabric was a soft, shimmering shade of gold. The top of the dress, above the waistline, was two layers: a delicate cotton lace with the Môti logo subtly blended into the pattern over a smooth satin liner of the same color. The bottom of the dress was a giant puffy rayon chiffon skirt, pleated and tucked into a rhinestone belt. As best as I could tell, it was a party dress. I set it down gently on the table next to me.

Next, I pulled out a cream and gold knee-length evening dress. The skirt had a similar shape to the first dress, but the material was a little different. It seemed to be some kind of nylon, but a little duller and with a slightly less exaggerated shape. The top was a slim, fitted satin blouse underneath a tiny bolero jacket with gleaming acetate trim. Rhinestones lined the collar of the jacket and, inside, a Môti label was almost entirely torn away from the fabric. I folded the dress as neatly as I could and set it down next to the first one.

The rest of the box contained six more dresses, all similar in look and feel and materials. Had I seen any of these dresses on my aunts or maybe my mother's friends as a toddler? I couldn't be sure. The fabrics triggered sepia images in my mind, but I couldn't tell if they were memories or imagination.

A large manila envelope was at the bottom of the box underneath the dresses, dusty and stained with age. Envelopes or folders like this were in most of the boxes. I picked it up and gently pulled out a set of photographs from the runway show where these dresses had debuted. There they were—all six of them, worn by glamorously thin women with perfect, egg-shell shaped hair and porcelain white skin. Two of them wore pillbox hats and every one of them had on gloves that went up past their elbows. The pictures were taken on the runway with the clapping audience all smiles and nods in the background. The Môti logo hung high above the models, flash bulbs crowding the edges of the runway.

It was a perfectly frozen moment of glamour from well before the age of Facebook and LinkedIn. I smiled and wondered what the models would have thought if they knew that fifty years in the future, someone born on the same day as these pictures were taken would be preparing to scan them into a giant database and render them immortal in ones and zeros. I wondered what their lives were like, if they had long modeling careers, or if they went off to marry some rich Parisian banker after a season or two. Had they eventually grown old and happy with a dozen children? Were they still alive today? I thought back to what they would have known for technology in that time. Just the basics, not much more than radios and televisions. Maybe they had read something in *Newsweek* about one of the giant room-sized computers built by the government or IBM, but probably not. I shook my head. "If you only knew," I said out loud to the empty room.

I glanced through the rest of the stack of photos and laid them all back down in the box along with the dresses, and closed it. I returned it to the pile out by the elevator and pressed the down button. Enough nostalgia, I thought to myself.

Alfonse was our project leader in name, but after our first few meetings he began taking a bigger role in overseeing the entire museum. He was spending more and more time in the attic with me, watching as we went through box after box of Môti history. He proved very helpful in providing insight into the nature of the designs and how they fit together and evolved from one season to the next.

Sometimes he was cold and other times he was easy going, but I learned to work with him. If I asked his advice, he was friendly and helpful. If I seemed to require anything more than direction, I got a tense, bristly response. He was not a technical person, and I would be surprised if he had used more than the email function on his cell phone or laptop. So I made a habit of presenting him with fully baked plans for different parts of the project that required just a yes or no on some of the details.

He had an uncanny ability to turn up out of nowhere. Like a cat, he materialized at random, seemingly from thin air. I would be working on something, deep in thought at my desk when I would suddenly feel a presence over my left shoulder and turn around to find him staring at whatever I was working on. He always wore approximately the same thing, a safety pinned tee shirt and some type of tight pants—the safety pin was his signature piece that summer.

"I need your help on something a little unexpected," he said to me one morning, appearing as he did. I had my nose buried in my laptop revising several lines of code that had been giving me trouble for the last week.

"What's up?" I asked, happy for the distraction. I turned around to see him standing in the middle of the room holding a huge blue plastic box. He was flanked on either side by two very handsome young interns whom I hadn't ever seen before. They stood as straight as Marines at attention, both holding giant blue plastic boxes identical to the one in Alfonse's arms.

"Luca Sparks is what's up," Alfonse said.

"Sorry. Luca who?"

"Luca Sparks, the famous photographer. I want to open the museum with an exhibit of all the work that Sparks did for Môti."

"And who is Luca Sparks?" I asked. One of the interns rolled his eyeliner-laden eyes at me. I wanted to cuff him.

"Luca Sparks is only the most important photographer of the twentieth century." Alfonse set the box down on my desk and rummaged through it for a second, pulling out an old issue of *Vogue* from sometime in the nineteen nineties. He flipped through the pages until he came to one in particular. "This one," he placed the photo down on the desk in front of me. "This one is a Luca Sparks photo."

"Okay. How will I know his stuff in particular?" Until now we'd been sorting through and organizing things based on their place in Môti history, not by magazine, writer or photographer.

He leaned in even closer, grazing my right shoulder with a loose fold of his tee shirt as he grabbed the photo off the table and held it out in front of us. "You can always tell his work."

"You can?" As uncomfortable as I was, I was curious what he meant.

"It's the way he uses light. On their faces." He pointed to the three models in the picture. "They have an angelic quality to them.

You can't put your finger on it, but something about their expression looks like they're from another world. Only it's not their expression, it's the way the light in the photograph plays off their features. Sparks is a genius at that. It sells clothes like crazy."

"Oh," I said, unsure of what Alfonse expected me to say.

"This was his first shoot," he said about the photo in front of me. "At least his first real commercial shoot. He had been hanging around Paris and New York a lot in the late 1980s, doing all kinds of arty stuff. He liked to call himself post-Warhol. *Vogue* gave him his first break."

I looked closer at the photo, three women out in front of a host of others emerging from what looked like a decrepit garage, their glistening bodies draped in plaid gowns. One of the front women held a tire iron, another held a wrench, and the third held a bag of potato chips.

"He was so serious. He had a reputation for long shoots. He was relentless on the models and the crew. They say he once went for eighteen hours on set. Because of the unions, they were supposed to switch out the crew and the models, but no one in their right minds would ever leave a Sparks shoot."

"How come?"

Alfonse shrugged. "It was a matter of necessity, really. If you left his shoot, he'd never hire you again. If Sparks wouldn't work with you, pretty soon no one else would either."

I nodded. "It sounds a bit draconian."

"Whatever it was, he was brilliant. They say he invented the grunge movement with one single photo spread." I could feel Alfonse's breath on my face, and it sent a wave of chills down my back. "He's a local, but he doesn't take photos anymore. Had some kind of breakdown. Now he just spends his time hanging around in cafes and bars here in Paris. I run into him all the time."

"Really? A local?" I could hear the forced sense of blasé in his voice, but I knew instantly it was an act. Paris was all about connections. I had no doubt that Alfonse would do whatever it took to see and be seen with even a formerly famous photographer. I wondered if the whole premise of a Luca Sparks exhibit was anything more than a play for personal attention.

"Yes, a local. I want you to find everything you can by him. You can start with these boxes." The interns each stepped forward and placed their boxes in front of my desk, then stepped back to where they had been standing before. "Then you can look through some of the other boxes from the 1990s and early 2000s."

I looked around the room. "Alfonse, that will be like finding needles in a haystack. In a couple of months when we've cataloged everything and tagged it, yes, this would be easy to do. But looking for it specifically right now will take us off task. It could put us way behind schedule."

"I don't care about that. This is very, very important."

I let out a deep sigh. "I'll try, but I don't know…"

"Don't try, just do it." He turned on his heel and marched over to the elevator, trailed by his interns.

"Oh, and by the way," he turned around. "You were in the blog."

"The blog?"

"Yes. The blog." He squinted at me. "You don't read the blog?"

"I read a couple of different blogs. But I'm not sure which one you're talking about specifically."

He chuckled. "You really are a newbie to this industry, aren't you?"

Before I could respond he continued. "The blog—Runway Confidential. It's everything you want to know about the Paris fashion scene. I'm surprised you didn't notice. Our little project was featured last week."

"The museum project?" I was stunned. "Really?"

"Yes." He gave me that look again, somehow creepy and condescending at the same time. "It wasn't the most flattering post, and, of course, it didn't mention you personally, but it did say that Môti was 'moving into the 21st century' by digitizing its historical collection. I was mentioned briefly in the story, not that I like to see my name online. It's really an invasion of privacy, but that's the price of working in such a visible position in the industry."

He looked very much like he *did* like seeing his name in Runway Confidential, or whatever it was called. When I was silent, he eventually continued on his way towards the elevators.

After he left, I sat staring at the picture. I couldn't help but notice the light in a new way. It began to come alive for me in waves. At first, I noticed the models in the foreground, the snarl of the lips, the loose curl of hair flopping down over an eye with a motion of its own. Then the color of her dress came to life against the backdrop of the grey-brown deteriorating building, all of it working together to bring something off the page.

It wasn't about an event. It wasn't like news photos or even vacation photographs that seek to capture a series of memories. This was about bringing to life a feeling, an emotion, an ultra-saturated experience that would be impossible to find in real life. Here it was perfection, here it was a movie star experience on a page. I found myself wondering what it would be like if I could somehow step into the moment of the picture.

CHAPTER NINE—PARIS IS A SMALL CITY

Paris has a strange luster all its own, a glamour that pulls people together and pushes them apart in waves of love and luck quite unlike the natural properties of any other city on Earth. One cannot possibly spend any substantial length of time in Paris and remain unaffected by those forces of nature. They are just beyond our control and understanding. The city's plan for each of us is as much a mystery as the city itself, and to ask why we feel the way we do in Paris might as well be to ask why its night sky is such a rich shade of purple.

I've listened to people talk about Paris, either directly to me or in overheard conversations, and the sense of mysticism is universal, though some smile happily when they talk about memories of Paris and others seem to wane and grow smaller, as if eclipsed by some trace of fear or passion. Paris finds what is deep inside us and steers us on a path towards it, for she is the goddess of coincidence. We can bury what we like, but things have a way of surfacing on their own there, as the city brings people together on the wind of chance encounters.

As if to prove out Alfonse's words like a prophecy, I actually met the infamous Luca Sparks on the fourth of July. I won't deny that his photograph in *Vogue* had sparked my interest, something I hadn't felt in looking at a photo since that night years ago when I'd seen the Mapplethorpe print in that stifling Greenwich Village gallery. But it had been weeks since Alfonse had trudged into my office with his interns and asked me to find everything I could by Sparks. I scrambled to meet his request over the following days, only to be told by the end of the week that Alfonse had changed his mind and wasn't going to open the museum with a Luca Sparks exhibit. I hadn't held a grudge for the unnecessary diversion; I just re-buried myself in the original work to the point where I'd almost forgotten about it.

So, while my country was celebrating its independence with fireworks and hotdogs, I was finishing up a small dinner alone at a sidewalk café I had adopted as my weekend office. The place was just a block down the street from my flat, tucked into the corner of an elegant side-street building with bright red and white awnings. A deep mahogany bar took up most of the space inside, but no one ever sat in there, at least not this time of year. Everyone was packed out onto the window and sidewalk tables. I sat at one of the outside tables, with a mostly-eaten cheeseburger and my second glass of wine in front of me. I was typing away on my phone and making notes in a small paper notebook I carried everywhere.

It wasn't that I needed a place to go. Either my apartment or the Môti office would have been fine, but after spending most of the time during the week in the attic library of Môti and not really having enough room to do much more than sleep in my apartment, I wanted to be somewhere else. I looked down at my wine glass and wondered what Ellie and the boys were doing at that moment.

It was too early for the fireworks yet, but I could imagine her packing up a basket with food and supplies. She would have thought of everything from Pepsi to an extra set of hoodies for the boys. They would head down to the Marina green or maybe Fort Mason to watch the fireworks, and they would spread out one of the boys' old quilts that had Matchboxes or superheroes on it. Ellie had saved a few such blankets in the top shelf of our laundry room for just that type of occasion. I smiled to myself as I imagined her on her tippy toes pulling them out, all of them tumbling down on her as she tried to grab just one. But the smile faded from my lips and a slowly growing pit in my stomach began to consume me as I thought more and more about my absence.

I shook my head and took a final sip of the lukewarm wine in front of me, making an effort to push the mildly depressing thoughts of home out of my head. The sticky heat of the day had given way to a pleasantly warm evening with a little bit of a breeze to cool things off. The night was perfect for sitting out and watching people on their way home or heading out for a night on the town. I laid my phone down on top of my notebook and just watched the sidewalk scene around me, trying to let my mind wander at least for a few minutes. I could afford just this little bit of time, I told myself.

The place was full of the typical summer crowd of German and American tourists with their obvious girth, chomping away at *foie gras* and pointing at maps of the city. I saw the odd pairs of businessmen, always in twos and always sitting together with little more than glasses of wine and sometimes little plates of cheese and bread between them. Their love affairs were with money—not with the food or the wine—and breaking bread together was too intimate an act for these shepherds of industry, even if they were French.

A couple of lovers sat at a table just inside the window, staring into each other's eyes and playing footsies, barely touching their plates of food. There was a table with a pair of old women who must have come into the city for the day. We all sat in our places, each a separate little part of the restaurant tableau, watching and carrying on our business as the young waiters moved across the floor and out onto the sidewalk, back and forth swerving around the tables, the conversation rising and falling, an ambivalent tide of sound.

But as graceful as the waiters were, there were only three of them. Perhaps that was enough for a normal crowd, but they were having a hard time keeping up that night. They buzzed around seating people and taking orders, and they ended up leaving several tables, mine included, for long stretches of time without attention. But this didn't seem to bother anyone except for me. One of the things about Paris I was still getting used to was the slow pace of table service. It runs at a different cadence than it does in the States. In New York or San Francisco, the waiters are instantly on you and stopping by constantly during your meal. I've always thought their goal must be to get you out of the restaurant or bar in as little time as possible.

No sooner do you finish your last bite or drain that last sip of wine, than your check magically appears at your elbow with a "no rush, whenever you're ready." In France, I found the waiters took your order, then you were lucky if they showed up at all during the meal. They generally left you alone unless you specifically beckoned them, and even then only appearing after a few minutes of letting you wait. At first I thought this was rude, but after a while I learned to try to enjoy it. I called it the forced savor.

My phone buzzed suddenly, yanking me away from my thoughts. Andrea had texted me to let me know she'd just made another hire back in San Francisco, but she was having trouble with the visa paperwork. I drew in a sharp breath and exhaled loudly. When I finally did look up again from the phone, my jaw was clenched. I'm sure I was scowling.

I glanced past my empty glass of wine, searching for one of the waiters, and that's when I first noticed him. He was a stranger to me then, but something about his face made me think I had known him for a very long time. He sat smoking a cigarette, the smoke drifting up through light blue eyes the color of pond ice. And they were set directly on me. When he noticed me looking back at him, he smiled like we were old friends, like he'd seen me across a table a thousand times before, and I'd just somehow returned from a long walk.

In that moment, I wondered if we had actually met before. After all, why would anyone be looking at me like that here, in Paris? I searched my memory, but I couldn't place him. Suddenly, I wondered if maybe he was a pickpocket sussing me out. I quietly felt my pant pockets for my wallet and my phone and panicked for a quick second when I couldn't feel my phone, until I realized it was in my hand. I felt suddenly self-conscious of the scowl on my face. I relaxed as much as I could, but it didn't matter; I later found out that he'd been watching me for almost ten minutes before I looked up and saw him.

"You look like you're having a very bad night," he said. I'd expected his voice to be icy like his eyes, but it wasn't. It was smooth and mellow and sounded more like the smoke curling around his head as he exhaled. It bothered me at the time that the two characteristics I had noticed first about him were so discordant. The sharp ice of the eyes and the silky tone of his voice were somehow just wrong together.

"San Francisco. Work," I said back to him, holding up my phone as if that was all the explanation that was required. "They're making me a little angry tonight."

"The price of anger is failure, you know." He raised his eyebrows and smirked at me as he ashed his cigarette in the tiny ashtray at the center of his table. "Ellwood Hendrick."

"I'm sorry?" I asked, unsure if I'd heard him correctly.

"Ellwood Hendrick," he took another long drag off of his cigarette, which I had now noticed was one of those awful dark French cigarettes that lack the antiseptic American smell of smoke. They are somehow grittier and earthier, romantic in the way only foreign cigarettes can be romantic. But the romance was lost on me. They made my stomach ache, and it was one more thing I instantly disliked about him. "It's a quote." He watched me for a moment and then laughed, a short, mischievous chuckle that made me want to like him even less.

"Sorry," I said back to him, looking around for the waiter, who, like the entire army of French service staff, had evaporated when needed. "I don't think I've read anything by him."

"No, I can see that. No time left for reading books when you're reading the phone so much," he nodded towards my phone "—the text messages?"

I stared at him blankly.

"I've been watching you now for some minutes, and you are doing nothing but reading them. Angrily reading them." That smirk again.

"It's my work." I said, beginning to be a little uncomfortable with this intrusion into my evening.

"Ah, yes, the work," he sighed. "Me too. I used to have lots of the text messages."

"Really," I said, looking back down at my phone and turning the screen on. "Not anymore?" I asked, beginning to ignore him as I clicked through the three new messages from Andrea.

"No, not so much any more."

A distant tone in his voice somewhere between remorse and relief pulled me back and made me look up at him again. I couldn't help myself. I knew Andrea was waiting for an answer from me. I thought about it for a second and then put my phone down. "You don't work anymore?"

"Oh, no," he said "I still work. I just don't do the same thing that I used to." Then, after a few seconds, "I used to take pictures."

"Pictures?" The word had such a funny ring to it coming from him. Maybe it was his accent, but it sounded almost childlike the way he cradled the word when he said it, as if he had his arms around it.

Our waiter finally reappeared to deliver a plate of oysters to the table at the end of our row, and I managed to catch his eye as he passed by on his way back, waving slightly at him. He nodded to me efficiently on his way inside but didn't stop.

"I am sorry," he said leaning back and crushing out his cigarette. "It's nice to meet you. I'm Luca." Something about the name clicked in the back of my mind, but I ignored it. He leaned across the table and reached out his hand. I stood up a little so I could reach over, and we shook.

"Ian," I said, sitting back down.

"You are from America?" He pulled another cigarette from the pack lying on the table and lit it.

"Yes," I said, laughing for the first time that night. "But I won't apologize for it. *On peut parler français, si vous le souhaitez?*" I was brave and a little ridiculous; my French had steadily improved from listening to the daily chatter at the Môti office, but I was far from fluent. I was just annoyed at how often I'd been sidelined in the past few weeks through language.

"Bien sûr!" He smiled at me. "I should have guessed. You don't look like a tourist. But if you don't mind, I'd like to practice my English. I don't get many chances anymore. And why, by the way, should you have to apologize for being American?"

I shook my head. I hadn't realized until that moment how defensive I had come to feel here. Everything I did or said was wrong. What I ate, how I walked, even the way I ordered my coffee seemed to turn heads and engender looks of pity. It was always too big, too loud or trying too hard. Nobody ever said this, at least out loud. People were constantly talking over me or looking at me and considering whether or not they should speak in English. I felt like a child or a mute, unable to be part of the conversations or unwanted when I tried to contribute something in the little French that I was learning—and I *was* learning. I was able to pick out more and more of those conversations at work or on the street.

"Is it possible you're being too sensitive?" he asked, as if he had sensed what I was thinking?

"Sensitive?" I pondered the word, wondering if it translated the way he meant for it to. I may have grown aggravated by living in a different place, a different culture I always had to try to be a part of. "Yes, I suppose."

"The French," he said, "we are not always like this. This is Paris and it's a little like New York in the way we think we're the heart of everything. Outside in the country is better sometimes, the people are nicer."

I laughed. "That makes sense, I guess."

Our waiter finally reappeared, this time with a single glass of red wine on a tray, which he promptly placed down on the table in front of me. *"Oh, non, Je voulais que l'addition s'il vous plaît..."* I frowned.

"Now that is American," he said, then to the waiter—*"Un vrai Americain, n'est-ce pas?"*

"I was going to ask for the bill," I said to him, slightly uncomfortable, partially because I didn't know what he was getting at and partially because I figured he was silently judging me for my accent or my manners.

"Yes, and now you are angry again," he said. "Only an American would expect the check and be unpleasantly surprised when a glass of wine showed up instead. Where are you going so fast on a Saturday afternoon? Eh? Sit. Enjoy. I'll join you for another." He nodded, and the waiter disappeared again. After weighing the options, I figured he was right. What did I have to go home to? A small rented flat with one channel of English television and a mountain of work. I smiled and took a sip of the wine.

"Fine," I said, relaxing a little. "So, what do you do?"

"What do you mean 'what do I do'? I told you, I take pictures. Well, at least I did."

"What kind of pictures do you like to take?" I asked. The waiter brought him his glass of wine and set it on the table. He took a sip and watched me across the rim of the glass.

"What do you think of our French wines? How do they measure up to your American winemakers?"

I shrugged. "I'm not really an expert on wine. But I think they both have a lot to offer."

"Fair enough," he said. "You're clearly not taking a side, but fair enough."

I took a sip of my new glass of wine and looking across the table I found it hard to meet his stare. "Why won't you answer my question about the pictures?" I asked after a few seconds of silence.

"There isn't much to say about it, really. I took pictures. I lived in New York for a while. Chicago too. It was usually a gallery opening that made me move to a new city. Then I'd maybe teach some classes there. I did some commercial work. I even did a music video once."

I was confused at that point. "Wait, you were a professional photographer?"

"Yes." He had a patient look in his eyes, as if he ran into this type of situation all the time. "I told you that. What did you think I meant when I said I took pictures?"

I'm not sure why I hadn't taken him seriously when he first told me. After all, I'd just spent the last two weeks cataloging and scanning pictures professionals had obviously taken. But it hadn't registered with me that someone I would meet on the street would ever be a photographer. A banker, a bookstore clerk, an advertising executive—all those were normal. But a photographer? It didn't exist in the realm of realistic occupations for me. I considered maybe this was a side occupation, some sort of hobby.

"I don't know. I guess I thought you meant as a hobby or something."

"You thought I was a just a hobbyist?" His eyes seemed to soften as he took this in. "If I was still an artist, I would be offended."

"Still an artist?" I repeated his words. "What do you mean by that?"

"There are not many things I can mean by that, no? I mean that I used to be an artist. I used to care. I guess I still do care a little bit, but not about photography."

His voice was soft, lapping gently like waves on a beach, rushing in a little bit with a subtle crash of meaning every so often and then retreating. That spark of recognition clicked again in the back of my mind as he was talking. "Wait," I interrupted him. "You said your name is Luca?"

He nodded, a glint in his eye. I realized he knew what was coming next. "Yes, that's right."

"Luca Sparks?" I asked.

He nodded again, this time grinning from ear to ear. If he had given up being an artist, I thought, he hadn't given up the ego that went with it. I might have been reading too much into things, but it sure looked like he was proud of his name.

"As in *the* Luca Sparks?"

He continued nodding.

"Wow, that is amazing," I started to laugh. "Paris is such a small place."

He stopped nodding his head and looked at me. It was the first time all night that he seemed surprised. "What do you mean?"

"I am working at Môti." I contemplated explaining the whole project, but then thought better of it. "Well, I was just looking at some of your pictures the other day. They were telling me what a wonderful photographer you are."

"Ah," he said. "They, presumably, were the people at Môti?"

I nodded. "Yes, the historical design curator, Alfonse. He's a big fan "

"Ah." He sat very still for a moment, looking out past me into the street. "I know Môti very well. And you, are you in fashion?"

I let out a quick burst of laughter. "No." I shook my head vigorously and gestured at the tee shirt I had on. "Not even close to it. I'm working on a technology project for Môti."

"Ah," he smiled. "Then I know about you, too."

"You do?" I thought he was making fun of me again. "How?"

"The Confidential," he said, waiting for me to recognize the term.

"The what?"

"*Runway Confidential*, the blog. They did a post a few weeks back about Môti's technology project."

"Oh yeah." I was surprised. "Alfonse told me about that blog, too. I guess I didn't take him too seriously."

"Oh, the *Confidential* is very, very serious." He took a sip of his wine and raised his eyebrows in what I could only guess was a mocking way. "At least as serious as you can be about the lives of those in the fashion industry." He pulled out his phone and flipped through a couple of screens before handing it to me. "Oh wait." He pulled the phone back. "I'll translate." Before I could protest, he held up a hand. "Solely for the purpose of practicing my English."

He cleared his throat. "Môti digitizes its historic collection... Afraid you might have missed out on a bit of fashion history? Well, don't worry about it any longer, Soon the trendy people at Môti will be digitizing up all their archives, which go all the way back to the early 1900s (circa the birth of yours truly, because I am old as dirt). That's right, word on the street is it will all be searchable. However, you might be out of luck if you're not among the Môti elite. Only insiders will have access to the database. Sad clown."

"Well." I didn't know what to say. "They actually said 'sad clown'?"

He nodded. "So, you're scanning in all their shoes and dresses? To memorialize the fashion industry, huh? It sounds like you're very committed."

"We're also scanning in a lot of your photos too," I said. "But I'm doing it because it's my job. Not out of some commitment to the fashion industry."

"Oh, well that's good." He let out a long sigh. "I thought we might have to talk about fashion now. But I'm relieved that's not the case."

"Nope. No need to worry about that."

"But I'm curious. You said they showed you one of my photos. Which one?"

"Oh, well, I've seen quite a few of them now, but the first one I saw was that famous spread in Vogue. The girls with the tire irons?"

His eyes searched the street-scape, then suddenly landed on the memory. "Oh, right. The grunge set. Yes, I remember those now. What did you think?"

"Well, I don't know much about photography, but I liked the picture."

He raised his eyebrows and turned his head ever so slightly. He picked up the cigarette pack in front of him and thumped it against the palm of his hand, nudging one out. "Do you mind if I smoke?" he asked. I shook my head no, even though my stomach turned to think of the dark stench, and so he continued to light it.

"You haven't told me if I was good or not?" He inhaled deeply on the cigarette and let out a billowing cloud of smoke.

"I'm sorry?" I said, confused because his tone sounded a little bit like a question and not a question at the same time.

"Usually people tell me if they think I am good. You said that you liked my work. The difference is important to me."

I nodded, taking in the breadth of his comments. I had never stopped to differentiate between the two statements. "I guess, maybe in English they mean the same thing?"

"Do you think they do?" he asked. "That would be such a disappointment."

"A disappointment?" I echoed. "How is that a disappointment?"

"Let's take one question at a time," he said. "Let's keep with the difference between 'I like your work' and 'you're good.'"

"Fair enough," I said, a little unsure of where he was going with this.

"If you like my work, it means something to you. You've personalized it. If you think I'm good, it means nothing to you.

You're passing judgment on my skills as a photographer, and the truth is that you probably don't have any real credibility to do so."

"You're awfully opinionated about your art for someone who no longer considers himself an artist," I said. "I guess I see your point, though. There is a difference between those two statements. But the heart of both of them is validation." I took a sip of my wine, readying myself for the next round of the conversation. "Why did you quit?"

"I don't know exactly." He stared at me, the smoke curling up around his face and off into the night. "I had so much passion for it for so much of my life. When I started, it was all I ever wanted to do—I'll tell you about my first camera some time, but not now. For many years, I just practiced and practiced. I would spend a whole day just shooting pictures. I'd work on composition and experiment with lighting. When I finally got my own studio, I spent every waking moment there. You couldn't pull me away from the camera."

He smiled at the memory. "Of course I did what I needed to do to get by. I did weddings and all kinds of parties. I did corporate head shots, anything. But none of that was painful for me. If it involved the camera, I didn't mind doing it."

"Then it just all started to go wrong. The more successful I was, the less it meant to me. It started to be something I was doing for someone else." He took a deep sip of his wine. "You know that question I just asked you? The one about do you like it versus is it good?"

I nodded.

"You said you liked my work. That means you recognize it's only your opinion, and it exists outside of the work. Too many people were telling me I was good."

I shrugged. "And that was a bad thing?"

"Yes." He slapped his hand on the table. "Don't you see? It's not about validation, it's about control. They don't get to say if I'm good. They don't get to say if the work is great. It's my work, I get to say. But you can't know that when you're young, so you allow it. One day, you wake up in a world where it feels like everyone else owns you because of the very thing you love to do." He took a deep breath and let out a sigh, shaking his head and ashing his cigarette into the small black ashtray on the table. "It's not a good place to be in. That kind of world is not real."

He took a long drag, exhaling a plume of smoke up into the evening sky. "Anyway, I found my mind drifting during shoots. I wanted to make new things, but I was just doing more and more things for money. And when you do these things for money, nobody wants anything experimental. They want something that is, well, pardon my ego, but they want something that is 'Luca Sparks.' And so I was just doing the same thing over and over again." He took a breath and stubbed the half-finished cigarette out in the ashtray on the table. "And so I just quit."

He was silent for a moment, a triumphant look on his face.

"It wasn't even a big catastrophe for me by then. I didn't care. You see," he continued, "by the end, taking pictures was just an identity, just something to be anchored to. I couldn't find the art in it any longer, only glory and a vague sense of place that it gave me. But as another one of your American writers likes to say, 'people can't invent their moorings any more than they can invent their parents.'"

"Baldwin," I interrupted him.

"Correct," He smiled at me, and his eyes lit up. "And in the end I had to let go of that mooring because it wasn't real for me any more." We were both silent for a while, each of us sipping our wine and looking out across the square into the night. The evening had started to come alive as it does in Paris on weekends. The tourists were still out, but not in the same numbers. The ones wandering along the streets with their bags of scarves and books and trinkets shaped like the Eiffel Tower were headed back to their expensive hotel rooms to change for dinner.

But the Parisi, the natives, were starting to come out in bigger numbers, school kids and teenagers out on some small window of liberty, young professionals heading out into the night, stopping at the sidewalk cafes and bars for a quick drink before a party or a date. I took a breath, trying to take in all of it. I loved the energy of that time of night. The evening was fresh with so many possibilities, it could become whatever you wanted it to be. Even if I was only headed home to a sparsely furnished flat, millions around me were headed for adventure tonight, and watching them was enough to feed my soul for a moment.

"You're smiling," Luca said. I turned to find him staring again, those eyes so cold and warm at the same time.

"I love this time of the evening," I said to him. "When the day becomes the night. It always makes me feel young again."

"Mon dieu, c'est magnifique, mais tu n'es pas si vieux."

"Well, thank you." My face flushed a little. I wasn't prepared for the compliment, and I felt a sense of warmth rush up just below the surface of my cheeks. "But I fear I am pretty old compared to most of this city and most of my world sometimes."

The waiter, who had been scarce the entire time, finally, nervously interrupted our increasingly silent conversation with a look at first me, then Luca. *"Et maintenant l'addition?"* he asked.

I looked at Luca and then down at my empty wine glass. "Yes," I said. "I think I would like the bill now."

"Bien sûr," said the waiter, and he laid a check down first on my table and then in front of Luca.

"Come, I'll walk you home," he said after we had finished paying our bills.

I smiled, unsure of whether or not to take him up on his offer. My face must have given away my concerns because he smiled back at me and nodded. "I am not looking for an aperitif, nor am I going to take your wallet. I will walk you only part of the way. I want to show you what I'm working on now."

"I thought you said you weren't taking pictures anymore," I said as we headed down the street away from the river and towards the Boulevard Saint-Germain with its broad sidewalks and elegant leafy trees. The soft hum of the traffic scurrying along was more of a lullaby than the static it had seemed earlier in the day.

"I'm not. I'm painting," he said, the emphasis smacking down on the first syllable of the word, making it sound as if 'painting' was derivative of pain.

"Oils?" I asked. "Something big?"

He laughed. "Something big? Yes." Then after a few seconds, he added, "It's a house."

"A house? I don't get it."

"I am working as a painter. I paint houses now. It is the perfect occupation for me. I told you I can't stand to look at photographs of anything anymore. So now I just look at walls and fill them with color. It is very, very relaxing for me. The house I'm working on is right here." He gestured to a grand old granite building on one of the side streets just before we got to the larger boulevard. "I know it's dark, but if you look through the windows there, up at the top of the window right in the corner of the room where the streetlight shines in, you can see the molding. Can you see it?" His voice sounded like a child's.

"Yes," I nodded, squinting through a darkened window to see what he was pointing at.

"That is what I worked on today."

"Well," I said, "I like it. I don't know if it's good, but I like it."

He smiled at me and shook his head, and we continued to my street in silence. After a few more blocks, he turned to me. "My house is this way, so I am going to leave you now. But I'm sure we'll see more of each other."

"I'm sure we will." I stuck out my hand to shake his, but he looked down and laughed.

"Oh no, my friend. This is Paris." He ignored my outstretched hand, leaned in, and kissed me lightly on each cheek. *"Bon nuit, Ianto,"* he said, and he walked away. Something struck me as odd about his goodbye, but I didn't piece it together right away. It took me a few seconds before it dawned on me that he had called me 'Ianto,' the nickname only my parents and Ellie had ever used. It was an accepted nickname for Ian, but not a common one. I watched as he walked away, thinking how strange the evening had turned out to be.

"Bon nuit," I repeated a moment later, remembering to speak only when he was about fifteen yards away. I stood for a little while, watching his figure retreat and grow smaller against the backdrop of the glimmering Paris night. There was something about him that

I could just not capture in words, something exciting and almost dangerous. If you'd asked me to compare our lives that evening, I would have said we had nothing in common. The one thing that I have learned since then is those who have passion have it in common. It doesn't matter how different their vocations are. Finally, I turned around and started back towards my own apartment.

PART THREE: CLOSER

Perhaps Tina Barney was an accidental photographer. No one will ever know for sure. It's rumored she picked up photography as a distraction, something to pass the time while she waited for a real mission in life. Her photos, however accidental they may have initially been, changed the way the world viewed family. She captured relationships in a bold, plastic and colorful way that expressed the universality of family—the love as well as the friction and imperfections of it.

CHAPTER TEN—CLOSER TO WET

It rained the second week in July. Huge, elegant storms, the remnants of a pair of Atlantic hurricanes, blasted through the northern central part of France and sat down on top of the City of Lights and stayed. I spent most of the days going through the mountain of boxes in the attic. Each one gave me a sense of archeology, a glimpse back into some year of the last century. Of course, we were fully staffed by that time, so the place was not as quiet during the day as it had been when I'd first arrived. While having a crowd around took away some of the magic of the boxes, I found the buzz of people comforting. It calmed my frenetic sense of needing to meet a deadline.

Occasionally, I would glance up from my work and look out of the giant windows of the Môti attic at the water pouring down. Rain is different in Paris than it is in San Francisco. In San Francisco, the rain rinses the city. The streets feel clean, they glisten with a dark luster that refreshes the gritty alleyways and the broad avenues of the city. Rain in San Francisco feels like starting over. The crowds dissipate and the city seems empty and untouched, as if it belonged solely to me. But in Paris, things are older and not as easily moved to rebirth. The rain dulls things in Paris, but it does not restart them. It mutes the colors of the city. The pink and blue sky turns to a dark grey, and all the buildings along the Seine fade to shadows on a sooty horizon.

That week I missed my first return trip back to San Francisco. I had scheduled the trip home before I'd even left for Paris, but I knew that I wouldn't make it as early as my first day on the job at Môti, there was just too much to do.

"You missed Gary's last game of summer baseball today." Ellie's voice was thin and emotionless over the phone. It was late on Friday evening in Paris, and I was still at the office, sitting hunched over my laptop and trying not to speak too loudly. "But I'm sure you forgot about that already."

That burned. The fact that she could deliver a line like that in such a flat voice just made it worse. "Hey," I said softly, "that isn't fair."

"Isn't it? We're not on pause, you know, Ianto. Just because you decide to take off for three months doesn't mean we all go into suspended animation."

"Ellie, please. Don't do this."

"Don't do what, Ianto?" She sounded for a couple of seconds as if she was going to continue, but she stopped abruptly and the line was silent.

"Are you still there?" I asked.

"Yes."

"Look, maybe Gary and Robin can come over here for a week or so like we talked about."

"And what, sit in your apartment while you work? Don't you think that would be even worse for them? To be ignored at close range?"

"Ellie…"

"No, Ianto, I'm not trying to be cruel, I'm just trying to be realistic. Look, I know you feel bad about this, but taking this assignment is a choice you made."

"We made," I interrupted her. I was not going to take the full brunt of the decision.

"No, not really. But still, you feeling bad and wanting to give Robin and Gary a treat is nice, but think about how they'll feel when they get over there and you don't have time for them."

"Could you all come?"

"You mean so that I can mind the kids so you don't feel guilty? No, Ianto. We live in California, not France."

I couldn't think of anything to say to her.

"Look, Ianto. Do what you went over there to do. We'll figure things out over here, okay?"

"I miss you, Ellie. I miss all of you guys." I swallowed hard and forced myself to smile.

"I miss you too, Ianto." I could hear the irritation in her voice. It wouldn't matter what I said now. The conversation was over. She would hang on the phone for a few more minutes if I did, but she was done talking. I knew that tone in her voice, the leave-me-alone tone.

As we said our good byes and hung up, a deep sense of emptiness filled me. The distance between us was growing, and it was not related to the ocean and continent that separated us. I felt things slipping farther and farther away from me, and I was powerless to stop them from here. I looked at the time on my phone and decided to head home.

Outside, the dim light of a cloudy late afternoon played on the wet granite buildings and sidewalks, reflecting back a diffuse layer of radiance. The rain had turned to a lazy drizzle, and the cool, damp air felt fresh on my skin. I tried to think of other things as I walked towards my apartment that evening, anything to take my mind off the call with Ellie.

My route took me along the river, past several of the magnificent bridges that defined the city. I thought about all the water that moved below them, from the beginning of time until today, not a drop of it the same, none of it traveling the same route twice. I turned right and crossed by the *Ile de la cité* and stood for a few moments looking up at Notre Dame. It was beautiful this time of day, even against the backdrop of the gray sky.

I continued over the river and up past the little café by my apartment where I frequently ate, and I recognized his face in the window, half buried in a magazine. Luca looked out from behind the drizzle-covered windowpane at just the moment I was passing by. He folded the magazine closed and smiled at me. I smiled back, and he waved his hand, motioning for me to come in. I thought about it for a few seconds and decided to stop.

Inside, the café was steamy and warm. The air conditioning cranked away above the door, but its modest efforts were useless. My tee shirt and jeans were damp from the rain, and I could feel the material sticking to my skin. I glanced around for Luca, but as soon as I did, my cell phone buzzed against my leg. I paused among the polished brass and oak tables and pulled the phone out to see a text message from Ellie with a photo of Gary from his game earlier today. I smiled at the picture, hearing his squeaky voice in my head, embarrassed that his mom was taking a picture of him yet again. I made a mental note to text him back this evening, then slipped the phone back into my pocket. I looked up again and spotted Luca's table towards the far end of the café. He was already watching me as I made my way through the soggy restaurant to him.

"I see you have not made much progress in separating yourself from that phone," he said as he placed the magazine down in front of him.

I smiled and nodded. "Well, this time it's not just work."

"No?" He arched an eyebrow. "This time you are looking at the rest of your life through this device? Tell me, how does it look through there?"

I pulled the phone back out and turned it so he could see the picture of Gary at bat. "I see what I'm missing," I said, "and it makes me sad."

He leaned forward to look at the picture more closely. "Your boy?"

"My youngest. Gary." I looked at the phone again. "I think I have officially made Worst Dad of the Year Award."

"Ah," Luca shook his head and put his hand on my wrist. "Well, sit here." He gestured to the chair across the table from him. "We can be sad and miserable together."

His hand on my wrist felt foreign, a form of intimacy without the weight of implication, a simple gesture from another culture that didn't carry the same boundaries of physicality that my own did. He looked up at me with a deliberate innocence in his eyes. I was alone, and I had nowhere to go, and I thought that he must be alone too. Aside from my conversation with him a week ago, I hadn't talked to anyone outside of work since I'd been in Paris. So I sat down in the chair across from him and made up my mind to be social.

"So," Luca smiled. "How did he do at the match?"

"Sorry?" I said, disoriented.

"Your boy, in the picture. How did he do at the match? Did he win?"

"Umm," my mind went blank. I had just read the message, and I couldn't remember a thing. The street was still for a few seconds as I thought about the question. I could hear cars in the distance, snippets of other people's conversations, even the bells in a church somewhere behind us. But I did not know if Gary had won the game or not. I didn't even know how he'd done. I thought back. I was sure the text message that contained the picture must have said. Ellie was nothing if not descriptive when it came to our kids. She would have included something like that in the text, I was sure of it.

"Sorry," Luca said. "I'm making it worse. I should not have asked."

"No," I waved a hand in front of my face, dismissing the imaginary block. "It's not that. I just... Never mind, it's not important. I think I'm just starting to see the light in a couple different parts of my life."

He shrugged. "Light is important. I should know, I'm a photographer. Or at least, I was."

I laughed, thankful for the distraction. "Yes, I suppose you would know better than most of us about light." The seconds ticked away, and I felt as if I had to say something, but I couldn't think of anything to ignite the conversation. "I'm sorry, I guess I'm just not very talkative all of a sudden."

He shrugged. The seconds turned in to minutes, and he was either as uncomfortable as I was or he just knew it would be easier for him to talk than for me. "It's always about the light, isn't it? Light is central for the photographer. It's central for life," he smiled a broad, ear-to-ear grin. "But it's never what you think it is."

"What do you mean?"

"Well," he hesitated for a moment, fiddling with the magazine, now folded up in his hands. "You see, light isn't the same for everyone. We all see it differently."

He looked at me, his head lowered in expectation. But I didn't know what to say, so I simply shrugged my shoulders and blinked.

"I will let you in on a little secret." He pointed two fingers at his eyes. "These are the enemies."

"The enemies? What?"

"The eyes. They are the biggest enemy of the photographer." He smiled and took a sip of his wine. I nodded my head a little, but I wasn't following him. How could the eyes be the enemy? It didn't make sense. After all, weren't they the one thing that told the photographer what to see, what to take a picture of? My questions must have shown in my face, because he smiled and started over again. "Let me explain. The eye does so many things that the camera cannot. For instance, look over there." He pointed to the street scene in front of us.

"It's beautiful, no? This slice of life? The reflection of the street life in the shop windows, the children playing over there," he pointed across the street. "Over here is an old woman with a hundred years of life on her face. And the beautiful light of the sunset is coming in across the building there."

"Yes." I took in everything he said, following his finger as he spoke and pointed out the tableau in front of us.

"But the camera, it won't see all that. You take a picture of this because you love the light or the beauty of the children playing. The camera won't get any of it. Unless..."

"Unless what?"

"Unless you specifically focus it on something. Focus only on one part of this. The camera can only see a very small part of this with any meaning."

"Oh."

"Of course, once you figure out what you want to do, that changes things. The camera and the eyes, they get along then. But, until you've made up your mind about what you want to do, the eyes are just frustrating to the camera."

I thought for a moment. "Where is your favorite place to take pictures?"

"Hmmmm, what a question." He sat back in his seat and ran his hands through his hair. "What do you mean specifically?"

"Well..." I hesitated for just a second, a little self-conscious that I wasn't using the right language. "Where is the best light? Where is the light just perfect for you?"

He shook his head. "Nothing I just said made any sense, did it?"

It was my turn to sit back in my chair. I still had no glass of wine, but I was getting increasingly comfortable with myself. I didn't care if I sounded like I didn't know what I was talking about. "I'm not saying that you don't make sense. And I refuse to entertain the idea that I failed to understand you. Instead, I'm asking a question that I'm really interested in. As a professional photographer, you must have a place you like to shoot in because of the light, right?"

He looked at me in silence for a moment, a slight wrinkle in his nose. Gradually, his face relaxed and he began to lean forward. "In my opinion, the best light is in Spain." He smiled at me as he said it. "In Spain the light takes on a romance of its own."

"A romance?" I shook my head.

"Yes, absolutely. There the light is brilliant, like the way you feel during a love affair." His chair scraped against the tiled floor as he adjusted it underneath himself and leaned in further, placing both elbows on the table and folding his hands beneath his chin. "Have you been to Barcelona?"

"Um, no. I haven't."

"Do you know much about Gaudi?"

"Well," I hesitated. "Not really. I mean, I know who he was."

"Then you know about the Sagrada Familia? No? It's the cathedral in Barcelona that's not finished yet, his most famous work?"

I nodded, trying to figure out where he was going with this. "Yes, I've never been but I know what you're talking about."

"Gaudi was the expert on light."

"I was wondering where this was going."

"It's true. He knew we need light to see, but too much of it blinds us. A little like love, no? Like romance. They say when Gaudi was planning his famous cathedral, he was very specific about the stained glass windows and how much light was to be let in. When people asked him why he only wanted to let in so much light, he said that light plays a very special role in churches. Just enough light and you have illumination; too much and you can't see. It blinds you. He said it was like that with life too." He glanced at my phone and then back at me. "If you are, as you say, seeing the light in parts of your life, you might want to be sure you are not looking for so much light it blinds you."

I waited a moment, taking in his story. "I think that's a charming metaphor, but I'm not sure it works here."

"Well, perhaps if I knew more about the situation."

"No, I don't want to talk about that right now. I just want to give my head a little bit of a rest."

"Of course." His voice was softer now, and I couldn't tell if I'd injured him with my abrupt unwillingness to talk more about myself. We lapsed into silence again, the table between us an open plain with nothing but Luca's empty wine glass and the magazine he'd been reading. "You know what?" he finally said.

"What?"

"I think you should come out with me tonight."

"Out with you?" I smiled. The tone of his voice made it sound like a secret adventure in a kid's book. "Out where?"

"Out in Paris," he shrugged. "I don't know where, I just know where we'll start. Let's see who's out and about. Come on, let's get out of this place, I will show you the real Paris."

I blinked. "You paid already?" The waiter still hadn't arrived at our table.

"Yes, I paid," Luca said. "We're free to go."

"Fine," I shrugged. "Let's go."

CHAPTER ELEVEN—COMMUNISTS AND WINE

We stepped out of that little café and headed down the street in a direction I had never been before. "We're never eating at that café again," Luca said as he tugged on my arm and steered me out of the path of an oncoming bicyclist.

"Why not?" I asked.

"It's awful." He pursed his lips together in what looked like something between disgust and concentration.

"Why were you there tonight then?" I asked.

He slowed down for a little bit and turned to me, putting his hand gently on my shoulder as if I were a little boy. "Waiting for you, of course." He looked at me and then laughed before turning back to the street in front of him and speeding up again.

"You knew I would be there?"

"I know you're a creature of habit, so yes. I knew you would be there again. I figured it was on your way home from work, so I watched for you."

"You were watching for me?"

"Well, yes. I felt bad for you after our first conversation, stuck in Paris all alone with nobody but those Môti fashionistas to talk to all the time. I knew you must be going crazy. I thought I should rescue you."

"Rescue me? Hmmm." Despite his explanation, I still felt a little weird knowing he had been watching for me.

"Would it make you feel better if I said I was hoping to see you?"

I thought about it for a moment. "Yes." Luca steered me around a broken glass on the sidewalk. "I guess I would feel a little better about that. But I still don't really believe you."

"Fine. I had no idea if you would come, but I figured my only chance of meeting you again would be to try the same restaurant where I first met you."

"But if you don't like that café, why were you there last week?"

Luca let out a loud exasperated sigh and looked up at the sky. The drizzling rain had at last let up and a few strands of the setting sun pierced the blanket of clouds above us. "Why do you Americans always ask so many questions? Why this? Why that? How many colors can the sky be?" He gestured up with his hands. "Enough is enough, huh? No more questioning Luca. Besides, we're almost there."

I gave up on the questions and simply followed him. The café turned out to be not too far from the rest of my little world in Paris. Only it was down a different street, a left when I would have taken a right, a right when I would have gone straight, and then an abrupt turn.

"Here," he said, pointing down and across the street. "We are eating here." He dragged me down the rest of the alleyway, past the dank walls of a centuries-old church plastered with graffiti. We dodged a group of off duty construction workers as we crossed the cobblestone street and ducked into a small wooden door with the word Café DeTra. "And then we will drink somewhere else, if we feel like it." He shrugged. "Or maybe we just stay here."

The windows of the Café DeTra looked up to the street, giving the place a basement-like darkness that pressed in on me as I walked through the door. Luca turned to me as if sensing this and gave me a reassuring look. "Don't worry," he said. "We will sit out back."

"Out back?" I asked, wondering if we'd find a set of poker tables in a dark room with sawdust on the floor. But out back turned out to be a small flagstone patio with several white wrought iron tables squeezed together among giant concrete urns of rosemary and lavender and roses. Little white tea candles glowed and glittered on top of each table, and two or three large umbrellas stood sentry among the tables and plants keeping the place dry in spots big enough for people to dine in. Strings of tiny white Christmas lights crisscrossed the yard in a random pattern, illuminating the restaurant in a soft aura of celebration. At the center of it all, an ancient chestnut tree rose majestically above the place, its graceful branches arching gently down like a setting hen, over the entire patio. The effect was dazzling. It was less of a restaurant and more of a secret garden.

"You would never find this place, eh?" he asked, turning around, no doubt, to see the look of surprise on my face. "It's not for the tourists of Paris. It's for the people who live here."

He was right. I looked around and saw a mix of old and young, but no one in a suit, nor in an American football jersey. I smiled. "It's amazing. I never would have guessed this was back here."

Luca nodded at the waiter and led me to a seat close to the back of the patio. "This is the place that my father used to like to come," he said as we sat down, "when he would come to Paris to visit me."

"Did he visit often?" I asked, watching as Luca signaled the waiter with a gesture of two fingers. I must have given him a look without realizing it, because he explained to me.

"They only serve a few things here. They know what I like. I just ordered us two glasses of wine, which I hope you like too. If you don't, well, I guess you can blame me. This place used to be chic. You see the big glass doors and the columns?" He pointed to the alabaster columns on the ends of the outdoor bar. "There was a very fancy place that tried to make it here, but it failed. There are not the right clientele in this neighborhood, and rich people don't like to walk down steps to go out to dinner. They like to walk up them."

"Really," I mused.

"Yes, really." he said, the serious look still on his face. "They want to feel as if they are eating above the rest of us. They want to feel safe where they are, that no one from the great unwashed masses will sneak up and steal a morsel from them."

"You sound like a bit of an old-school communist. A Marxist, even," I said to him as the waiter arrived with our drinks and set them on the table in front of us. The wine was a light pink color, not something I would have normally ordered, but I thought better of protesting. To do so would be to insult Luca. A few rogue strands of late afternoon light pierced the leaves of the chestnut tree on the edge of the patio and danced on the wine, making it a mottled ball of pinks and yellows and whites. It stole my focus for a few seconds, looking a bit like some sort of rare gem. I thought back to what he'd said earlier that evening about light and how we all see it differently, and I wondered if this was as beautiful to him as it was to me.

"I wouldn't be ashamed of that," he said. Then, seeing the lost look in my eye, he prompted me, "of being a communist. I wouldn't be ashamed of it. I think we need more people with ideas like that who know what is really happening and who aren't afraid to talk about it."

I nodded slowly and thought a moment before I responded. "Don't you think that is the trouble in Europe these days? Too many communists and not enough capitalists? Who is going to keep the machine moving?"

"Ah," he said to me, letting out a long sigh and shaking his head. "And what is so very critical about the capitalists? How do they keep things moving? By keeping too much for themselves and not sharing enough with the rest of the world?"

"All right, all right. I don't want to talk politics," I said, holding up my glass of wine. "I don't love the communists or the capitalists. I just think there needs to be a better balance of both or else no one is incented to work, to create value."

"Capitalists do not create value," Luca said, raising his glass up to mine. "But I will toast you to balance, even if we don't agree on exactly what it is." We clinked glasses and I took a sip of the wine. It tasted the way old oak leaves smell in the late fall: dry, deep and just a little earthy—not the sweet, syrupy taste I'd expected from a pink wine. It was good, and I looked at the glass as I put it down, surprised at the discovery I'd made and suddenly very thirsty.

"You never answered me about your dad." I reminded him. "Does he come to see you in Paris often?"

"Ah," Luca waved at the air again, that gesture that seemed to tell his stories for him. "He used to, back when I was just getting started up here. He was worried about me a lot, I think." A sad smile spread across Luca's face.

"It makes you sad to talk about it?" I asked.

He took a deep breath and looked up towards the leaves of the chestnut tree as if searching for something in its branches. "No, not sad," he said after a moment. "Happy in some ways, to remember how much he cared. I miss those days sometimes. I was poor, but so many things inspired me back then. I think my father saw that when he came up here. He worried about me—not that I would be thrown out of my room, but more that I was living too fast and never resting. I think it was hard for him. I was so focused on my work that I had no room for anything else in my life, and sometimes I wonder if he felt like he couldn't reach me in those days. All I wanted to do was take pictures, and all he wanted to do was spend time with me. I was too young to see it, but he could. So he came up to Paris as often as he could, and he followed me around as I took pictures all day.

"He was—is," Luca corrected himself. "He is a good man." He was silent for a few seconds before he continued. "I think maybe I have the same feeling as you when you talk about your sons. Fathers and sons. So much strength and so much sadness is in those relationships. We never feel like we've done enough, regardless of what side of the relationship we're on."

I waited, without saying a word. I knew he wasn't through and he was stopping only to let the air between the two of us settle and adjust to a new layer of intimacy.

"He is still with us," Luca continued after a few moments. "He is down on our family farm outside of Avignon." Luca let out a soft laugh. "Only now it is my turn to worry about him. His joints are stiff, and his back aches all the time, and he finds he can't do as much as he once could. But he still gets out of bed every day. He still walks around the place and does his chores."

"You grew up on a farm?" I asked.

"Oh yes," he said, taking a long sip of his wine. "It was not a great big farm like the ones you have in America. It was a small little farm with some olive trees and a couple of sheep, still big enough to get lost on as a little boy, and big enough in the last century for my parents to make a living on. But now the sheep are gone, and the olive trees are old and unkempt. My father gave it all up when my mother passed away. He has a few chickens he keeps in the yard, and he's got a little garden in the back that he grows in the summers." Luca let out another laugh, this time with more of a smile. "There is still drama enough in his life, though. He goes crazy trying to keep the chickens out of his garden."

I laughed, imagining what he must look like, an elderly man in overalls, maybe in worn blue denim, chasing around a flock of hens and shouting at them in French. "Do you get down to see him much?"

Luca nodded. "I do now," he said. "It used to be more difficult when I was taking pictures. I always had some place to be, some destination to go to and take pictures at, and I spent most of my time chasing that work. Now I just paint houses, and in between, I go down on the train to visit him. I bring him things from Paris that he likes: chocolates and sometimes fun tee shirts with crazy slogans or pictures on them. He used to love to find the most outrageous tee shirts when he would come up to visit me. He would buy them and leave them with me. He'd usually buy me a coat or a sweater, too, even if it was warm out when he visited. He made the mistake of coming once in the middle of winter and he saw that my rooms had no heat." Luca looked down at the table, lost in his past. "He really was a miracle for me in those days. I don't know how I would have eaten without his help."

"Were you in school then?" I asked, taking another slow sip of my wine and watching him.

"School? No. I learned pretty much on my own—no." He stopped mid sentence. "I take that back. I didn't learn on my own, I used to go through all of the stalls along the banks of the Seine. You know the ones I'm talking about?" I pictured the merchants at the wooden box stalls lining the river up and down on both sides. They were always open, selling souvenirs and books and compact discs full of Edith Piaf music. I had never really stopped to look at any of them, but I'd spent one or two Sunday mornings walking along the banks of the river, and after a while of passing by them, you begin to pick up little bits and pieces about the old ladies that sat out in front of the paintings and books and old tin signs for sale.

Luca must have seen the far off look in my eyes. "You are somewhere else?" he asked.

"No, no." I shook my head. "Just picturing the stalls along the river."

"Ah." He gave me a slight nod and raised his eyebrows. "Okay, I understand. Well, you know they sell all of the used picture books. And on some days when I had not much else to do except take more pictures and worry about finding the money to buy more film or finding a place to develop my pictures besides my room, I would wander down and look through those books."

"They must have loved you," I said. "Did you ever buy anything?"

Luca shook his head slowly back and forth. "No, not then. I was far too poor and practical. I knew some artists at the time who would spend their last franc on posters or books, but not me. I just walked through and looked. I am, as the Americans love to say, cheap."

"There's nothing wrong with living within your means."

He smiled at me. "Of course you would say that. It's so American."

"I won't argue with that," I looked directly at him. He had a glint in his eyes I didn't quite understand. "Where did you live back then?" I asked. "Back when you were cheap and young?"

He drained the rest of his glass of wine and reached across the table to put his hand on my forearm. His skin was cool and dry and a little rough from the powdery grit of plaster and paint. The gesture was not one of intimacy, although I realize now as I think back, it might sound as if it were. But it was more a gesture of *camaraderie*, almost as if he was looking for some connection between us that had to do with our separate pasts. "You know," he said without taking his hand off of my arm. "I lived in the part of town that I think is the best and the worst part of town at the same time. Do you know Montmartre?"

I nodded slowly, thinking back to something I'd read about the hilly artists' village on the outskirts of Paris. "I know a little bit about it."

"It's the kind of place that they call up and coming. You know what that is code for, right? It means watch your wallets and phones when you're there. But it's a beautiful place, set up in the hills just out on the edge of the city. The neighborhoods run from chic little storefronts and flower-boxed stone houses to the dingier back streets where the paint is fading and the sidewalks have no tourists."

"It sounds interesting," I said.

"Well, that's where I lived." He motioned to the waiter again with a flick of his wrist. "When I was starting out. I took a lot of pictures out there. There is a cathedral on the top of the highest hill in Montmartre, Sacré-Cœur. I used to climb up that hill and take pictures of it every morning. I'm not sure why," he said, finally taking his hand off of my arm. "I guess I thought things might change—the light was different every day of the year—not much, but in little increments. And I wanted to train my eye to notice the small differences." He was lost somewhere for a few seconds. By the look on his face, he must have been picturing the cathedral as he'd seen it every morning.

The waiter appeared again, this time with a bottle of wine. He was one of those sleek Parisian men you find in cafes and restaurants throughout the city. They have a grace I have never seen in my own country. Though sometimes elusive, when you do see them, they move as fluidly as running water around the tables on the floor, laden with plates of food or glasses of wine, and making the restaurant look as if it were a ballet. I hadn't quite finished my wine by that point, but he filled my glass anyway and did the same to Luca's. Only this time, he left the bottle before gliding off.

"One time," Luca continued, rustled out of his memories by the waiter or me, I'm not sure which. "One time, I took my father up to the cathedral at dawn. The walk up the hill was a little hard for him even then, but we trudged up together, him stopping every few minutes to catch his breath. We passed all of the people going home from the night and some of the ones coming out for the morning to go to work. My father, he said it was just like a changing of the guard, all these people coming and going. I always thought of it like the tide, but he was probably more accurate. Those who keep the city alive at night were handing things off to those who keep it moving during the day.

"We would keep going up and up the hill, slowly, so slowly I was afraid we wouldn't get to the top until lunchtime. But we made it just in time to see the sun coming up behind the large—how you call it in English—basilica?" Luca was by this time getting very animated, talking with broad sweeping gestures of his massive hands and a fire in his eyes. I nodded my head quickly so as not to interrupt his story.

"And it was a magical morning. The clouds were just right on the horizon, and the sky was a beautiful purple and red and orange the way it only looks in story books and movies." He stopped for a moment and took a breath, a deep, remembering smile spread out across his face. "My father loved it. He said he could see why I make my photographs. He said to me that it was my job to show the world the things like this. And that moment was so important for me, you know, because I knew that he understood my love for photography."

We sat in silence for a while after Luca finished his story, each sipping our wine and trying casually to avoid the other's eyes. I wanted to give him the privacy of his memories and, for his part, I think he felt as if he might have dredged up too much of his heart for sharing with such a new friend. But, as I was to learn, Luca seldom said things he didn't want to, and if he regretted what he'd said, he showed no outward signs of it. After a few moments, the waiter came back with a basket of bread and a plate full of cheeses, olives, and figs. He set it gently on the table between us, maybe sensing the quiet that lay in the air above us. I looked up to the waiter, and then finally at Luca, meeting his eyes again for the first time in minutes.

"Did you order?" I asked him in a quiet voice, not quite certain if I would be disturbing him or not.

"*Mais non,*" he smiled as he answered, much to my relief. He was back from whatever depth he had drifted to, his eyes shining brightly again, perhaps delighted in my newfound naiveté. "They know me here, and they won't let me order off the menu. They just bring me whatever they know is good on that night." He looked up at the waiter. He had a smooth olive complexion that made it hard to tell his true age. He could have been anywhere between eighteen and thirty. His eyes were a soft, gentle grey that looked a little like the eyes of a mourning dove, and when he looked back and forth between Luca and me, I could see the mind behind those eyes trying to figure out exactly what was happening at our table. "Sometimes I like what they bring me, sometimes I don't, but this way I always eat it."

"Always?" I asked. "Even if you don't like it?"

"Especially if I don't like it," he said.

"But, why?"

"What do you mean why?" Luca looked stunned. "Well, the answer is really quite simple. You see these people are experts at food. I know they serve me always what they think is the best thing in the restaurant that night, so I am getting their very best work. And food is like art. It is a creation. If I don't like something, then I am the one who is missing the point. So, I always eat the entire dish and every bite. No matter how much I want to spit it out, I don't. I savor it and think about the flavors, the smells, the texture of whatever it is in my mouth, and I try to figure it out, try to learn to appreciate it. Even if I don't like it, I know it's important to experience it."

Luca's words hit me like the answer to an impossible riddle. I don't know why, but he made me feel as if I had missed an important part of understanding life. I thought of my own approach to food, how difficult I was, how picky I was about what I ate. I thought about my home city of San Francisco and all of its five-star restaurants and the chefs who studied their whole lives to create works of art at those restaurants. They were always at the mercy of patrons who judged something too salty or too sour or not hot enough, as if those patrons would just as soon tell Matisse how to paint. Luca saw beauty in so many things I never considered beautiful. But more importantly, he saw the need for beauty and how many people routinely failed to see it.

I never told anyone, not even Luca, how that conversation sent me off on a secret quest to re-discover all of the foods I'd ever disliked. To this day, I make it a priority to try the most elaborate thing on the menu, especially if it sounds as if there's no way I could like it. In the weeks after that conversation, I thought of every food I'd ever disliked, and I tried them all again. I found a place where I could order liver and onions the way my mother had cooked it when I was young. The stench of the plate almost made me gag, and I could barely keep down the first few bites. But I forced myself to slow down and experience the flavor of liver and onions—not just force myself past it, but try to understand it. And I found Luca was right. Though I'll never like it and I'll never eat it again, that meal was something I had not fully tasted or fully experienced, and it gave me an oddly profound sense of joy and accomplishment to finally get to know liver. After that it was a slew of things: some fully cooked meals, others candies or packaged foods I'd never cared for, squishy fruits and fishy things like salmon roe.

But that night in the restaurant, when Luca taught me the secret of food, all I could do was stare back at him in awe. I couldn't form a sentence, so I just nodded. The waiter, who had been patiently enduring our conversation at the side of the table took the opportunity to break in and ask if we would be having dinner tonight.

"Non." Luca kept his eyes on me. "I think only the cheese today."

"No." I could feel my cheeks, much to my embarrassment, turning a deep shade of red. "I would very much like to have dinner tonight."

Luca studied my face for a moment, as if reassessing me in that strange detached way I was to witness time and time again over the next few weeks. After a few seconds, he nodded. *"Bien sûr,"* he said, carving out a side of the soft cheese in front of him and spreading it thickly across a rough piece of country-white bread he had pulled out of the basket. "We will be having whatever is for dinner tonight," he said to the waiter.

CHAPTER TWELVE—A NEW KIND OF DRUNK

That night at dinner, the conversation stayed mostly on current events and painting, with Luca explaining in detail the differences between semi gloss, high gloss and matte finishes. I listened to the excitement in his voice as he described how a room comes together with the right colors and textures, how palate could change the way people feel when they walk into a room. He spoke as if painting walls had been his calling, and I found myself wondering how anyone could not love paint as much as he did. The evening progressed in bursts and spurts of conversation, and soon the crowd around us began to thin out. We sat alone on the patio after dinner, drinking the rest of our wine. The two little tea candles in the center of our table had burnt almost all the way out, and I was starting to think about my bed in my tiny apartment. It had been a long day, and I was looking forward to going to sleep.

"Okay, now we're going to The Marigold." He pushed back his chair and tossed his napkin onto the table.

"The Marigold? What's that?" I didn't move.

"For a nightcap," he said. "It's a little bar that I know down the street."

"Oh, no." I shook my head. "I'm going home and going to bed."

"Oh, Ianto, no." He looked directly at me, his blue eyes shining brightly against the backdrop of the patio café. "It's only Friday, and so much is going on. You're in Paris, you're young, and you may never get a night like this again."

I looked back down at my hands. His eyes were so intent I found myself unable to hold his stare. "No, I'm not much of a night person."

"Well, you're from California, right?"

"Yes. What does that have to do with anything?"

"Well, it's nine hours earlier in California, so it's not even really night time for you. You can go out and still actually be an afternoon person where you're from."

I laughed. "Thanks, Luca, but I really shouldn't."

He took my laugh as a sign that I was giving in to his plan, and that was all he needed. "Come on," he stood up and crossed around to my side of the table, making a mocking gesture of pulling me up by my arm. "Are you going to make me drag you there, or are you going to cooperate?"

"So," I laughed again, looking up at him as he stood. There was something irresistible about him, even in the most superficial way. He had a juvenile energy that made everything seem more exciting. "You're kidnapping me? I just have to know for sure so that when the authorities finally do find me I can tell them accurately what happened."

"Hmmm." He grinned slyly and gave me another gentle tug, urging me to rise. "Kidnapping you and dragging you off to another bar for a nightcap? Mmmmm, maybe. Yes, I guess that is what I'm doing. But just for one or two more."

"One," I stood up. "Just one more drink—a nightcap, and then I'm going home. I am not staying out late tonight. I don't want a hangover." He smiled at me and even as I followed him out of the restaurant, I could feel the wine from dinner starting to hit me. My head was light, and my legs wobbled just a little uncooperatively. "One more is really all I can have."

"Ah, Ianto, you will learn, my friend," he said as we left the café and stepped out into the warm Paris street. The sun had finally set and the streetlights sparkled above us, washing the whole scene in a yellowish glow.

"What will I learn?"

"Not to argue with the night." He put his arm around my shoulder. The noise of the evening sidewalks filled my ears as we walked: the sound of a distant street corner jazz band, the blend of the passionate and mundane conversations taking place all around us, the buzz of far off traffic, and the clatter and bumping of the cars close to us as they slowly made their way across the evening map of the city. We moved through the streets past windows full of late night diners and street patios crowded with couples drinking wine and smoking.

We changed direction a few blocks down the street, heading left down a cobblestone alley where the buildings stretched over our heads, bridging the streets and blocking our view of the night sky. Halfway down the alley, Luca stopped abruptly under one of the bridge buildings and looked around until he saw a sliding warehouse door, the kind that you see at the back of theatres and on loading docks. As my eyes adjusted to the darker light, the word Marigold gradually appeared in large orange and red neo-Gothic letters on the side of the building above the door. I strained to listen and when I did, I could hear the hum of voices beyond.

"We're here," Luca said, pointing to the door.

I shook my head slowly. "What kind of place is this, Luca?"

"You'll see." Luca went through the door ahead of me, negotiating something with the doorman, who seemed to know him. He walked through and motioned back for me to follow him. It was loud and crowded inside, full of people shouting and laughing and spilling their drinks all over each other. Luca leaned into me and put his arm around my shoulder, steering me towards a zinc bar at the back of the room. He had a mischievous look in his eyes that only grew wilder as we walked.

"Have you ever had absinthe?" he asked.

"No." I looked around at the shelves of liquor behind the bar, trying to see the names on the bottles. "I think they just legalized it in the States, but I haven't tried it yet."

"Tchh tchh tchh." He shook his head. "I don't think you even have the real thing in America. I think you've got some watered down copy of it."

I shrugged. "I couldn't tell you."

"Tonight you will try the real thing." He motioned to the bartender with a raised hand.

The bartender looked like he could have been on either side of the bar. He was chic, with blondish brown streaks of thick hair falling down around his face in loose curls. He wore horn-rimmed glasses, a bulky off-white sweater, and tight jeans. His belt was buckled on the side of his waist, which caused me to inadvertently stare at his midriff until I caught myself and looked in the other direction. Hopefully before anyone noticed. He winked at Luca and gave him a quick nod as he finished serving another customer's drink. "Eh Luca? What'll it be?"

"Deux verres d'absinthe," Luca looked back at me. "This is a truly French experience."

"American?" The bartender gave a quick nod in my direction.

"Oui," Luca responded. "A new friend from the new world."

"You're introducing him to the Absinthe?" He stretched his face into a mock frown as he poured a greenish liquid into two glasses on the bar, and then set a slotted spoon with a sugar cube over each glass. Finally, he poured water from a pitcher behind the bar over the sugar cube into each glass, one at a time. I watched as the green liquid transformed into a milky white substance with the addition of the water. The bartender removed the sugar spoons from the glasses, glancing quickly down into each to inspect his work before finally pushing them across the bar to Luca. *"Bon chance,"* he said, flashing a grin at Luca. He turned toward another customer, not bothering to ask for payment.

"You're quite well known around here," I said, taking the glass Luca handed me.

He shook his head and nodded back toward the bartender. "It's good to know the bartenders. They're usually the life of the party wherever you go."

I held my tongue.

"What's so funny?" he asked.

"Nothing, really. I guess I just don't go to that many parties."

"Ah, well. Maybe you're the smart one." He stared at me for a moment as if he were trying to figure something out about me. *"Salut!"* He finally said, raising his glass and putting his hand on my shoulder once again.

I mirrored him and we clinked glasses. *"Salut,"* I said, and took a sip of the strange white liquid. It had a sweet, organic taste to it. I've heard it described as tasting like anise or licorice, but to me, it tasted like drinking a handful of dandelions. "Oh, wow." I wiped my mouth and put the glass down on the bar in front of us. "That's quite a drink."

"They call it the green fairy." His eyes were locked on me. "I used to drink a lot of it."

"Why's that?"

"I thought it would make me a better photographer." He seemed amused by the puzzled look on my face. "They say it has the power to unleash your inner creativity."

"Great. I'll need that for all the coding I have to do tomorrow."

"Ah." Luca shrugged his shoulders, turning so his back was to the bar and he was looking out over the crowd. "Even coding can be done with flair. I can't imagine how, but I'm sure it's possible."

"I'm sure it is." I watched him surveying the crowd. "Anyone you know?"

"A few women that I recognize." He frowned. "No one interesting."

I laughed. "You mean no one that you can talk to."

"And how do you know so much about me all of a sudden?"

"I can tell by that look on your face right now. It's a universal look. The only people you recognize here are people you've slept with."

He laughed. "You are presumptuous."

"And I'm right."

His lips tightened, and he tried to suppress a smirk "Fine, you are right." He drained his glass. "Hurry up with that drink. I want another."

Against my better judgment, I drained the rest of my absinthe and placed the glass on the bar. He signaled the bartender, who seemed to materialize instantly for Luca. After a few short words in French, the whole ritual of pouring the absinthe started again. I looked the crowd over as Luca and the bartender chatted. The music was loud, but almost no one was dancing.

They crowded the dance floor just standing in threes and fours with cocktail glasses and pilsners in their hands, chatting and bobbing their heads at each other in agreement or bewilderment or some other sentiment I couldn't identify. Finally, Luca interrupted my stare, placing another drink into my hand and clinking his glass to mine. "Salut," I mumbled.

"Salut." He took a sip and waited for a moment before he spoke again. "So what do you think of this little place?"

I was at a loss for words. "I don't really know what to think. It doesn't matter, does it? A drink's a drink at the end of the day, right?"

It was his turn to look out over the crowd. "I don't know about that." He put his hand on my shoulder. "All of these people are out here looking for love."

"So, it's a meat market." I felt the heat of his hand and struggled not to move away from him.

"Meat market?" He glanced at me sideways. I was sure he could feel my discomfort, but he didn't move his hand. "I think I understand what you mean. But no, it's not necessarily a meat market. It's not that they have to go home with someone. But they come here to be loved, to be looked at, to find someone to talk to, and yes," he turned just ever so slightly so he was looking at me almost straight on, "yes, sometimes to go home with someone. But it's more that they come here to shine."

"That's silly," I said.

"Silly?"

"Yes," I waved a hand out at the crowd, summarily dismissing them. "It's vain to go some place to be seen, to be noticed."

Luca shook his head slowly. "I don't agree," he said, locking his blue eyes on me. "I think it's incredibly important to know that you're appreciated, to know that someone thinks you're beautiful. Take yourself. Doesn't it matter to you that someone knows you're beautiful?"

"I'm not beautiful." This time I couldn't stop myself. I pretended to reach back to the bar for something and squirmed out from under his hand. "And it doesn't matter."

"Ah, my friend, you're not being honest. You have a wife, you have friends, you maybe have girlfriends. They all think you're beautiful." He kept his eyes on me the whole time he was speaking. His hand was off my shoulder, but he was edging closer as he spoke, and the air between us grew hot and charged with an energy that made the hair on my arms stand up.

I shook my head. "Well, maybe they like me or something, but I never thought of myself as beautiful, even in their eyes."

"Then you are either too modest or too foolish. In either case, you're bound to outgrow it someday. Hopefully, your lack of awareness will not cause you to miss out on anything in the meantime, eh?" He raised his glass towards me, only a little of the whitish liquid left in the bottom of it. "To *naïveté*."

I nodded and leaned back on the bar. "I'll drink to that." I could feel the edges of a strange drunkenness sneaking up on me. The center of my head was starting to slow down, but the edge of my skull, out along the top of my forehead and back around my ears was cool and sharp. I placed a hand to my forehead, and Luca looked over at me. I watched the shadow figures of strangers as they moved along the periphery of the room. The light was fading out around the edges of my eyes, gently transitioning to a rose color, and everything was starting to wobble and float just a little bit.

Luca watched me. "Ah, the Green Fairy," he said, resting a hand on my neck and gently massaging it. "Just relax and let it take its course." I shook my head, unable to comprehend what he meant. His words passed out of my mind quickly. I was too preoccupied with the way I was feeling to think much about anything specific. He seemed to read my mind. "The Green Fairy—it's what they call absinthe."

"I need to go home," I finally managed to say.

Luca shook his head at me and moved the hand on my neck around my shoulders, gathering me to him in a semi embrace. "Home already? When you're just starting to feel a little bit of life?"

"It's not life I'm feeling."

He leaned back and observed me. "Okay, maybe you're right. Let's get you home."

I did not know it, but that night was just the beginning for us.

❖

Luca's Paris was full of light, full of stars that shined at the zinc bars and polished tabletops of nightclubs nestled far back from the banks of the Seine. Starting that evening, he became my guide to the vast expanses of night in that ancient city. My days would remain the property of work, filled with computers and software and all of the dull-grey things we do in this life to make money. But that first night with Luca, I learned how to taste the world.

The next day I woke in my bed, fully clothed except for my shoes. I had no idea how I'd gotten home, or for that matter, how I'd even got my shoes off. For an instant, my heart raced, a small panic building from the pit of my stomach as awareness slowly seeped over me. I lifted my head off the pillow, but a wicked thumping between my eyes made me slow down. I looked around the room and seeing my wallet, phone and keys on the bedside, I relaxed. Next to my wallet and phone was a note and a glass of water. "Fun night. Drink lots of water. See you later, Luca." I lay back down and stayed there, staring at the ceiling and fighting the urge to throw up.

CHAPTER THIRTEEN—ADVENTURES BEGINNING

I stayed in bed for most of that Saturday nursing a cruel hangover. I'd had hangovers before but nothing on that scale. Dealing with the aftermath of an absinthe night was new for me. Not only did my head throb and my stomach ache, but a strange fuzziness enveloped my whole being, a disconnectedness that felt a little like I'd just gotten off a whirly ride at an amusement park. When I finally did wrestle my sore body out of the sweaty sheets, it was because I had to pee so badly I thought my gut was going to burst.

I stared at myself in the bathroom mirror, the dark circles under my eyes telling the story of the night before. I stood there for a few minutes, and then I went back to bed for the rest of the day, finally rising a little after five when I couldn't stand to be in that little bedroom any more. I wearily got myself dressed and left the apartment for a walk. The sun was still high in the sky at that point, and the brightness of the day hurt my eyes.

That afternoon as I walked along the banks of the Seine, the bright granite stone walls bathed in the yellow glow of the late sun, I thought about the evening before with Luca. I kept picturing his eyes, looking out over the crowd. I kept feeling his hand on my shoulder, and I kept thinking about the sour herbal taste the absinthe left in my mouth. Our conversations kept playing in my mind, and I knew he must see the world in a different light than I did. He saw all the colors and objects and shapes making sense in a different way than me. While I only saw how things fit together, he saw things as not having to fit anywhere. To him, what mattered was that there was beauty, that was the symmetry. In my world of technology and engineering, the simplest form of something was always the most elegant. But the same wasn't true for his world.

I walked for miles that afternoon, taking in the sun, watching the way it came to life on the river as the day waned, sparkling and dancing in sheets of tiny glimmering specks. I noticed the couples holding hands, oblivious to the rest of the world, practically bouncing down the sidewalk. I watched the children lined up along the edge of the river with huge chunks of chalk in their hands, drawing on the pavement. I watched the old men fishing off the banks of the river, casting and casting and never catching anything. Their little white buckets stood empty by their sides, full of hope and water and not much else. The fish of Paris were either smart, elusive, or imaginary.

I'm not sure at what point I decided to find a bookstore. At some deeper level, out of sight from the rest of my brain, I needed to learn more about this person who had thrust himself into my life so unexpectedly. I stopped at a Gibert Jeune along the Boulevard Saint-Germain right where it meets the Seine. I stood in front of the giant yellow awnings looking in at the stacks and stacks of new books for only a second before I went in.

I didn't stop to browse. I went directly to the photography section, navigating as best I could with my limited French, and I scanned the spines of the books until I found his name. He was there in force. No fewer than twelve books full of his photographs lined the shelves of the small section. I flipped through each of them, finally settling on one that had a significant amount of text as well as his pictures. I wanted to learn about who he was and what other people had to say about his work. I bought the book and left with it tucked under my arm, not sure what I would get out of it, but absolutely sure that I could not go on not knowing about this person.

I spent all day Sunday reading the book. I forgot about the work I had piled up to do that week. I forgot I had planned to start the week ahead by getting some of that work done on Sunday. I forgot to call home. I forgot Gary had a soccer game that day. I forgot to eat. I sat out on the balcony of my tiny apartment and read the story of Luca Sparks and watched as it unfolded in the small sample of his work that the publisher had included. I looked at the lighting and the colors and the staging in his work. I looked at the commercial pieces and the artistic ones.

I read with wide eyes about his galleries in New York and Chicago. I read about the time he attended a party with Bill and Hillary Clinton and spilled red wine on Hillary's beige dress because he thought the lack of color was unflattering to her. He'd then taken out his camera and snapped dozens of shots of her. The book included both his pictures and some pictures taken by bystanders watching the whole scene unfold. He was probably the only person in the universe who could have gotten away with that. How the Secret Service hadn't dragged him off and locked him up was beyond me.

I finally finished the book as the sun was setting over the rooftops of the city. I set it down on the concrete deck of the balcony and stretched my hands up to the sky. My back ached, and my butt was sore from sitting, but my hangover from the day before was gone, and I was immensely grateful for that. I felt a little like I had spied on a new friend, that by reading this book, I'd somehow deprived Luca of the chance to tell me about himself in his own words. But then again, something told me that the Luca in this book was the public one, the Luca that belonged to the world. The Luca I'd met was a different person. This thought gave me a little relief. If that was indeed the case, Luca still had a lot to tell me about himself.

Monday seeped into being, dragging me slowly back to the Môti offices and to a pile of work that hadn't moved since Friday. It was building blocks for me that morning, a slow focus on the first job of the day followed by the next job and the next and then the one after that, until the time started to have a cadence to it that moved along. By the afternoon, time was passing quickly, almost in a hurry, the way it had before the weekend.

Late in the day, I called Andrea to check in with her and let her know how the project was going. "How is everything back on the West Coast?" I asked, cradling the phone in the crook of my neck as I flipped through print outs of several options for the User Interface

Design. I'd reviewed them all that morning, but I hadn't made up my mind yet which format to go with.

"Well, besides the fact that I can barely move, and I need to pee every three seconds, things are fine."

"When, exactly, are you due?" I was only half-focused on the conversation. "It has to be close now."

"Very, very soon." I could hear her shuffling papers on her desk. "What are you still doing at work?"

"There is just so much to do here," she said.

"You don't want to be at the office when you pop, do you?"

"When I pop?" she laughed. "What, are you twelve?"

We talked for the better part of an hour, catching up on work and everything else that was happening in San Francisco. I continued to drift as I listened to her, glancing through things on my computer and occasionally fiddling with the odd stacks of paper on my desk, when I found myself looking down at a stack of photos. After a couple of seconds, I recognized them as a set of Luca Sparks prints.

"Are you listening to me?"

"Yes," I said. "I think so. I mean, I got a little distracted for a minute by something here."

"What's wrong? You sound different," she said after a few seconds of silence.

"Just now? No, sorry. I just uncovered a few things I was supposed to catalog over the weekend, but I forgot."

"No, not just now. You've sounded weird through this whole conversation."

"Sorry, I guess I'm distracted."

"You should come home for a little while, Ian."

"Jesus, Andrea, for real? I'm over here because you asked me to take this job on, not because I wanted to be here. It's not like I'm on some friggin' holiday." I took a deep breath. The explosion surprised even me. "I'm sorry."

All I heard was silence on the other end of the phone for a few seconds followed by a heavy sigh. I gritted my teeth. "No, I'm the one who should be sorry, Ian. I didn't really think about how hard this would be for you."

"It's okay. I'm fine."

I spread the Luca Sparks photos across my desk with one hand as I waited for her reply. This shoot must have been taken some time in the late 1990s. The model, a guy dressed in dark motorcycle pants with a bright yellow turtleneck, was standing under some high tension wires in front of a black 1960s Lincoln, holding a clamshell cell phone. The model had impossibly high cheekbones and a hungry look in his eyes, and something about his face blended in perfectly with the industrial-desert scene behind him. Yes, I thought, he would be perfect for a cell phone marketing campaign, but this campaign had been for the clothes. I stared at the pictures, the garments blending into the background, as if you'd expect someone standing in the middle of a desert under power lines to be wearing that outfit.

"Are you sure?" Andrea jolted me back to the present.

"Yes, I'm sure. I'll be fine. I'm just behind right now, and it's stressing me out a little."

"And Ellie?"

"She's fine," I lied.

We wrapped up the call talking about business items, timelines, and budget details for the Môti project. We stayed away from anything personal. We finally said our goodbyes and hung up. I sat back in my chair after the phone call, staring up at the chandelier for a few moments.

I looked back down at the photos spread across my desk. This time I noticed the stark beauty of the whole picture—the barren landscape and the sweep of light in the model's eyes. He was just a boy, really. He couldn't have been more than twenty two at the oldest, but Luca had captured something in his face that made him part of that landscape and separate from it at the same time. The vacant look in his eyes was both intimate and distant.

I imagined Luca taking these pictures, and I wondered what he must have done to create this. How had he managed to elicit such beauty out of a background I wouldn't have stopped to look twice at? The combination of light and expression in the boy's face and, I don't know, something more, sparked a sense of curiosity in me that bordered on attraction. That's what I couldn't understand. There was something almost ethereal about his photos that I couldn't put my finger on, and similarly, there was something more about him.

Something changed inside of me that afternoon, sitting alone in that attic storehouse after my phone call with Andrea after everyone else had left for the day. I felt it in the base of my spine, like a circuit breaker flipping, a jolt of decision.

I wanted more of the feeling I got when I looked at that picture, more of the curiosity, more of the overwhelming excitement for life that I felt in Luca. I wanted to experience that great big expanse of life I had glimpsed the weekend before with him. I was sick of phone calls with bosses and files full of code that had to be sorted and photos that needed to be cataloged. I was sick of the unimaginative world that I had just weeks ago found so much order and peace in. It seemed stale and motionless to me now.

It was four thirty. I straightened up my desk, grabbed my keys and wallet, and left the office for the day. I started in the direction of the apartment but veered off down the street Luca had walked me down a week or so ago after our first meeting. I wandered a few blocks, tracing my steps back to the construction site he'd shown me, the house where he was painting the ceiling moldings. On the walk over, all I could think about were our conversations that first day and then again on last Friday night. I kept replaying bits and pieces of the things he'd said. I wanted to know more about him. I wanted to know what about this man had made him give up. I wanted to know what made him lose that drive and never ever want to take another picture like the one with the boy in the desert.

I realized I was out of breath, and I slowed my pace as I approached the street where the construction site was. I looked around, and the buildings were the same as the ones on my street a few blocks over—that is to say they were the same as the homes you see all over this part of Paris, tall stately stone buildings that rise for four, sometimes five floors and then dovetail into a slate or tin Mansard roof resembling the arc of hands pressed together on either side of a bible. Each roof pointed toward the sky with four or five rows of tall French windows, some with small balconies, others with just a rail across for safety.

Suddenly it was right in front of me. One of those homes, like all the rest on that street, but with scaffolding set up above the front door and a worker's van in front of the place. I hadn't thought about what I would say at this point, what I would do. Should I go knock on the door? I didn't know. I felt my lack of planning collapse in front of me. I should have at least thought about what this part would feel like. As it was, I stood there on the street in front of the house, waiting for something to happen and feeling increasingly stupid with each second that ticked slowly by.

Sometimes the world acts in strange ways, though. If you wait for the right moment, things fall into place. As I stood on the sidewalk across the street, staring at the house, Luca walked out the front door. He was dressed differently than when I last saw him, this time in white canvas overalls and a white cap. He looked dusty, even from across the street. He had plaster on his face, and his overalls were stained in places with streaks of different colored paint. He was with another worker dressed exactly the same as he was, and they were chatting rather loudly in French as they left the building. He spotted me immediately as he walked through the front gate and out onto the street, and he looked a little surprised. He squinted his eyes in a double take and slowly waved to me. I waved back. He leaned into to the man beside him and said something I could not hear, but it was punctuated by a loud and friendly *"a tout"* from the other man as he nodded to Luca and looked briefly in my direction before continuing along his way.

Luca smiled at me and crossed the street to where I was standing. *"Ça va?"* he said, just as if he had expected me to be there. "How was your day?" he asked, shoving his hands into the pockets of his overalls.

"Ça va." I returned the greeting, suddenly glad he was so casual and hoping he didn't think I was a little bit crazy for showing up at his work place unannounced. I thought briefly about how out of sorts I would be if someone I'd met a few nights ago showed up at my office. I tried to shrug off the awkward feeling. "I hope it's okay that I stopped by. I thought it would be nice to grab a drink some time, and I didn't know how to get in touch with you, except to stop by here." I could feel myself starting to turn red, a sense of heat rising around my neck, under my collar. But he didn't seem at all put off by my behavior. He just stood there looking at me, the unwavering smile still on his face.

"How about now?" he asked, curling his lips up slightly at the corners of his mouth, in an expression that I couldn't quite decipher.

"Sorry?" I said, caught off guard, not ready for his reply.

"That drink? *Que diriez-vous maintenant?* Is now good? Because I could use a drink now."

"Uh, yes." I swallowed, and the swallow turned into a smile. "If you're sure. I didn't mean to barge in on your afternoon."

"Barge in?" He repeated my words to me. "Is that an Americanism?"

I laughed, aware of his eyes on me. "Yes, I guess it is. It means that I didn't want to interrupt your afternoon if you had other plans."

"But I have no other plans." He put his arm around my shoulder as if we were old friends. "What did I tell you the other night? When a drink shows up, you should always be happy. And for today's lesson, when a friend shows up with that drink, you should be twice as happy, *n'est-ce pas?"*

I couldn't help the sporadic feeling of happiness that seemed to flood my entire body at that moment as I fell into step with him. "We're friends then?" I could feel the heat of his arm across my shoulder.

"Well, you tell me. You're the one showing up at my work." He looked forward, tilting his head and crinkling his nose up into a look of mock concentration. "There are only two types of people that show up at work—clients and friends. I assume you don't have a room you want me to paint. No? In that case, you're not a client. You must be a friend." He chuckled. "Besides, I don't introduce just anyone to Marigold absinthe," he said, referring to our Friday night drinking binge.

"All right." I started to laugh. "It's official. We're friends." Then looking at him, realizing again that he was still in his work clothes. "Do you want to change out of your work clothes?"

"Ah," he said, waving a hand at the idea. "That's not important. But tomorrow I will be prepared. Tomorrow, I will bring a set of play clothes so I will be ready to go out when you come around."

"Tomorrow?" I raised an eyebrow.

"Yes." He shot me a devious look and the sparkle in his eyes seemed to change their shade of blue just a hair. "You will come again tomorrow, no?"

"Yes." I thought for a moment how natural this felt. "I guess I will," I said, and we walked along the street heading in a direction I hadn't yet explored in Paris.

❖

That night we ate at the same small café, Café DeTra, out on the patio underneath the giant chestnut tree. The same set of elegant Parisian waiters looked up and nodded to us as we walked in, and I wondered what they saw working there all day, day after day watching the lives of the regular customers play out in front of them.

"You know," Luca said, noticing how I was watching the waiters as we sat down. "These four are all part of the same family."

"The waiters? I figured."

"Notice how the work is never divided up equally among them? That's because it's all based on hierarchy." He pointed to the youngest one, the one who waited on us last time. "That's Raymond. Nine times out of ten when we come in, he will wait on us. Mark my words. He's the youngest, not more than nineteen or twenty at the most, and he is the lowest man on the team. His *patron*, the old guy sitting at the bar with the two older waiters, is actually his father, and his name is Gerard." The older man Luca pointed to had some considerable heft to him. A pair of dark eyes stared out at the world from underneath a neatly trimmed head of white hair. "He's there, in that same corner of the bar at all hours of the day, and he's always got a half-full glass of something—always at exactly the same level. In the morning, it's espresso. In the evening, it's red wine.

"The other waiters, they're Raymond's older brothers. The family owns this place. Has for generations." He lowered his voice and leaned in to me. "The brothers are almost always standing on either side of the old man, looking as if they had just bitten into a piece of bad fish. They're not particularly nice men. Before Raymond started at the restaurant, they had to do all the work. Now they just sit there most of the time, moving their way up the family ladder by waiting for the old man to die. If you ask me, neither has much ambition beyond that immediate corner of the restaurant."

I looked at the four of them: the three sitting at the bar and Raymond running the tables and taking orders from behind the bar. He had the same dark complexion and brown eyes as the other three, but he was still in his youth and everything about him had a shine or a snap to it.

"Occasionally," Luca continued, "if the place gets especially busy, which happens from time to time at dinner and sometimes right after work, the two older brothers start helping out behind the bar or with some of the tables. But that's all. Never more than they have to." He shrugged.

That was only the second night I'd ever been to Café DeTra, and it was all still a marvel of color and sound to me. Watching them was like watching an elaborately choreographed musical number; only without an orchestra. The music was just the hums and whispers of the crowd against the percussive banging of dishes, and a television playing French music videos far off in the distance of the kitchen. I sat opposite Luca and wondered why I felt so easily at home in this place.

"So, Luca," I asked after Raymond had, without bothering to ask us if we wanted it, brought us a bottle of the same pink wine we'd had the time before. "You mentioned something the other day about your first camera. You said you'd tell me about it some day?"

He took a sip of his wine. "I found it by accident deep in the south of France where I grew up." He raised his eyebrows and opened his arms in an expression of mock drama. "And that is how it all began."

I laughed at his theatrics. "Well, tell me about it. Seriously, what was it like? Did you have an instant attraction to the camera, or did it take you a while to figure out what to do with it?"

He looked directly at me for a moment as if evaluating something. Finally he took a sip of his wine and nodded his head. "You want to know about me, huh? About how things all started? Well, okay." He put down his glass of wine. "I think I might have mentioned that my father's farm was part of a small village outside of Avignon, a collection of sun-baked brick and mortar buildings probably as old as the Earth itself, but no one knows for sure." He stopped. Something about his own words had jolted him, and he looked at me differently then, as if gauging something about my intent. "I don't want this to be some sort of interview. It's not, is it?"

"What?" I shook my head, surprised to feel a little bit hurt. "No." His arm was resting on the table, and I found myself reaching over and touching it gently for just a second before I realized what I was doing and pulled my hand back. "I just want to know a little bit more about you. But if you don't want to talk about growing up, that's okay. We can talk about something else."

"No." He stared at me and then his face softened. "I'm sorry. I've just been asked that question so many times by people who didn't care what the answer was. I should have known you wouldn't have asked like that."

He took a breath. "My village," he eventually continued, "was a place for forgetting."

I looked at him but said nothing.

"It's hard to understand, but the people in my village just couldn't remember things. At least that's what it felt like when I was a child. I always wanted to know things about the past. Not big things, just little everyday things, like had the church always been that color? When had the olive trees been small and who had planted them? Who built the little bakery in the center of the village? Some children ask why the sky is blue or how come birds can fly, but I was obsessed with knowing what things had been like before my time."

"You were just inquisitive," I said.

"Yes, that's the right word. I was inquisitive, so much so that I became something of a village nuisance. The more I asked about the past, the less anyone wanted to speak to me. They would just wave and tell me that things were the way they had always been, and that I should get back to my chores." He laughed at himself. "Well, that was just so strange for me. Every day things seemed different to me. The sheep were in a different part of the field, the olives were further along on the trees, the wind had changed direction. In my eyes, everything was new each day when I rolled out of bed. How could these people think everything was the same today as it had always been? Didn't they have eyes and ears?

"In my young head, I made up elaborate explanations for this. I imagined maybe it was some sort of collective guilt about the Second

World War or something deeper in our little past. Maybe it had to do with the Avignon Popes. But in the end it was just me, a small child wondering why the rest of the world didn't share my sense of curiosity about things." He took another sip of wine. "Anyway, that became part of what made me want to take pictures so badly in the first place. You can't forget something if there's a picture to remind you, or so I thought at the time.

"My parents' house was a few kilometers outside the little village down an unpaved road that ran through some old olive groves and lavender fields. I used to like to take pictures of the olive trees. They were so squat, and their branches were tangled on themselves, and I loved the way the light played on the leaves and shined—that *is* how you say it right, shined? It's a weird word in English." I nodded, anxious for him to continue the story. "I loved the way the sun shined through the gnarled branches of the olive trees. The light was good there, especially just at dawn. I would lie down on my back with my little camera and take pictures looking straight up through the branches. And that was kind of hard to do because my camera at the time was a Brownie."

"A Brownie?" I hated to interrupt him, but I'd never heard that name before.

He chuckled at me, which made me feel just a little self-conscious. I shifted in my seat and took another sip of the wine, trying not to let anything show on my face. But he reached over and patted my arm briefly before he continued. "The Brownie, yes, it's an American camera from Kodak. They made millions of them from around 1900 all the way through the 1960s. It was a very good little camera, just a little black box really. If you've never seen a Brownie, it's about eight centimeters by ten centimeters by ten centimeters. They were matte black with silver lining on the edges—the earlier ones were. Later, they got more streamlined. Mine was almost new when I found it in my father's shop. It still had some of the yellow Kodak paper clinging to the sides of it."

"I thought your father was a farmer?"

"Ah, yes," he nodded. "In his workshop, in the barn. It was just up above his workbench, perched there on a small shelf waiting for someone to find it. I was sitting with him one day watching him fix something on a mower blade. I was around five years old or so, and he had flown into a rage earlier that day when he hit an olive stump with his lawn mower. It was the first time I had heard any English words. My father used to swear only in English. He told me later that was because he didn't want us to know what he was saying when he was upset. But the only words he knew in English were the bad words, and I think he said them in English because, well, honestly, because the swear words, they just sound better in your language." He winked at me.

I smiled back and nodded in agreement. "You've got something there. Cussing in English is a lot more emphatic than in French. It must be why Americans are always running around upset," I added. "But the Brownie?" I asked, trying to get him back on track with the story.

"Yes, the Brownie." I couldn't tell if he had forgotten his place in the story or if he was just glad that I really wanted to hear more. "Well, as I said, I had spotted this little black box on the shelf above my father's bench and I asked my father, 'Papa, *qu'est-ce c'est ca'*? He looked up from his mower blade, this giant man with his big, greasy, callused hands. 'You see everything, eh Luca'? he said, smiling down at me."

Luca's face transformed as he told the story, his pale eyes shining and his own mouth stretching out into a generous expression of joy at the memory of his father. Those eyes, that face, so emphatically from a different part of France or maybe Europe altogether, but definitely not the olive skin and brown eyes typical of southern France. I pictured those eyes as a little boy, peering up at that camera on the shelf above him.

"'Is it part of the lawn mower'? I asked my Papa." Luca continued, laughing at himself this time. "My Papa just smiled at me and shook his head. He told me that no, it wasn't part of the lawn mower, it was this thing called a camera. You can laugh," he said, pointing his glass at me and taking another sip. "It's funny, I know, but I was just a five-year-old farm boy, and I had no idea what a camera was or why you would need one. Yes, we had a few photographs in our home, but they were always of old people sitting very still.

"Well, my father, he pulled the camera down, and he showed it to me, popping the top of it open…" He stopped for a second, searching my face to see if I was following him. "You see, on the early Brownies, you would pop open the top of the camera and look down into the box to see the picture you were taking, like this," he made an open box with his hands to demonstrate.

"There was no adjustable lens until later. So my father, he showed me how to work the camera. There wasn't much to it. They were set to a certain focus. I think it was about eight feet. It was American, so of course everything was in feet and inches, which makes no sense at all to me." He waved away the American measurement system with his hand. "And the aperture was not adjustable, either. But those little cameras took pretty good pictures, all things considered. Of course, as soon as my papa showed me how to use the camera, I couldn't put it down. Imagine my delight a couple weeks later when he and my Maman finally broke down and bought me some film for it, eh? Then there was no getting my attention away from that little black box." He paused. His eyes were somewhere else, remembering, I guessed, the little boy he used to be, running around with his camera and capturing the world one snapshot at a time.

He didn't seem to want to go on much after that, so we finished the meal mostly in silence. He asked me a couple of questions about my home to try and bring the conversation back to life, but he seemed to lose focus when I answered. I left him after we finished. He wanted to stay at the bar for a while longer, but I had work to finish up. We agreed I would stop by on my way home from work again the next day, just to say hello, and I headed back to my apartment.

CHAPTER FOURTEEN—THE FIRST PAPARAZZI

The next day, I arrived at work to find a print out on my desk. It was from the *Runway Confidential* blog. Someone had taken the liberty of translating it into English for me. It read:

"Spotted: Luca Sparks snacking at Café DeTra—with a new friend. The famous photog, who hasn't taken a photo since he abandoned the business years ago, has been laying low for a little while. But tonight, he was out on the town in what looked to be painter's overalls. A new fashion statement? Come on Luca, why are you teasing us? Pretty soon, all the princes of Paris will be out and about in carpenter's smocks."

I re-read the post two or three times trying to figure out how someone would know I was the one out with him. I finally figured that someone from Môti must have been at the café and seen us there together. Alfonse, perhaps. I folded the print out several times and set it in the trash.

After that evening, I saw Luca more and more often. We started to go out almost every night. During the middle of the work day, I'd find myself looking at a photograph or digging through a shelf of garments in the Môti attic, and some color or smell would set off a memory. I'd start replaying a conversation from the night before in my head. Most days, by the middle of the afternoon I found myself wondering about what might be in store for that evening. What wild bar or nightclub, what insanely beautiful view of the city, what intense conversation would consume us that night? At those points,

I was almost unable to concentrate on my work. But then I would reel myself back in and force myself to focus.

Four thirty or five o'clock would roll around, and I would feel so confined in that attic space that I just had to get out. I'd grab my phone and my wallet and head over to the construction site at pretty much the same time. He sometimes brought his play clothes, as he liked to call them, and he would change in the back hall of his work place. And we would go sit in one of those casually elegant sidewalk cafes along the small side streets of the Saint-Germain-des-Prés, or we might occasionally wander off to the Marais or maybe the 11th arrondissement, where there were several cheaper, rowdier bars.

On those nights, we were younger than our years. We would consume huge amounts of cheap liquor, and we would move away from the safety of wine and drink cognac and whiskey and sometimes even martinis if we were feeling particularly extroverted. We also moved away from the safety of wine conversation to the depth of whiskey and martini talk, subjects like life and death and love.

At first I was surprised with how young I had become in so short a time. Night after night of outlandish adventure can be an aphrodisiac, even in the most platonic way. Life had gone from a series of computer screens, soccer games, and nights full of quiet arguments over the dishwasher, to a flood of colorful bars peopled with beautiful Parisian women and loud music.

"What do you think happens when you die?" he asked me on one of those lost nights. We were sitting at a dive bar on the edge of the 11th arrondissement that had become one of the most popular places in Paris that summer. It was packed, and we were wedged in together at the end of the bar, scrunched up against an ancient American jukebox full of Edie Piaf and Chris Isaak songs. The floor was sticky, and the bar was so narrow we barely had enough room for our drinks.

"I don't know." I watched his face, looking for more meaning behind the question. "I've never spent much time thinking about it."

"Ah," he laughed. "For you, it's just the end of the program, right? You just finish up with some final line of computer code, and then that's it. All done, huh?"

"No." I felt a little stung by his suggestion that I was too shallow to contemplate my own death. "I just think it's a little bit morbid."

"It's not morbid." He was playing with a white paperboard coaster on the bar, tearing it to shreds. "It's part of the cycle of life. I just wonder if we get the chance to see all of it together, from a distance. Do we get a few seconds to reflect on how our whole life fit together, before we're whisked off into heaven or hell or the next life, whatever you believe in?"

I nodded, buying myself time to think and letting my mind drift in the soft glow of the whiskey. We were never particularly careful with our conversation, and I think that's one of the things I loved about Luca. We talked about anything and everything, and I never knew where the subject was going to go. It undoubtedly included elements of the fantastic and elements that were strangely boring. Our words would flow with such ease from one extreme to the other. We just didn't know where or how a particular talk would lead us. "I think it depends on the circumstance," I finally said.

"Eh?"

"Yeah." I finished my glass of whiskey and beckoned the bartender to bring us two more. "*Avec des glaçons, s'il vous plait.*" I turned back to Luca. "I think that some people go so fast, they don't have the chance to see it all. Others are so focused on dying, they can't see their life. I bet only a few get the chance to see things in the bigger picture on their way out."

"Hmph." He looked at me, his eyes boring deep into mine, as if trying to see something in the back of my skull. "And do you think you'll be one of those who sees the bigger picture?"

I was very glad the whiskey and ice came in that instant. Otherwise, I might have been compelled to think longer before I responded to him. But I simply picked up my glass and took a swallow before saying, "Only time will tell, Luca. Only time will tell."

Looking back over that period in my life, I'm always surprised to realize how short a time it was. In total, it couldn't have been more than five or six weeks we spent carousing out at the bars and cafes of Paris, but it felt like years and I remember it like it was an eternity, an unending field of ambivalence. Occasionally, I would start to worry I was spending too much time out and I would be tired and hung over the next day at work. Luca would smile at me and say, "come on, live it up, Ianto. You might as well experience all those things you are turning into ones and zeros for Môti!"

He was right. The fashions and the photographs we were archiving for Môti were all about beautiful people having fun in beautiful places. It was a cycle of emotions for me. At points along the way, I stopped and thought about how lucky I was to be out in such a beautiful city, laughing and experiencing life like this. But then the feeling would fade. That's when the first seeds of guilt began to slowly sew themselves deep under my skin. I'd worry about something at work or my family or something else until Luca ordered another drink, and we would start talking again and that worry would ebb temporarily.

Night after night of careless drinks and passionate conversation can be food for the soul, or it can begin to be something else. Those nights can become a seam ripper slowly clipping apart your life, thread by thread, until you feel your very fabric coming undone. But this takes time. It doesn't happen right away. At least it didn't for me.

And the arguments. Luca and I would fight over anything. Our discussions were frantic and passionate. They would often end with both of us throwing our hands in the air and threatening to strangle each other before collapsing into a set of high fives, or, on our more drunken nights, fraternal bear hugs. That was the nature of our relationship. I can only speak for myself, but it felt as if we had both found someone to be passionate with rather than something to be passionate about. I realized during those nights I had never really gotten into a heated, truly heart-bound conversation with anyone before—the kind that start at seven in the evening and go on for hours, until you look up and it's almost daybreak.

After a few weeks, Luca started making it a habit to come over on the weekends to collect me for a night out somewhere. He never called ahead of time. I don't think he even had my number. He just dropped in, picked me up, and off we went. So I wasn't surprised to hear his familiar step on the stairs followed by his voice one Saturday evening.

"Ianto," he yelled from out in the hall, before he even got to the landing. "Get dressed." He rushed through the door of my apartment without bothering to knock, a bluster of breath and sound. He knew I always left it unlocked when I was there. And I was there, sitting on the faux-leather IKEA couch, iPad firmly cradled in my lap, trying to get through some reports I hadn't managed to finish the previous week.

He spotted the iPad the minute he stepped into the room. "You're working, aren't you?"

"Just going through some red tape," I said, putting the tablet aside but not bothering to get up.

"It's Saturday, what are you doing working?"

At that moment, he finally stopped moving and stood still long enough for me to notice him. Gone was the casual Parisian hipster, aging out of coolness. Gone were the stylish jeans and the loose button-down shirt he usually wore. They had been replaced with a black Armani suit, and a tight, shiny pin-striped shirt underneath. His hair was slicked back in a mound of gel, and the barbs of his typical five o'clock shadow had been neatly trimmed along a fiercely masculine jaw line. In his hand he held a garment bag, which he promptly set down on the couch next to me.

"What happened to you?" I asked, still not moving.

"I want to see a show tonight."

"Oh." I swallowed and looked at the garment bag. "Are you leaving that here?"

"No." He let out a loud sigh. "I figured you might not have a suit, so I picked something up for you."

"A suit?" I unzipped the bag a couple of inches, just enough to see the dark fabric inside. "I take it that means I'm going with you?"

"Yes, you're going with me." He moved the bag over and made room for himself to sit down next to me. "Michelle is in town, and she's asked me to go to her show tonight."

"Who's Michelle?"

"Stop asking questions and go get dressed." He pushed me up off the couch. "The runway show starts in a couple of hours, and I want to get there a little early so we can go backstage."

"Okay." I reluctantly rose and picked up the garment bag, carrying it with me to the bedroom, where I dropped it on the bed. I stared down at the bag for a few seconds, a mix of feelings filling my head as I stood there. No one had ever brought me something to wear before.

I slowly pulled off the tee shirt I'd been wearing for most of the day, noticing the small coffee stain on the front of it for the first time. I unzipped the garment bag all the way and pulled out a black Môti men's suit. Set inside it was a glistening white shirt of the same brand. I recognized both garments from the video displays in the Môti lobby. They were this year's line, and they wouldn't be on sale in most stores for another month or so. "Luca, where did you get this?"

"I picked it up today. I'm pretty sure it's your size."

"Picked it up where?"

"Again, you with the questions." He sounded exasperated. "Stop asking so much. Just put it on and get washed up. Don't forget to put some gel in your hair."

"Gel?"

"I put some in the side pocket of the bag for you."

I turned the garment bag over and unzipped the side pocket. Sure enough, just inside was a small toiletries kit with hair gel, cologne and a couple bottles of assorted lotions. "What's all this other stuff?"

"It's for your face. I'll show you when you're done getting dressed."

I pulled on the shirt and buttoned it. It was exactly my size, tailored to a perfect fit. The pants and the jacket were the same—cut as if they were made for me. "Luca, I don't know about this."

"I know you don't. That's why I brought it for you. You work for Môti now. You can't go to a runway show wearing some tee shirt. It would be like spitting in their face." I heard his footsteps crossing the short distance from the couch to the bedroom door, which was already slightly ajar. He pushed it fully open. "It looks good on you." He walked over to me and adjusted the collar of the shirt. "There." He patted down the breast of the jacket. "Now the gels?" he asked, laying a hand out flat in front of me.

I grabbed the toiletries kit off of the bed and placed it in his hand. He unscrewed the top of one of the jars and bumped a little bit of the white creamy liquid into his hand, then placed the bottle back in the kit and laid it on the bed. Before I knew what was going on, he worked his hands together, and then he rubbed the stuff onto my forehead and cheeks. "Stop making that expression," he said. "This will give you a matte face. Photographers will be there. You don't want to be greasy."

"What is it?" I asked as he massaged my face.

"It doesn't matter what it is, just stay still."

So I did. I stood still for several minutes while he worked a series of different creams into my face and my hair, remaking me into something I didn't understand. When he finished, he stood back and looked at me and after a few seconds, finally nodded in approval. "*Voilà.*" He gestured for me to look at myself in the mirror. What I saw shocked me. There stood someone with my likeness who looked about ten years younger than me. The suit not only fit, but through some black magic trick, it gave me a perfect chest and broad shoulders. It slimmed at the waist, tapering in to give me a Superman stance that resembled some action hero movie star, not me. Whatever creams and goops Luca had rubbed into my face and hair had done their own magic. I looked scrubbed and polished in a way I had never imagined possible.

"Perfect, eh?" He beamed with pride at what he'd made out of me. His words drew me out of my stare, and I looked at him. His eyes held mine for just a few seconds before he quickly looked away.

"Uh…" I searched for words. "Yeah, perfect." I finally broke the stare and glanced down at my naked feet.

"The shoes are in the bottom of the bag. I trust you have socks?"

I was almost embarrassed to answer him. "Not Môti socks."

He laughed. "Hopefully no one will see your socks tonight."

I sat down on the edge of the bed and put on a pair of socks and the shoes he had brought, while he wandered over to the balcony and looked out over the rooftops. The late afternoon light was starting to wane, turning everything to gold the way it did in the summer.

"So who is Michelle?" I asked again as I tied my shoes.

"Michelle Matthews."

"Oh." I grimaced, recognizing the name of one of Môti's most popular models. I'd cataloged several of her shoots over the past few weeks. I gave Luca my best 'I should have expected that' face.

"I used to shoot her a lot." He wandered back into the room and sat down next to me on the bed. "She's been through a bit of a rough patch lately, lots of tabloid stuff, but she's a good friend."

"Anything I should know before we go?" I said, finishing my shoelaces and sitting back up on the bed. I could feel the warmth of him sitting next to me.

"Like what?"

"I don't know, like what to say, what not to say. Is there anyone I should avoid? You know, I assume this is wing man duty."

"Wing man duty?" He looked at me and scrunched his eyebrows together. "What is wing man duty?"

"I, ah…" I was at a loss for words. I'd never thought about how to explain the concept of a wing man. "I guess it's when you go somewhere with a friend, and you are expected to help them out."

"Help me out?" He still didn't understand.

"You know," I nodded my head. "Make you look good…to Michelle. …And the other women there… You know, help you get…social."

He was silent.

"Laid, Luca. Help you get laid. A wing man goes with you, makes you look good, talks to the women you don't want to talk to so you can talk to the ones you do want to talk to."

"Ah," his head went back in almost jovial laughter. "Ah, okay, okay, okay. Now I understand. No, Ianto." He shook his head and put a hand on my knee in an almost paternal gesture. "I don't need a wing man, but thank you. That is a very nice thing to offer." His eyes seemed full of mirth. I could feel the grip of his hand on my knee, and I was just a little uncomfortable. I didn't understand what was so funny or what had prompted the gesture of his hand on my knee. Thankfully he stood up after a couple of seconds and walked back towards the door. "No, I think this will just be fun tonight. I think you will like seeing the other side of the industry, too." He turned and looked back at me. I was still sitting on the bed. "We should go now. We'll grab a drink on the way and get there early to visit backstage."

I nodded and slowly rose, following him back to the living room and gathering my wallet and keys before we headed out for the evening.

Luca had hired a car service that night. I tried to hide my surprise at the car sitting in front of the door to my building. In fact, I walked right by it, headed to the subway, when Luca cleared his throat, and I looked back to see the driver opening the rear curbside door for Luca. I shot Luca a questioning glance, confused for a moment.

"It's hot out," Luca answered the look on my face as he motioned with an outstretched hand for me to get into the car. "We don't want to sweat in these suits and arrive with giant armpit stains."

"I thought you said you wanted to get a drink on the way?"

"There are drinks in the car," he smiled at me.

I shrugged and murmured a brief, "Okay, sounds good," as I climbed in and sank back in the air-conditioned coolness and black leather seats of the sedan. We rode in silence in the back of the giant Citroen, through the small neighborhoods stretching from my apartment to a huge tent set up on the lawn in front of the Eiffel Tower. It would have taken us no time at all to walk or take the subway, but Luca was right, we would have been sweating. He flipped open a small cabinet in between the seats and pulled out a glass bottle of what looked like scotch. He poured two glasses and handed one to me. We drank in silence and I watched the buildings whiz gently by as the car maneuvered down the Boulevard Saint-Germain.

"Um, Ianto," he said as we neared the giant tent, the Citroen slowing to a crawl behind a long line of cars. "There may be a few photographers when we get out. Just ignore them. Don't wave or acknowledge them at all."

"What do you mean, like *paparazzi?* Where are you taking me Luca?"

"It's nothing, really. But this is kind of a big show here in Paris. It's for a benefit, so they've gotten a lot of the press here. Don't worry, though. They're nice to me, and they won't get pushy. Just don't talk to them or wave or anything, and don't answer any questions they ask. Okay?"

I nodded and stared out the window as the Citroen pushed closer to the front of the tent. I began to notice the flashes, and I could now hear the noise of the crowd through the blacked out, insulated windows of the car. My skin began to tingle as we approached the entrance, and my stomach started to grumble. An hour or so ago, I was sitting at home on my couch, thinking about maybe going to a bar or grabbing a small supper out on the street cafes of the Saint Germain. Now, in an unexpected twist, I was headed to what was increasingly looking like a celebrity event.

We finally stepped out of the car into a sea of camera flashes. I crawled out of the back seat first, standing up among the noise and the cameras, dazed at what was happening to me, lost for a second until Luca stood up behind me and put his hand on my shoulder.

"I'm sorry about this," he whispered into my ear. "I should have warned you more clearly about this part. There's really no way around it."

"It's all right," I whispered back to him. "It's just that I never think about you as famous."

He smiled at me. "I'm not famous. This is for everyone else's fun, not mine."

I wasn't sure what he meant, but I didn't have time to ask him anything about it. He had gone from an easy grip on my shoulder to steering me towards the front of the tent. "Let's get moving," he said. "They've already got enough pictures of us."

But as we began to move toward the door, the shouting got louder. Unintelligible questions erupted from all corners of the crowd. Mostly they were in French with a few in broken English, but I couldn't really make anything out. Luca pushed me onward, moving a little faster as the shouting continued.

"What are they asking?"

"Nothing, just stupid press questions. Ignore them."

The inside of the tent was plastered in the blue, white, and red of the French flag. Toward the back of the room, a long raised runway draped in white satin ran between rows of tiered seats covered all in black fabric. Lamps shaped like huge glass tubes hung from the canvas ceiling, and little groups of bar tables were clustered around the front of the tent with an already-crowded bar off to each side. I was still a little unsure what benefit this was actually for. I just knew hundreds of people were decked out to the nines in dark suits and sparkling dresses. They stood around in little klatches drinking cocktails and wine and beer. I looked back at Luca, hoping for some guidance, but he was busy, scanning the room.

"Let's head back stage." He gently guided me toward the back of the room. As we moved, I spied the runway, a long raised platform in the middle of hundreds of folding chairs.

"Where are we sitting?" I asked, mostly because I didn't know what else to say.

He shook his head and ignored my question. "I'll show you later. But right now, I want to find Michelle." He dropped his hand from my shoulder, and we ducked behind a couple of curtains, and the scene changed. Gone were the socialites milling about with martini glasses. Here we were in the center of a frenzy of backstage activity. Racks of clothing, naked models mid-change, starkly pale stage managers dressed all in black with headphones draped over mops of dark shaggy hair. I glanced over at Luca, and he was looking around searching for something.

"Luca!" a woman's voice called from somewhere out of sight. We both turned at the same time. A couple of clothing racks gave way to reveal a woman in a bathrobe, practically tied into a high chair with an army of people working on her hair and makeup.

"Michelle!" Luca shouted her name and headed over to the chair.

Michelle tried to remain expressionless for the makeup artist, but I could tell she was excited to see him. Little by little she gave into that excitement and her somber, placid face gave way to raised eyebrows and deep-set dimples that made her look much more beautiful than she ever did in photos. The makeup lady stood back grumpily and frowned at her. Luca grabbed the arm of my sleeve and dragged me over to the chair with him.

"Air kiss," she said when we arrived.

Luca leaned down amid the hair and makeup bees and kissed her just above the surface of her cheeks, once on either side.

They started chatting immediately, but I couldn't focus on them. I was drawn to everything happening around me. I watched, mesmerized as people ran around shouting and crying, carrying hordes of dresses and skirts and shirts, and boxes of makeup and shoes. Everywhere I looked, I saw cyclones of colorful fabric and emaciated models.

"This is my friend Ianto," Luca said, pulling on my sleeve again and pulling me into the circle of hair and makeup. "He is fixing Môti up with computers for their archive of garments."

"Hiya," she said, a slight East End London accent tinting her voice.

"Nice to meet you," I replied and reached out to shake her hand.

She looked at me and giggled, a slight breath of a laugh, almost a whisper in the center of all the chaos around us. "A gentleman." She gave me a look that was at once charming and embarrassing, and I was instantly self-conscious. She paused for just a second before she reached up and took my hand, forcing a hair stylist to step aside. "It's very nice to meet you. Luca says you're brilliant."

I could feel myself turning red. "Well, I don't know about that."

"Don't be shy, darling. If you're brilliant, be brilliant. There's no time in this life for shy." She looked back to Luca for a second before the stylist pounced back into position over her bangs. "Isn't that right, Luca? I seem to remember some famous photographer telling me that on my first shoot."

"Was that your first shoot?" Luca shrugged.

"Yes, it was. And you were right. There is no time for shy."

Luca nodded briefly before being cut off from her by another hairdresser. In the brief moment Luca's view was blocked, Michelle looked directly at me and winked. My face went blank, and I turned around to look behind me, thinking she must be winking at someone else, but nobody in the army of hairdressers and makeup artists was making eye contact with Michelle. When I looked back at her, she frowned, but only for an instant. As the hairdresser moved out from between her and Luca, her face lit up again and she flashed a brilliant white-toothed smile at Luca.

"Luca, be a love and go and grab me a Diet Coke and vodka, will you? Not too much vodka, just a little. You know how I like it." She pushed away a powder-brushed assistant who was attempting to dust her face. "My nerves are a little on edge."

Luca hesitated for only a second, looking over at me as if to ask if I would be okay on my own. Michelle noticed his glance. "Go. He'll be fine. I'll look after him. I promise. Besides, what's the worst that could happen? You'll come back, and they'll have put some eye shadow on him by accident. It wouldn't be the end of the world."

He looked over at me again.

"Luca." She reached out and slapped his leg gently. "Vodka please. Now." She smiled up at him again.

"Okay, I'll be right back," he said, leaning down and quickly kissing her on the cheek.

As soon as he walked away, she leaned over towards me. "So, what's going on with him?"

"Sorry?" I said, a little surprised at the question. "I'm not sure I understand what you mean?"

"What's going on, you know?" She waved a hand in a giant circle in the air. "What's he doing? Why is he ignoring everyone else in his life these days?"

"Going on?" It felt as if she was accusing me of something, maybe stealing all of Luca's focus.

"Well, I've been away, so I wouldn't know, myself. I've been on a shoot in London and before that, Hong Kong." She paused for one of the makeup artists, a short, slightly overweight woman with glitter on her face, to apply a new layer of lip-gloss. "But all I've heard since I landed is how Luca has disappeared out of sight. Nobody has seen him in weeks. He hasn't been to any parties. He doesn't answer his friends' texts. What has he been doing?"

"Um." I paused, trying to figure out exactly what she was asking. "I'm not sure I know what you mean. I think he works during the day and then at night we go out, sometimes to dinner but mostly to different bars and clubs."

"Hmph." She looked at me, her eyes traveling from my head to my toes and back again. "You go out? As in, just the two of you?"

"Yeah," I swallowed, feeling as if I might somehow be telling on Luca, although I couldn't imagine why anything I was saying would be confidential. "I don't really know anyone in Paris."

"Yes, darling, but you see, Luca does. He knows tons and tons of people. He's one of the most famous photographers in all of France. And for the past few weeks, he has dropped almost completely out of sight. Until tonight, that is. He shows up here with you on his arm."

I coughed loudly at her words and looked around self-consciously. "I'm not exactly 'on his arm,'" I said.

"Really?" She tilted her head slightly in what could only be mock curiosity.

"Yes, really."

"You were invited to this show?" She closed her eyes as the makeup artist dusted each lid with a pink and red powder.

"Well, no." I stumbled over my words. "I guess he wanted to come to see you and he asked me to go with him."

"Uh, huh." She leaned her head farther back as the makeup woman continued to dust her lids. "And that Môti tux that you're wearing, the one that doesn't hit the racks for another two months, that's yours? You just happened to come across it somewhere? Perhaps on eBay?"

"In case you forgot, I work at Môti." I stepped back and turned slightly so I was half looking away from her.

"Don't get defensive, love." The makeup lady finished her eyes, and Michelle opened them and blinked a few times as she adjusted to look at me straight on again. "I think it's wonderful that he's found a new friend. It's just a little unusual for him, that's all. He doesn't usually..." She hesitated.

"Doesn't what?" I asked.

"Well, honestly, he doesn't usually like other…"

I leaned forward and opened my hands in a broad, questioning gesture, encouraging her to complete her sentence.

"People," she said softly. "He doesn't usually like other people. As friends."

"Uh-huh," I said, matching her volume and tone of voice. I wanted to say more, ask more. I wanted to know what she was so carefully trying to figure out. But Luca had suddenly reappeared from behind the curtain, carrying with him a tall glass of Diet Coke and Vodka.

"Sorry it took me so long. Those lines are crazy at the bar," he said, handing the glass to Michelle. She took it from him, holding it in her hand for a few seconds before taking a small sip of the bubbly liquid.

"Thank you, Luca. You're the best."

He leaned in and kissed her. As he did, she seemed to notice something about him. She squinted her eyes just a little bit. "Luca?" she said.

"What now, dear Michelle?"

"Nothing, love. I was just wondering if you might have a cigarette I could steal?"

"Um, no, actually." He looked up at me quickly before looking away, then down at Michelle again. "Sorry."

"Oh." She made a fake pouty face. "You always have smokes, and I could kill for one right now. It's so unlike you to be out."

"I, um, I actually quit." He rolled his weight up onto the balls of his feet, then back again. I probably wouldn't have noticed that move on anyone else, but it was a nervous move and it was so uncharacteristic of Luca to be nervous.

"Really?" She looked directly at me, then back at him. "How long ago did you quit?" But before he could answer, she waved a hand in the air. "No, let me guess, it's been a few weeks or so." Then, turning to me. "Ianto."

"It's Ian, actually."

"Right, it's Ian, except for Luca. For Luca, it's Ianto. Got it." She rolled her eyes. "I don't expect you have a cigarette? No, you wouldn't, would you? Because you don't smoke." She looked back at Luca for a moment then back to me. "Funny how some things just happen to turn out, isn't it?"

At that moment, I couldn't take my eyes off her. She had such an intent look on her face. I felt like a teenager who had just gotten caught sneaking in after curfew, but I couldn't figure out why. She was right. Luca had smoked incessantly the first time I met him, but never again. I don't know why I hadn't noticed it before.

"Indeed." Luca smiled tightly at her. "I've always said you're nothing if not observant."

"No," she corrected him. "You always say there's no time in life for being shy."

"Well," Luca stepped back out of the way of the makeup team, giving them room to work on her. "We really should let you get ready."

"Sounds good, love. See you after the show."

And with that, we were off, back behind the curtain and into the throngs of people searching for their seats. I noticed a few of the designers I recognized from work, but no one I knew well enough to say hello to. I thought that maybe, for a brief second, I'd seen Alfonse out of the corner of my eye. But when I turned to look at him full on, he was gone. We eventually found our seats, clearly marked with Luca's last name.

Later that night after the runway show, I stood by Luca's side watching what seemed like thousands of handshakes and air kisses. Cameras flashed as he leaned in time after time to smile and say hello to people. They crowded around him and pushed each other out of the way, each reluctant to make room for the next.

It was as if everyone in Paris either wanted to meet Luca or wanted to know where he had been lately. I stayed a step behind him, largely ignored by the rush of the crowd. Occasionally someone would glance over at me for an instant and say a very brief hello, reluctant to shorten their moment with Luca. A few times Luca introduced me, saying only that I was on the Môti team. People would politely nod and say a few words to me in French, to which I responded with a series of bewildered but polite hellos and instantly forgot their names.

But Luca was as eager to get away from the handshakes and kisses as I was, and we made our way backstage as soon as we could, slipping out through an open flap in the back of the giant tent. As we stepped out together into the warm summer air, we both exhaled giant sighs of relief at the same time. I looked over at him, giving him my best 'what the hell was that?' face and we both started to laugh.

"I'm sorry about that," he said. "I forgot how intense these things can be."

I nodded, still a little overwhelmed by the experience. "I've never been mobbed by a crowd of fashionistas before," I said. "It's kind of crazy."

"Come on," he said, shaking his head and putting his arm around my shoulder. He pulled me toward him as if we were soldiers just emerging from battle. I could hear the wind through the chestnut trees lining the park and the noise of the traffic, but it was almost soothing compared to the chaos of the fashion show. We began to walk in step across the damp lawn of the park, and he directed us away from the tent. "The night isn't over yet. There are still the after parties."

"Oh, no." I shook my head. "I'm done with the crowds. You go. I can get myself home."

"No, no, no." He shook his head. "Ianto, remember what I said about living a little. Besides." He squeezed my shoulder. "I'll take you to the good after party, it will be nice. Maybe even a little quiet."

"Uh-huh." I didn't believe him. "Do I get to be in the receiving line again?"

He chuckled and leaned into me as we walked. "No, Ianto, no. This will be a small party. Very quiet, I promise. Very relaxing."

"Okay." I let him lead me away from the tent.

We walked the length of the great park behind the Eiffel Tower almost to the Military School, then veered off into one of the posh neighborhoods that line the 7th Arrondissement. The night was warm, and we talked very little. A stillness came up between us then, or maybe it was just still compared to how loud the night had been up until then. Now that we were out of the rush of the fashion tent, I could think through the details of the night—the glamour, the faces, the electric energy of passion all around us. Perhaps it was just me who felt the stillness as I was digesting everything. Luca kept walking, his eyes intent ahead of us as if everything was the way it should be.

The party we ended up at after walking for several blocks was up in a penthouse apartment overlooking the river. The place was a giant den with leather armchairs and miles and miles of paneled and gilt walls and a library full of weathered old books. It was the kind of home you expected to be smoky and dark, even when the lights were all on. And he was right. It was quiet, but it wasn't small.

The place was filled with glitterati. Everywhere I looked, I saw models from the show or Môti designers, or minor celebrities, or just dozens of other people somehow loosely attached to the fashion industry. Waiters in tight-fitting tuxedos flooded the place, carrying trays of drinks and brightly colored finger foods, wading through the sea of people all looking as if they should be in the next issue of *Vogue* or *GQ*—with rough eyes and a daunting coolness about them, dressed in crisp denim or worn-out canvas.

But Luca said he didn't really know anyone at the party. Despite a few more air kisses, we were mostly left on our own when we got there, so we found a spot and sat by ourselves at the end of a makeshift bar in the library, surrounded by the hushed hurricane of edgy chic that enveloped everything. One of the waiters had left us with a plate of oysters and a bottle of cold white wine, the kind that you can only find once because they make it in such small quantities that even the vintners miss out on it. I was happy enough to sit with him in that moment.

So I sat, breathing in this edge of a life that was slowly becoming the norm for me, and I watched Luca. He was scanning the room, his eyes darting from one person to another in the crowd, occasionally lighting up with interest. His eyebrows would rise in a curious expression, only to go flat again as he continued glancing about. And I found myself wondering what was going on inside his head.

"Luca," I asked, suddenly remembering the earlier conversation with Michelle. "How come you quit smoking?"

My question seemed to pull him in to focus. He looked across the surface of the bar toward me, but he couldn't look directly at me. Instead he glanced over my face and rested his gaze on my right shoulder. He traced his finger along the side of the wine bottle. The glass was damp with perspiration, and he began to slowly rub the label off. "I don't know." He shrugged. "It's not really a big deal. I've been spending a lot of time with you and you don't smoke... so, I guess I just fell out of the habit of it." He looked directly at me. "That's all. I don't even know if it was intentional."

I nodded at him and took a sip of my wine but didn't say anything.

"Would you prefer I start again?" His face slowly came to life, his blue eyes dancing in the muted light of the room.

"No." I shook my head slowly, remembering the rank stench of the thin brown cigarettes he had burnt through, one after the other, on that evening when we had first met. "No, that's okay."

He laughed gently at me and reached across the bar to put his hand on my forearm, a gesture he often made when we were out drinking. "Ianto, you are sometimes a funny guy."

"Funny? How so?"

"I don't know." He seemed lost in something. "Just funny." He stared at me for a moment, and the strange look on his face, in his eyes really, made me think he was appraising me like he might a photograph. At that moment, his phone buzzed. He reached into his jacket pocket and clicked it off, but ten seconds later it buzzed again, and again. Finally, the moment broken, he pulled out his phone and looked at it. His eyes were suddenly cross.

"What is it?" I asked.

"Nothing," he said, waving his hand dismissively.

"It's not nothing." I shook my head. "You don't get mad at nothing. What happened."

"It's that stupid blog."

"*Runway Confidential*?" I couldn't help a short laugh. Ever since I'd moved to Paris, it had become an increasing part of my life, this serial drama-documentary on the lives of the French fashion industry. "What now?"

He shook his head and handed me the phone. I read the post silently, my French now good enough to understand it. "Luca Sparks lights up the night with a new pal at the Paris Benefit Fashion Show. Who is this mysterious and handsome stranger? We're not sure, but judging from the accent, he's definitely American. Multiple sources reported that he hung around the star snapper all night, even ducking back stage for a little tête-à-tête with super model Michelle Matthews. The two slipped away early though, reportedly to one of the many after parties. Pals or more? Has Sparks finally found a spark in his love life?"

"Wow," I said, handing the phone back to him. "That's kind of creepy."

His eyes traveled down my face, from my forehead to my chin, and he seemed to be taking me all in, evaluating me and trying to decide what to make of my response to the post. "What if something like that were true?" he finally said.

"What do you mean? It's not."

"But what if it were?" He looked at me so directly, I felt like I wanted to hide, felt like the boldness of his eyes would make me shrivel up and disappear. "You are a very beautiful man," he said. "No, don't look like that." He touched my chin gently and pulled me back to meet his gaze. "I don't mean just pretty. Though you *are* handsome. No, Ianto, there is much more. Your soul is so deep, such a mystery to me. Covered up in all that California gloss, there is someone really amazing beneath it. And I can't help it if I find that very interesting. Can you blame me?"

I followed his eyes as he leaned in across the distance between us, leaned into me until our noses touched, leaned in even farther than that. And it felt like we remained there suspended in time, so close I would have sworn it was the nearest I'd ever been to another human being. We waited for each other, both on guard, both waiting for the other to make a decision. He had come this far. The rest of the risk was not his to take.

Finally, I yielded. I let him press his lips against mine, and a new old feeling rushed in to fill my stomach with something that had been dead and buried for decades. His lips jolted me back to those few hours in New York so many years ago with Vince. The roughness of his skin against my skin, the feeling of power behind his dry, parched lips caused my head to spin. A current moved through Luca's body into mine. My face tingled with stitches of heat, and I wanted to open my mouth and let the kiss happen for real. But I didn't. I leaned back and stared at him.

Our eyes were locked and I, in my bewilderment, couldn't look away from him. His eyes said nothing though; I was out, alone, but not in a cold way. If I read anything from him it was a tome of patience. When I finally broke away from Luca's gaze, I noticed someone else staring directly at us from across the room.

She was an older woman, very unlike the hordes of air kissers who had crowded us earlier at the fashion show. She was probably about sixty-five or maybe seventy years of age, in a short silver-sequined dress and a monstrous tiara. A jet-black wig was plastered to her head, strands of the fake hair caked to her forehead and cheeks with giant beads of sweat. She held a beer glass in one hand and a clutch bag in the other, and she was staring directly, unapologetically, at me. Maybe she was staring at Luca and me both, I couldn't be sure. But when I looked in her eyes, I saw unabashed recognition. She placed her beer down on the table next to her, slowly raising her hand and giving me a thumbs-up gesture.

I realized instantly what she was looking at, and it shocked me—not because of what had caught her attention, but more because I hadn't recognized it myself until now. But there was no mistake; I was certain about what I saw in her eyes the way you're certain about a particular signal you would get from a traffic cop or an airline attendant.

This woman had traces of delight spread across her chapped lips and thirsty eyes, and she seemed as if she wanted to drink us in. I saw from the look on her face she thought Luca and I were lovers, and it scared me. I could tell by her eyes she was happy for us, and that may have been the thing that frightened me the most because it hinted at the possibility of a love affair ahead of me that I hadn't anticipated. I suddenly knew Luca was mine to have or to lose, and both outcomes were equally impossible to me.

Luca was still staring quietly at me, unaware of the old lady. I left him alone, silent in my discovery, as I considered how I must look to her, how Luca and I must have seemed to her. We must have looked like a new couple just starting our life together. It slowly began to sink in how stupid I had been over the past weeks, how much of an idiot I had been not to recognize this for what it was, and how impossible that I'd let things get to this point. I had let this friendship, this relationship, go for a very, very long time without a rudder. But worse than that, I realized, was I had been content to live in the middle of confusion.

That night was the end of my early days with Luca, the days that had no weight to them. Up until that point, our relationship wasn't heavy or terrestrial. I felt no consequences to wandering the nights with him—until that evening, until that woman had shown me by her stare what I was, until Luca had leaned into me and pressed his lips against mine, and I saw what I was playing with. I knew at that moment I had to escape. I could feel it in the pit of my stomach like a thousand voices shouting at me.

CHAPTER FIFTEEN—TRYING TO STOP

Towards the end of July, I returned to my home for the first time in more than two months. I sat still in the window seat as the plane taxied in from the runway, and I watched as the hills of the peninsula came into view beyond the runway, nestled beneath a giant bank of summer fog. I shivered, imagining the coolness of the air outside. Home was the only place in America where the summer was cold.

Ellie and the boys greeted me as I walked through security, and I had never been happier to see three people in my life. I grabbed the boys around their necks in a giant hug, and they each squeezed back. They had grown even in the months I had been gone.

"How was it Dad?" Robin let go of my neck and grabbed my roll-aboard suitcase.

"It was good. I missed you guys, though."

"Can we come and visit?" Gary asked.

"We'll see," I said. "Your Mom and I need to talk about that a little bit first."

"What's to talk about? You should just buy us tickets back with you."

Ellie stood back away from the crowd of hugging, a look of happiness on her face that made her even more beautiful. I leaned in to kiss her and she kissed me back. I felt the hesitancy in her lips just below the surface. I looked at her briefly as I pulled back from the kiss, and she turned away.

"All right everybody, let's get Dad's stuff to the car, what do you say?" She spoke brightly, and her voice was strong and brisk. "There's a Giants game tonight, and we don't want to get stuck in traffic, do we?"

The boys headed off in front of us, each fighting for control of the roll-aboard. "Hey Gary," I called, sliding the strap of my computer bag off of my shoulder. "Can you manage this one for me?"

He smiled and bounced back towards me. "Yep, sure thing Dad." No sooner had he grabbed it off my shoulder and caught back up with his brother than I saw him lean in and say, "I got the important pack."

I chuckled to myself as I watched them shoulder and elbow each other, Robin trying to dislodge the oversized bag strap from Gary's shoulder and Gary in turn sticking his foot in front of the roll-aboard's wheels to trip up Robin.

"They seem good." I leaned into Ellie.

"They're doing okay. They're glad to see you." I could tell by the vagueness in her voice she was somewhere else.

"And how about you? Are you okay?"

"Yes, I'm fine."

"I'm not convinced." I let the boys get a little farther ahead of us and then stopped and turned to her.

"I don't want to talk about it, not here."

"What?"

"Ian," she said, a stillness between us in the middle of the rush of the airport. "You have to go back." She put her hand on my chest and looked away for a moment in the direction of our sons. "And when you do, whenever that is—next Monday or Tuesday—then I will have to deal with the reverse of this. It's fine, it's just difficult."

I nodded and stood looking at her, not knowing what to say. "Well, let's make that trip to Paris a reality, then. I want them to come and visit me, especially while school's out."

"We'll talk about it later." She moved her eyes in the direction of our sons. The boys had put some serious distance between them and us. "Come on, let's catch up with them or they'll try and start the car on their own."

Ellie smiled at me and I laughed, glad for a little bit of a break from the seriousness of our conversation. But as we walked towards the car, her tenseness didn't dissolve.

The weekend at home was a quick one, but I made it a priority to stay away from work. I didn't check my email once. We spent the time together as a family, starting with breakfast at our favorite spot down in the Marina. We walked from our house, each of us bundled up in sweatshirts and scarves against the cool San Francisco summer morning. At breakfast, I got the updates on summer baseball and the classes the boys would be taking next year at school. Between bites of French toast and hash browns, Robin even managed to fill me in on the how the Giants were doing so far this year.

Breakfast was followed by an afternoon at Fort Mason Park throwing the ball with the boys. Ellie peeled off at that point, taking advantage of a free afternoon to herself; something she hadn't had since I'd been gone. The sun eventually decided to come out shortly after noon, and by one, the park had warmed up to a blistering seventy degrees. We shed our sweatshirts and left them in a pile as our game of catch evolved into monkey in the middle. Finally, we collapsed in a lazy pile and sunned ourselves while we watched the park fill up with the typical weekend Marina crowd of shirtless guys throwing footballs and Frisbees.

I did my best to make sure it was an almost normal couple of days. Things between Ellie and I remained a little strained, though. I could see she was trying. For dinner that Saturday we had tacos, a meal that required everyone to participate. I got to chop the onions while Ellie grilled the hamburger. Gary and Robin chopped up tomatoes and lettuce and shredded cheese, putting each thing in mismatching bowls and placing them neatly in the center of the kitchen table. Robin had pulled together a playlist for the evening on his iPod, which wasn't too bad. I suspected that his mom had set a few ground rules, such as no rap or hip-hop. I smiled to myself as I chopped, imagining how that conversation must have gone.

That night at the table, the conversation focused on what my life away was like. I told them it was mostly boring work stuff, the same in the States as it was in Paris.

"You don't do anything fun?" Robin said in between bites of a massively splintering taco.

I shrugged. "Not really." I took a bite of my own taco and tried to rescue a set of rogue tomato cubes that tumbled out of it. "But I did meet someone famous at dinner one night," I added, thinking about Luca.

"Oh, yeah? Who?" Gary chimed in.

"A photographer, Luca Sparks." The boys looked back and forth at each other and then me.

"Who's that?" Gary asked.

"He's a famous artist," I said. "A photographer. His stuff is up at the MOMA."

"He's not famous." Robin said, a note of disapproval in his voice.

"Where did you meet him?" Gary asked, a little more hopeful there might be something to this famous liaison.

"I had dinner with him a couple of times."

"A couple of times?" Ellie looked up.

"Yes." I swallowed. "He's working on a project near our office. I bumped into him one night, and he decided to show me around the neighborhood a little bit."

"Oh." She finished chewing a bite of taco and swallowed slowly.

"Did you go to the Eiffel Tower?" Robin asked. I was thankful the conversation moved on.

"No," I said. "I figured I'd wait and see if we couldn't work out some time for you boys to come over and see me, then we could do it together."

"Only if you take the time off work." Ellie looked directly at me. Her tone was friendly, but she sent another message with her eyes.

"Yes, of course." I returned her look.

"Cool," Gary yelped.

"Only the oldest can go," Robin chimed in, "right Dad?"

"No." I reached over and tousled the top of Robin's head. "Stop teasing your little brother. You can both come."

"I'm not little," Gary chirped.

"Sorry," I turned to him. "Younger."

"So, this Luca," Ellie said, looking up from her paper. It was Sunday morning, and the boys were still sleeping. We were sitting out on the deck, bundled up in blankets against the fog and enjoying the quiet.

"Mmm?" I said, peeking over the business section.

"I've heard of him. He was really famous in the 90s, right? Didn't he do a bunch of Calvin Klein ads or something?"

"Yeah. He did a lot of the Môti ads, too. It's kind of funny because as part of the project we're working on for the company I had to upload and save quite a few of his photos. I think I recognized a few of the dresses from your closet."

"Really?" She eyed me suspiciously. "That must mean that my wardrobe is out of date. I should really go shopping."

"Ha ha. I guess that's one way to look at it." I shook my head, fixing my eyes back down on the paper.

"I saw his name in one of those fashion blogs a couple of weeks ago."

My heart froze. "Since when do you read fashion blogs?" I asked.

"Since it's the center of everything you're doing right now." She looked a little hurt.

"The French ones?" I asked, my suspicion getting the better of me.

"No," she laughed, the hurt evaporating from her face for a moment. "Just the American ones. But they've all been talking about him lately."

"They have?" I asked.

She nodded. "There was a piece about him at some fashion show a couple of weeks back."

I swallowed a sip of coffee slowly.

"Is he nice?" she asked.

"Um," I hesitated, thinking for a moment. "I guess. He's really interesting."

"Does Môti still work with him?"

"No." I shook my head. "I'm sure they would love to, but he's not working anymore."

"Yeah, the blog mentioned something about that. But I thought you said he was working on a shoot near your office?"

I drained the last of my coffee. "He's working on a project near the office, but it's not a shoot. He's painting something." I don't know why, but I didn't want to tell her that he was painting a house. I felt embarrassed about that detail for some reason. "He doesn't do photography any more."

"That's too bad," she said. "It would have been nice for you to get to see him in action."

"Yes, it would have been cool." I tried to focus on the paper again, but I couldn't. I kept thinking back to that night at the party after the fashion show, with the woman staring at Luca and me. I wanted to erase it from my mind.

It's true, I guess, that when you know someone as well as Ellie knows me, you're able to pick up on things that float under the surface of what is said. I know now she could pick up on things just by the way I looked at something or the lines in my face when I spoke. I am, perhaps, guilty of not being that perceptive. I finally folded up the paper and set it on the table between us. I got up and gently kissed her on the forehead and then went back inside to take a shower and get ready for the day.

CHAPTER SIXTEEN—MY REFLECTION

I made it a point not to see Luca when I arrived back in Paris. In fact, I promised myself I wouldn't ever see him again if I could help it. Things were happening inside my head that I needed to put a stop to, and I knew I wouldn't be able to do that unless I separated myself from him entirely. My plan was simple: stay busy, stay focused, and remember who I was.

The Môti attic changed from a prison to my safe house. I kept to a routine of staying late at the office, burying myself in everything I could, then bringing as much work home as possible. The walks back to my apartment at night were treacherous because I knew he could find me then. His work site was so close to my apartment that I feared running into him at every turn. I kept my head down on those walks, avoiding the sidewalk cafes, looking only at the pavement in front of me and trying to think of nothing except getting home.

I did whatever I could not to think about him or the glittering, spectacular nights that had marked my previous weeks in Paris. They were bright, I told myself, but they burned too hot for someone like me. I was not wired for that kind of life. I told myself forgetting him was for the best, and I tried not to let myself miss him. Still, sometimes during the days, I found myself staring out the windows thinking about the way he would reach across a table and touch my arm, or the way he smelled at the start of the evenings when we'd meet up at the Café DeTra.

Despite everything that was going on in my head, I didn't really think I had changed much. But those around me at the office started to look at me differently. Alfonse, my self-appointed mentor on the project, made it a point to stop by my desk twice a day to "check in" and make sure I was doing all right. I noticed a look on his face, the same look others gave me, only his was more pronounced—the sad eyes, the tight-lipped smile, the face that seemed to feel sorry for me and embarrassed all at the same time. Philippe and Roony, the two Môti tech guys, even tried to go out of their way to say nice things to me.

Around this time, I started to get really good at French through no conscious effort. I had learned some bits and pieces of the language in the first couple of weeks there, enough so that I had been able to utter a few words at Luca during that first meeting in early July. But this was different. I was really starting to understand the language without having to think about it. At first, it was just odd words, but slowly little bits and pieces of what people were saying around me started to make sense. Then I could catch phrases and eventually I could understand long pieces of conversations. The office started to come to life in a different way for me.

Of course, I kept my new understanding a secret. I felt at the time a little bit like an archeologist, uncovering a strange, previously undiscovered civilization. I now understood the banal conversations every office has—"Where is the paper that I ordered?" "Did you take my sandwich out of the fridge?" "My computer sucks." These little snippets were interesting to me only because I could decode them now. I found what people would say because they thought I couldn't understand them far more interesting. Phillipe and Roony would drone on about their wives, their kids and occasionally about the latest episode of the *Big Bang Theory*. They spoke in French because their English was so limited, not because they didn't want me to understand them.

But the designers were different. They would talk about me when I'd enter a room as if I wasn't there. "Here he comes, sad again, like someone broke his heart." "Oh, poor Americans, they always fall in love in Paris." "But this one is married, no?" They would stop their conversation after a few seconds, and then address me in English. "Hi Ian, we were just talking about the weather this weekend. It's gonna be nice, no?" I would shrug and look blankly around the room at whoever had been speaking. "Not sure," I would mumble in English, and then I'd leave the room regardless of whether I'd gotten whatever I had originally been after.

It didn't bother me that they were talking about me. I think that happens to all of us in every office. What mattered to me was what they were saying. Did I really have an aura about me of someone in love? Perhaps I had actually changed.

Luca finally broke my self-imposed exile about a week or so after I returned. He didn't call or text me. We never did that sort of thing, and I'm not sure he even had my number. I didn't have his. But he must have eventually sensed something was wrong because late in the afternoon that Thursday, a week and a half after I returned, I had a visitor.

"Ian, there is someone here to see you," the receptionist said over the speaker on my phone.

The attic had emptied out for the afternoon, and I was alone. I was in the middle of running a series of tests on a new scan and search function I'd installed on the platform and had piles of test photographs stacked up all around my desk. "Who is it?" I looked up from my screen and rubbed my eyes.

"He won't say, but he says you have missed several appointments with him, and he's here to make sure you don't miss your appointment tonight."

Luca, I thought, resting my head in my hands. I should have known I could not run away from this so quickly. I took a few seconds to collect my thoughts, wondering what I could do in that moment. What if I refused to see him? Would he understand why? Would he somehow know I was refusing to see him because I was scared? Or would he think that something had gone wrong, that he'd screwed something up or that I was frustrated by something he'd done or not done? If I refused to see him now, he wouldn't come back. That much I knew. The night of the fashion show would end up being the last time I ever saw him.

"Send him up," I finally said.

He appeared a moment later, leaning on one of the ancient shelving units, tapping his finger gently on an aged wooden plank full of boxes. A lock of his sandy blond hair hung down over his eyes, and his face was blotched and red, as if he might have been running a few moments ago and had just now caught his breath. He had changed out of his work clothes, and he wore a pair of new blue jeans with an untucked faded red Brooks Brothers shirt.

"Knock knock," he said softly. "Anybody home?"

I smiled at him. "It's not home, exactly, is it?"

"I don't know," he glanced around as if searching for something. "You maybe sleep here? That's why I haven't seen you for the past few days?"

I was silent. I could think of nothing to say.

Luca noticed the photos spread out all over my desk, and he moved closer to look at them. Picking one of them up with a casual hand, he said, "Tell me, what do you think of this guy?" He turned the photograph so I could see. It was a picture of a lean male model with hollow cheeks. He was deeply tanned with dark eyes and full, pouting lips. In his right hand he held a bottle of cologne.

I looked up at Luca and then back at the door. I shrugged. "You know I don't know anything about photography or fashion."

"I want your opinion of the model," he said. "It's not really fashion, is it? I mean he doesn't have any clothes on. What do you think when you see this? What strikes you about the picture itself?"

He looked at me dead on for a few seconds before he placed the picture down on the desk in front of me. "He looks hungry," Luca said, glancing down at the shot. "And he does not want anything to do with the bottle of cologne in his hand."

"Huh?" I was puzzled.

"Look at it. I know you can see something wrong, but you can't say exactly what it is. The problem with the photograph—and trust me, I know when there is a problem with a picture—the problem is that the model is *en désaccord* here."

He was now leaning over the desk in front of me, his hands spread out wide as he stared down at the photos I had been working on. I think he sensed I didn't understand what he was saying.

"I think," he continued, "that in English you call it discordance. He is hungry, there is want, but he is not hungry for the stupid bottle of cologne in his hand. Whoever took this photo is trying to make a picture that shows desire and the object of desire, but that is not what is happening here. They are showing desire, and an object that the model obviously doesn't want. He is looking only bored and still hungry. A little like you." He looked at me with those ice blue eyes, accusing and forgiving at the same time, not moving an inch.

The air was still between us, as I absorbed his words. I'd barely noticed, but I was visibly shaking. It wasn't until later I looked back on that moment and knew exactly what hung in the balance. I had to make the decision I'd been avoiding since the evening of the runway show, and I had to make it in those few seconds. I knew what he was talking about. I knew the hunger that he was referring to, I just hadn't known to recognize it for what it was. I tried to buy myself more time. I tried to stall. "I'm not sure what you're talking about, Luca...I'm not sure what you mean." I looked at him. "What do you mean?"

He met my eyes as he turned the picture back so it was right side up to me, then he gently pushed it towards me. "Bored and still hungry," he repeated. "Remember that first night at Café DeTra under the chestnut tree? Bored and still hungry. It is what happens when you refuse what life brings you."

Of course he had to bring that up, the secret of food, the secret of experiencing what was put on your plate. I shivered as I remembered that evening. "I hadn't really thought of that," I said to him, looking back down at the picture.

"That is the trouble with Americans. Sometimes they think too much, and then other times not at all."

"It's not just that, Luca. I don't understand this. I don't know what this is supposed to be. I thought we were friends, and now it seems like it's more than that. I don't know what that means or if I can deal with it."

At that moment he leaned in to me, slowly, easily, so gently and so gradually that I saw it happening before it even did. His lips reached mine and pressed against my mouth. I was powerless to stop it. I didn't have the will or the want or the determination. I let the kiss happen. His mouth was strong, and the feeling of his stubble against my chin was electric. He tasted like lemons and butter and salt.

Then, almost as soon as it started, it was over. He pulled back and stood across the desk from me, staring into my eyes. The feeling of guilt was almost immediate, splitting out from the pit of my stomach. I looked out across the attic, beyond the shelves, knowing no one was on the entire floor but still craning my neck to see if anyone might have seen what just happened. Luca followed my gaze and shook his head.

"Let's go for a drink," he said, sweeping the pictures over to one side of my desk.

"I can't go for a drink now. I have to work."

"Later tonight, then?" He looked at me, then past me and out the window.

"Okay," I said. "I can meet you around eight."

"You know," he said, not taking his eyes off whatever he was staring at out of my window. "This is new for me too."

"Oh?" I said. "I didn't know."

"I had a wife," he said.

"You didn't mention her."

"I haven't told you everything about myself." He pursed his lips in a sad smile. "Anyway, it doesn't matter. She's no longer with us."

"I'm sorry, Luca."

He swallowed and then straightened up and moved slowly towards the door. "Well, so am I, but I was lucky to have had her. I know enough to know when I'm lucky to have something. It was a long time ago, anyhow." He stood still for a moment before continuing towards the door. "I should go. You are busy."

"See you tonight, then?" I asked.

"If you want. I'll be at Café DeTra, under the chestnut tree."

Part Four: The Affair

In 1976, William Eggleston was one of the first photographers to have color photos accepted as art. He showed us things as if in a diary, not as if we were seeing them in a newspaper. He captured the in-between moments of life, and he put them in front of us to see as our own. He makes the viewer reflect on his own life.

CHAPTER SEVENTEEN—RELATIONSHIPS

I kept my word and met Luca that evening at the café. He was sitting under the chestnut tree on the patio, exactly where he said he would be.

"You thought I wouldn't be here," he said as I sat down. He must have been there for some time already because he had a half-finished glass of rosé in front of him. "To be honest, I was wondering if you might not show up."

I was at a loss for words. Was he turning the situation around? I looked down and noticed my hands were still shaking. They hadn't stopped since his visit to my office earlier that afternoon. "I wanted to come," I said. "But you're right, I almost didn't."

The waiter brought me a glass of the same wine Luca was having and disappeared without a word. We sat looking at each other for a few minutes until he slowly picked up his glass and saluted me. I toasted him, and as we drank, I searched his face, looking for some sort of direction, some idea of where to go next.

"So, what shall we talk about?" He watched me as I lifted a trembling hand to drink the wine. I had to put it down quickly. I thought about just drinking the whole thing in one gulp. It might help me to relax.

"What is this?" I asked after a few minutes of silence, both of us watching each other.

"This is nothing," Luca finally said. "This is two men having a friendship, and that is all."

I looked away from him.

"That's what you want me to say, isn't it?" He closed his eyes as he said it.

"I don't know what I want."

"Well, it's time to make up your mind, Ianto." For a moment he seemed as if he were deciding for certain what he should say next. If there was indecision in him, as there was in me, it had dissolved at that second. "I know what I want." His eyes were soft in the patio light, but an intensity in his face made the edges of all his features hard. "This is not me either, Ianto. I do not fall in love with anyone, let alone men."

I felt the heat rising from my neck up through my cheeks and to my ears. I was afraid people could hear us, and at the same time, I didn't care. I was more afraid of what he was saying and of what I was feeling.

We sat for a few moments. He did not take his eyes off me. His face glowed with what seemed a combination of fear and courage. He tensed and relaxed his jaw, and I could tell these words weren't easy for him to say. "But that is what's happening. For me, anyway. I am falling in love with you, and I don't want to waste this—whatever you want to call it—I don't want to waste it. Do you?"

I sat there, unable to move, unable to breathe. My heart pounded, and I felt like I was going to throw up. I knew I should get up and leave that table and walk away and never turn back. I pressed my eyes shut and made up my mind that's what I would do. I would back the chair away from the table and run. I willed my feet to push back from the table, but they didn't.

I didn't push away and run because somewhere deeper inside of me than that part that wanted to run was a different, more primal part of me that couldn't resist the person across the table. Somewhere in the deepest part of who I was, I wanted him. I wanted to touch him, to feel him close to me. At that moment, I could see it. All the uneasiness of this friendship, all my reluctance to talk about it with my family, all the things I had seen in the eyes of people who looked at us in bars and on the street. All this had been me trying not to run away from something the way I had run away from Vince so many years ago after that frenetic night in New York City. I had hidden all of this from myself, but I saw it now. I saw it as clearly as day.

I did not run away that evening. I stayed. And when Luca, after my long silence, decided to reach across the table and take my hand in his, I did not pull back.

"You're shaking so much." He caressed the palm of my hand between his thumb and fingers. "Are you cold?"

"No," I said, in a moment of truth that was raw and rare for me. "I'm just scared."

That night I saw his apartment for the first time, although not much of it. It was dark when we arrived, and he did not turn the lights on as we stumbled through the door and he led me to his bed. We embraced almost as soon as the door closed behind him, and I found myself collapsing into his arms. From that second on, I couldn't get enough of him. His body was a magnificent discovery—the lines, the curves, the strength in his movements. I hadn't realized I'd wanted it so badly. It was so much different than the night with Vince. Vince and I were rushed college students, neither of us with any experience. We were just finding our way around each other's bodies. Luca and I came together after a lifetime, and we mapped each other physically in ways that I didn't know could exist.

By the time the sun rose the next morning, and the first pale orange rays of light shone through the windows, I had seen more of Luca's soul and more of my own than I had known there could be. I lay in bed that morning with Luca still asleep beside me, staring at the room around me. His bedroom was vast and metallic and empty, despite the collection of furniture strewn haphazardly around it. Large modern windows lined one wall, leading out onto a steel-railed balcony overlooking the river and the Eiffel Tower.

The other walls were plastered from floor to ceiling with paintings and photographs and maps. The bed, a giant object with no headboard or footboard, stood in the center of the room, an island with only the two of us on it. Various articles of furniture were loosely placed around it: a nightstand, a bureau, a bench, none of them touching the walls. A chrome rolling rack with clothes on hangers was shoved over to one side of the room, and the floor was strewn with pairs of jeans, a few shirts, socks, and belts and underwear.

After I'd stared at the place, I closed my eyes and committed it all to memory as best as I could. Then I stood up and walked over to the balcony, still naked from the night before, and looked out over the city, wondering what I'd gotten myself into.

The days beyond that night are lost to me. I got through at work, but I don't know how. Things went slightly smoother than they should have. I wondered later if what we had in those days was something I had missed in my life before Luca. I searched inside myself for the answer to that, if it was just him or if I had tried to leave a broader part of who I was behind years ago. Either way, it didn't matter.

We would go back to my place or his after a night of drinking. It would just be for a nightcap. Every time, I told myself it would be just a drink. Then he would look at me with that hunger in his ice blue eyes, and he would grab me roughly by the shoulders and I would fall again into his arms, helpless against the sea of softness and hardness and the passion it surfaced in my soul. We would stay in bed for hours in those days, tangled in damp sheets, a bottle of wine or cups of steaming coffee between us, talking then making love then talking again.

Each day started the same. I woke up next to him, and at first, felt the warmth of his body, followed by the inevitable guilt of what had happened the night before. Every day as I walked to work, I swore to myself it would be the last time I let that happen. I would not go home that evening. I'd go to a hotel or I might just stay at the office. But then I knew he would come and find me like he had before when I'd returned from California. We might then have some discussion about life and Paris and there would be wine, and I would feel like I was connecting with someone in a way that I never knew was possible. And then there would be the physical part of it. He would touch me, just a hand on my shoulder or his thumb on my chin, and I felt like I was being touched for the very first time in my life.

❖

The realization of what I was doing did not dawn on me at first. But I think it was always somewhere in the back of my mind, this steadily growing awareness of my family and an identity that existed for me in another place half way around the world. In the early days after we started sleeping together, I was able to push this awareness to the outer edges of my mind. It obeyed me for a little bit, while we were out together in the bars and cafes or when we were wrapped up together in the sheets of my bed or his.

But then that awareness would slowly seep back into the center of my consciousness, and I would find myself sitting alone on my balcony staring out across the skyline of the city, or walking by myself along the river just to get the space I needed to breathe and soothe the growing pit in the bottom of my stomach.

"Don't you have any friends?" I asked one night as we strolled along the Seine. We were just outside the Hotel de Ville, a building that always made me feel a little hopeless. It was such a grand building, and nothing important really happened there, or maybe it did in some far off distant past that I had forgotten or neglected to learn in history class. We were walking down the river towards the Eiffel Tower, and the setting sun was hurting my eyes just a little bit as it turned everything into an orange-reddish glow.

"I do," he said. "I have lots of friends."

"In Paris?" I nudged him gently in the shoulder. "How come I never get to see any of them?"

"Oh, I don't know," Luca said. "I guess because you are so busy most of the time and when I do see you, I want you all to myself."

We walked along for another several yards in silence. "I wouldn't mind meeting some of them," I finally said. "Really, I would kind of like it."

He nodded, and we walked a few more blocks before he spoke again. "This weekend, when you have not so much work the next morning, we'll go out. I'll call my friends, and we'll have a little party. Maybe at Café DeTra? Friday?"

I nodded. "That sounds good." But I don't know why it mattered to me at all. I didn't really need to know his friends. In fact, the more I thought about it, the worse an idea it seemed. The last thing I wanted was more people to witness this. But somehow I needed witnesses. I wanted—no, I *needed*—to know this was real, that it was happening. Because inside of me, I still felt as if I was hallucinating most days. The hours I spent at work only seemed like a glimpse of the shoreline, and I was adrift at sea, unable to find my footing again.

I still spoke to my boys almost every other day during those weeks. We had put a plan in motion for them to come and visit me towards the middle of August before they went back to school for the fall. But I spoke to Ellie less and less. Looking back, I don't know if that was her doing or mine. I am sure it is ultimately my fault. Even if she was talking to me less and less, it's because she knew something had changed in me.

"You don't know yet, do you, when you're coming home?" she asked me one night when we were talking on the phone. I sat on the bed in my apartment, alone. The city was strangely quiet, without sirens or loud crowds outside like usual. Maybe because of the silence I could hear something in the back of her voice, something I had been hearing more and more when I spoke to her during those days.

Her tone had a slight softness, as if she were speaking with a sore throat, trying to get the words out without hurting herself. It nearly brought me to tears that evening, and I pulled myself together and told myself silently that I would stop this thing with Luca. I would end it, and it would all be over with and I would go back to the States, and we would be a family again. But then a voice inside of me, a voice beneath that one that I swore off Luca with, told me Ellie and I could never really be what I wanted us to be again.

"Home," I repeated her last word, bringing myself back to the conversation. "Well, the go live date for the project is scheduled for the second week in September, so not long after then. I may stay here a week and clean things up a bit. Maybe the twentieth of September?"

"Can we go away then?" she asked. "Just you and me. We'll get someone to watch the kids or maybe send them to my sister's. We can go somewhere nice and warm where we can spend a few weeks together. Maybe Hawaii?"

"I would like that," I said, my lungs seeming to collapse on themselves under the weight of my heart.

"Ianto," she asked after a few seconds of silence. "Is anything the matter?"

"No," I reassured her too quickly. "Everything here is going fine."

"It's just that you sound different."

"I do?" I thought for a moment and wondered what she might be hearing. How did betrayal sound in a voice? "How so?"

"I don't know, a little like you have something on your mind."

"Yes, well, this Môti project I'm working on. It's kind of obnoxious right now. So many moving parts and everything."

I sat on the edge of my bed after the call had ended, the phone in my hand and my throat so dry I couldn't swallow.

"So, you wanted to meet my friends?" Luca peeked around the corner of a shelf in my attic work space. He looked so innocent at that moment, more like a boy than a man, with wide eyes glancing back and forth to see if he was in trouble.

"What are you doing here? Who let you in?" I finished an email I was working on and pressed send.

"The receptionist loves me. I can tell she knows who I am, but she's too embarrassed to say anything."

"Great." I thought about how this would reverberate through the company.

"Anyway, it's Friday today, like we said the other day. So I was thinking it might be a good night for you to meet them."

"That sounds great." My stomach roared at me in rebellion. How could I have been so stupid as to suggest this?

"Something wrong?" he asked. "You sound a little upset."

"No." I shook my head. "Everyone seems to think I sound funny. It's just work. Tonight sounds great. Where are we going again?"

"Café DeTra. Be there around nine thirty, and we'll have drinks and whatever."

I nodded and he gave me a look that made me think he might cross the room and kiss me. I could feel the heat rising in my cheeks in a combination of excitement and embarrassment at the thought of it. I wasn't sure where the entire staff had gone, but I knew they hadn't all left for the day. I wanted him to leave quickly. I wanted out of everything at that moment. But I just nodded my head. "Okay, that sounds great."

"Okay," he said back in the same tone. "Well, I guess I'll see you then."

Again, that glint of mischief in his eye made me think he might come closer in some intimate display of affection. But he didn't. He simply nodded and ducked back out of the room the same way he had entered.

I heard them later that afternoon, well after Luca had left. I was on my way to the bathroom, and I could hear a clutch of the designers gathered around someone's desk. It was Friday, so someone had pulled out a bottle of wine and a small group of them were having an impromptu happy hour. They didn't see me, or maybe they did. They still thought I couldn't understand what they were saying. But by that time, Luca and I had started to speak quite often in his native tongue. I stopped short behind the corner of the room when I heard giggling. They were saying how different I seemed these days, how aloof and mysterious I was. One of the women wondered out loud if what they were reading on *Runway Confidential* could possibly be true. They all nodded and guessed it probably was. I wasn't sure exactly what they were talking about, but I had a pretty good idea what it might be. I turned around and went back to my desk. It was time to leave for the day.

CHAPTER EIGHTEEN—LUCA'S FRIENDS

I had been wrong to assume Luca was a solitary person. That night when I arrived at the Café DeTra, he was seated at a table in the middle of the patio. The daylight had faded into the last ember of sunset. I noticed more tea candles than usual, ten or fifteen to a table, so that the patio had transformed itself into some giant birthday cake. I felt myself surrounded by the light and sound of the place as if the entire restaurant was an extension of Luca.

He was in the center of the crowd already, enmeshed in a tight group of conversation at his table. Luca was a single center of gravity, and the rest of us were floating out there, waiting helplessly to be pulled into his orbit. And every single last one of his friends were all beautiful. Most of them were in their twenties, if that. But not all of them. Some were a little older, a few, the ones actually sitting closest to him looked to be in their forties or even their early fifties.

He was beaming, aglow like all of the candles on the patio reflected at once in his eyes. I stood for a few minutes and watched him. This was a Luca I hadn't seen before. I had always had him to myself. I had always been the center of his attention. But now I saw that glint in his eye, that broad smile stretched across his face, those beautiful wrinkles in his forehead as he leaned in to focus all of his listening on someone else. Not just a single someone, but at least ten other people around the table, and more kept floating in from other tables.

I felt something in my chest as I stood there watching. Something I couldn't remember feeling for a very long time. So long, in fact, it took me a few seconds to recognize the feeling of jealousy. Luca's friends poured into the café that evening in a never-ending procession of what I could only call flair, and I was jealous as I watched this parade of beauty floating around this garden-room, restless and relentless in their youth and passion, all of it surrounding Luca at the center.

Where did that leave me? I was plain and a little goofy, nothing compared to these people. I felt my mouth go dry at the thought of having to speak to any of them in my ugly American accent with my stupidly minute vocabulary. I kept my feet planted to the flagstones beneath me. I wanted to bolt, to turn and run in the other direction, to leave this posh crowd and return to my files and folders and software updates. And just as I thought I couldn't fight the urge to run a second longer, he looked up at me and I was frozen. His blue eyes brightened and he shifted his smile from the broad public smirk to a private grin meant just for me.

I watched him stand up in the center of that room, emerging from the whispers and barbs of conversation like some sort of obelisk coming out of the sea, tall and gleaming in the light of his own personality. The crowd around his table looked first at him, and then followed his gaze to me.

"You made it," he said, holding his hands out toward me and sliding elegantly out from his behind his chair. He had a glint in his eyes I'd not seen before as he approached me, bumping into the backs of chairs and scooting shoulders out of his path as he made his way across the patio. He was smiling with every feature on his face. Even his nose seemed to turn up a little at the edges. He had the look of pride about him. Of all the grace and gregariousness that he was filling the room with, his pride in me struck me dumb.

"*My Ianto*," he said as he reached me, hesitating only for a second before leaning in and kissing me lightly on the lips. "I was afraid you wouldn't make it." The wonder I had felt at noticing his pride had quickly turned to a brittle nervousness when I realized our greeting was playing out in front of the crowd. I could sense the entire patio watching us at that moment, and I felt the pit of my stomach drop to the floor. I tried not to look around, not to think about the dozens of faces locked in on us, watching our every move.

"No, of course," I tried to find my voice. "Of course I wouldn't miss this. I've been looking forward to meeting some of your friends." A murmur went up around the room at my words, and I felt my face blazing red hot. I briefly noticed a camera flash in the background.

He could tell something was wrong, something was off in me. And of course, with his superhuman ability to know what others were feeling, he guessed. He leaned in and whispered so that only I could hear him. "Oh, you are shy. I'm such an idiot. I didn't even think of that. Are you okay?"

I nodded very slightly, forcing the edges of my mouth up in something that I hoped was a pleasant expression.

"To tell you the truth, I am a little nervous too," he whispered.

"You are?"

"Yes, of course I am. These people, they're my friends, they are like my family. And it's the first time I'm bringing someone to meet them since..."

"Since your wife."

He nodded back at me, mirroring the motion of my head.

"And the first time you've brought a man to meet them?" I added.

He waved his hand away, dismissing the idea. "They don't care about that." But I could tell he was a little worried about it. He looked at me and we locked eyes, sharing a private moment of nervousness, he and I together in the middle of that room full of people. Standing there with him felt good and solid.

After a moment, he straightened up, and in a louder voice, a voice he knew others around the room would be able to hear, he said, "I've got some people I want you to meet. Come, I've been saving your seat."

Luca's friends were exactly the people you would expect them to be, poets and painters and actors and models. They were from Paris, most of them, anyway. But others were from all over Europe and even a few from America. I did my best that night to participate in the conversation; I wanted so much to be a part of this vivacious, unorthodox, and agile group. But try as I might, it was hard for me to keep up with them. Even when I could understand the depth of what they were talking about, it was hard to find the words to participate the way I wanted to. It was even worse when they would stop and look at me with a glimmer of pity in their eyes and switch to English, thinking they were doing me a favor. I only felt like a child at those points.

But the wine eventually made it easier, and the conversation flowed more and more freely, until towards the end of the evening I found myself chatting with Michelle, the model I had met briefly at the fashion show with Luca a few weeks back. I was able to see her clearly now that she wasn't shrouded behind an army of makeup artists and hairdressers. She had exquisite cheekbones and the whitest teeth I'd ever seen. Her mouth was shaped like a strawberry and she had a way of saying things so that they sounded melodic, almost sing-songy.

"He is so beautiful," she said to me, taking an extra long swig off a tired glass half full of rosé. The glass was plastered with smeared fingerprints, hers and probably somebody else's. The glasses had been passed around so much by that point, we hadn't any idea whose had originally belonged to whom.

"Who, Luca?" I asked.

"Yes, silly, of course Luca. He loves you very much, you know."

I shook my head at the girl and tried to look away, but she pulled me back with her eyes. "You're scared," she said. "I don't blame you. I'd be a little scared of him, too. I know his reputation."

"His reputation?" The wine had long since lulled me into a state of relaxed dopiness. But I had a vague feeling tugging on the edges of my mind. The tone of her voice pulled me back into focus.

"So," she leaned into me, closing the space between us. Her eyeliner was a crisp shade of green, almost lettuce, and I wondered if she had thought about it very much before she chose it or if it had just been a casual thing; a tube she grabbed off her vanity or from somewhere in the depths of a giant purse that she kept at home by the doorway of her apartment.

"So, what?" I asked, refusing to shift my gaze.

"How is life going in the Môti attic? Are you finding lots of things?"

I laughed. No one, including Luca or even the Môti team for that matter, had bothered to ask me about what I had uncovered so far. "As a matter of fact, I'm learning quite a lot about the history of fashion."

She quietly placed her glass down on the table between us. She pursed her lips as if she wanted to say something, but wasn't sure exactly what it was. "Are you coming across any of Luca's photos?"

I wondered what she was getting at. "It always comes back to Luca with you, doesn't it?"

She remained silent for a few seconds. Finally, she shrugged. "So much of our world is about him, *n'est-ce pas?*"

"Maybe that's true, but it seems like you're obsessed with my relationship with him."

"Well, at least you're admitting there is a relationship now. That's progress."

She had a musical quality to her voice that I liked, even when she was saying something I didn't particularly want to hear. "Well, as a matter of fact, I have come across several of his shots. But, as you can imagine, that place is huge, and I'm still uncovering things. The other day I found a box from what I can only imagine was one of his earlier shoots."

She raised an eyebrow. "Really?" She took a slow sip of her wine. "What was in the box? Were there photos?"

"Yes, photos and a dress. A shiny metallic green dress, or what's left of it. I don't think it was packed very well. It can't be more than a decade and a half old."

"The photos, were they of two men and one woman in an ruined castle?"

I nodded.

"It looks like somewhere up in Ireland or Scotland."

"Yes," I said. "Beautiful place, right by the sea."

She looked a little surprised. "Really?"

"Yes. You know them?"

"Everybody knows them. They're called the Scotland Photos. They're some of his most famous work."

"You sound surprised," I tried to take in the look. I hadn't seen her stunned at anything, and it seemed a little strange on her.

"I'm just a little surprised at where you found those photos. He didn't take them for Môti. He took them for the MOMA. It was a special project he did. It was supposed to be his view on modern photography on the tenth anniversary of his first shoot."

"Really?" I said. "Well, maybe they loaned him the dresses for the models or something."

She nodded and seemed to lose herself for a few minutes in remembering. Her eyes glazed over a little bit as she stared at the tablecloth. "Maybe, but I doubt it. He sold a lot of stuff when he quit. His whole studio. He just left it one day. Never went back again. Finally after a while, the landlords asked him what they should do with all his stuff. He told them he didn't care. They could sell it or burn it, whatever they wanted to do, but he didn't want it anymore. So, they sold all of it at an auction. Môti must have gotten those photos then. And the dress," she added, "it's not ruined with age. If you look closely, you can see it is that way in the photos. Luca ripped it apart on the shoot. He liked it better that way."

I nodded.

She looked across the room where Luca had started talking to a short man in a black beret. "You would not have recognized him in those days."

"Really?" I asked. "Why not? Was he so different then?"

"Oh yes, he was a much different person. So focused, so alone inside his own head. The rest of the world was caught up in the magic of his photographs, but he—I don't know what he thought of it all. For a while, he went off the rails. He partied all the time. He was out until the day ended and the next one began, and he wouldn't rest. It was like if he stopped moving, the world would stop for him. Of course, I'm guessing at all this. All I know is what I observed. I was just a student then, but I was doing some modeling, mostly for children's catalogs and the like. But I had started to go out to a few of the parties, and he was always there, this essence of something bigger than himself, the personality that was, I don't know, really, just a singular presence in Paris.

"He had loads of girlfriends too, you know." She shot a glance directly at me. "All types of people wanted to be in his light. And he took everyone's pictures—all of them, dancers, actors, politicians, people who were just famous for being rich. Even Princess Diana would come and meet up with him every so often.

"Locked away somewhere in that giant apartment of his or maybe in some god forsaken barn in the south of France is a whole shed load of film. What they sold off from his studio was just the tip of it. I'm sure museums everywhere would love to get their hands on that stuff. He did put out a book with a lot of those pictures in it. Several books, actually. It always drew a lot of attention when he put out a book. Caused a little a scandal when he published some pictures of Tony Blair at a party in Berlin. Luckily for little old Tony he was well out of office by that time. You should look for that one. Lots of fantastic photos in that one. There's even a few of me." She let out an exaggerated sigh. "When I was just a girl."

"Anyway, whoever was on the scene here immediately wanted to be with him. But Luca, he never really got close to any of them, hard as they tried." She looked up at the patio lights and leaned back in her chair, a cold glint lighting up in her eyes. But then she glanced at my face and her eyes softened.

"Oh, Ian." She sighed and continued. "I didn't know him when he was really young, but a friend of mine said he was just like a little boy, really. Just a boy who was so very focused and just a little dark. But that changed gradually, and by the time I came onto the scene, he was very dark. I think he began to get bored with all of it. He started to travel. At first it was just on assignments around the world, but then it was for longer and longer periods of time. He would be gone for months, and then he would show up here again at some dive bar in the Marais that nobody had ever heard of, and within a month, that would be the place to be seen. Of course, then he would stop going there, but it would take months for the place to fall out of fashion again.

"It's hard to describe him beyond that. There is so much more, I know. But I don't really know how to say it. We all wanted a little piece of him, we all wanted to be friends with him. But for him, I think he didn't really care about that. I think his social life was just a way to get to the pictures he wanted to take. It was always just about the photos.

"What he did with his camera, it was beautiful beyond words. He could make people and things come to life without even trying. And it was all just air to him. He expected it, and at the same time, he focused on it. He never went anywhere without a camera. It was his only real companion. They say he has never loved anybody. That he can't. Not even his wife can, well could, get through to him..." She paused. "You heard about her, right?"

"Oh, yeah. Well, bits and pieces. Where did they meet?" I asked.

"Oh, well, nobody really knows much about that. He just returned with her after one of his long absences. The rumor is that he was in Miami filming a video for some pop star or something like that. I could never understand what he saw in her."

"You knew her."

"Yes, we all did. He didn't stop going out after he came back with her. She wanted a quieter life then, but he didn't. He kept going out to parties and nightclubs. Of course, she went with him. She didn't really wanted to go, but she was afraid to lose him. It's not her fault, really. She was just so dull and drab and I don't know, so American."

I coughed loudly.

"Sorry, love. I didn't mean it about you. I mean I didn't mean to imply all Americans are dull. It's just that she was one of those people who was so serious about the world."

I nodded in acknowledgement that she wasn't slighting my entire country, just those of us who were too serious. The lateness of the evening and the wine were starting to get to me. I massaged my eyelids, fighting to keep them open. "His wife? She died, right?"

Michelle nodded. "Yes, awful thing that happened to her. She bit it over in Iraq. She worked for an American news bureau taking pictures of the war. It was back in the early 2000s, but he didn't even notice that she was gone, not really."

"What?" The blurriness of the wine lifted for a second at her words. "How could he not have noticed? Why would people say something like that?"

"I know, it sounds awful, but from what I hear, he was working on a photo shoot when one of his assistants burst into the studio and told him the news. He nodded at her, and then picked up his camera and gave his lighting guys some new commands before he kept on shooting."

I felt myself becoming defensive on Luca's behalf. I felt some ridiculous ownership of him and his reputation, but I couldn't help myself at the moment. "Well, it was probably his way of coping. I mean, he probably held onto his routine just to keep from collapsing. I'm sure he was devastated."

She was silent for a few seconds, and then she nodded at me. When she spoke again, her voice had lost all of its authenticity. She sounded a little bit sorry for me. "I'm sure you're right. After all, I've never lost someone like that. I guess I wouldn't know what I might do."

I thought about Ellie for a moment and what she might be doing right this second half way around the world. I wondered if she knew she was losing me, that I was slipping slowly, ceaselessly away from her. I wondered what I would do if I was the one to lose her. I thought about her accidentally stepping out in front of a car or losing her footing and falling off one of the piers by our house. And in an instant, I realized the masochism of that thought.

I looked past the beautiful young girl that I'd been talking with, at Luca. His jaw line was defined by the light from the candle on the table in front of him. He was deeply engaged in some conversation with a newspaper reporter in a black beret. His eyes locked into the reporter's, intent on what the reporter was saying. They were carrying on in rapid debate over the future of the French language, each shouting at the other, but Luca's eyes glinted with happiness.

"Can I ask you something?" I said, looking back at Michelle.

"Now, who is obsessed with Luca?" She laughed at me with her eyes, then seemed to catch herself. "I'm sorry, that was cruel. Yes, you can ask me whatever you'd like."

"Why did he really stop taking pictures?"

She shrugged her shoulders. "He didn't tell you?"

"He mentioned something once about not wanting to meet everyone else's expectations. But the more I know him, the more odd that seems. He doesn't care what anybody else thinks about what he does. I can't imagine it would be different in his work."

She leaned in toward me. "They say that his heart is worn out, dead in the middle from taking all of those pictures."

"What does that mean?"

"You don't know that much about photography do you?"

I shook my head. "No, but I seem to be learning more and more about it every day."

"Well," she continued, "the photographer isn't just standing there snapping away at the camera. He has to create the scene, he has to work with the models, pulling out and capturing all of those emotions. He has to make the model feel all of it." She closed her eyes for a moment. "And Luca was one of the best at that. He could get inside your head and make you feel like the Queen of Sheba or Little Orphan Annie."

"Little Orphan Annie, huh?" I just couldn't picture her like that.

She nodded. "It sounds silly, love, but it's not easy, having to shape people's emotions day after day and having to witness it all. At the end of the day, the technicians, the lighting guys, even the model walks away from the shoot. But the photographer, he's captured more than the pictures. He leaves with all that emotion imprinted on his soul, day after day, year after year. Not all of them." She looked away for a second, in Luca's direction. "Some of them don't really care. They don't bother to make that kind of connection. And their work shows it. But Luca, he couldn't help but dive in. Every picture he took was an emotion, a memory. I don't think he ever really knew what to do with all of it after he put the camera down, so it killed him inside. He couldn't do it anymore, and he just quit."

"What about his wife, when she was alive? He couldn't share it with his wife, talk about it?"

She shook her head. "No. I don't know for sure, but I don't think Luca ever really connected with anyone. Until now."

"Now?" I had an uncomfortable feeling the conversation was changing focus to me.

"You've done something to him, opened up some part of him, Ian. Or should I call you Ianto now?"

I bit my bottom lip slightly, but didn't offer a response.

"No, I didn't really think I could call you that. You're Ianto to Luca, but not the rest of the world, and that has changed him."

"I see." I looked over at him again. He was still carried away in conversation with the bereted reporter.

"I wonder if you do."

I shifted my gaze back to Michelle.

"He's usually not like this," she said.

"Not like what?"

"Beaming. Happy. Laughing."

"What?"

"He used to never smile. Not before you came. Now he smiles all the time." She looked directly into my eyes. "Not that I see him all the time, only once or twice a month, sometimes a little more if I have a shoot near where he's working. But no, he rarely laughs. His beauty was dark, and we all fell in love with the mystery behind his face. The famous photographer who had buried his talent deep inside some wound. We all thought it was insanely romantic. But now that mystery is different. When he smiles…" She let out a jagged sigh, her breath full of wine and the lateness of the evening. "It's like a rare moon that you only see once in a great while, something that only the hippies and farmers know about."

I let out a nervous laugh. I took a breath and tried to regain some sense of balance.

"We need more wine," she said to me.

"More wine." I heard Luca's voice over my shoulder. While I had been locking eyes with the young model, he had wrapped up his conversation with the reporter in the beret and scooted over to the seat beside me. "More wine is always a good thing."

I smiled and leaned into his shoulder, letting myself go. He reached up and stroked my hair, pulling a few strands off my forehead. "We should go soon," I said.

"Yes," he agreed. "But surely we can stay for one more glass."

I nodded against his shoulder. "One more glass."

The model looked at Luca and then at me, and she finished the last swig of wine from the mottled glass in her hand. She held it up as if to toast us or ask for more wine, I wasn't sure which. But I pursed my lips and told myself one more time, that this would have to stop. But not tonight.

❖

"Ianto, you're brooding again." He sat across from me, staring into a cup of coffee, pretending to look at a *Le Monde* newspaper that had been crumpled up and smoothed out a few times before we arrived at the little café that morning. It had started raining the night before, and the dark purple storm clouds still lingered over the city, casting the morning in a dull gray dampness.

"I'm not brooding." I snatched a section of the *Le Monde* from in front of him. We were at brunch on Sunday, sitting sipping small coffees out of tiny cups. I was already hot even though it was only ten in the morning. I looked at him then out at the street, and the sourness of the morning must have shown through on my face.

"It was your idea to come out to breakfast. Do you want to go home?"

"No." I shook my head slowly. He was right. It had been my idea to go out for breakfast. We had spent the night at my apartment, and I had woken up to a bad hangover and a text alert from Alfonse letting me know that I had made it into *Runway Confidential* again. He had conveniently pasted the link to the post in his text message.

It read: "Officially an item? Sparks, who has been seen around town with a new American friend, threw an informal party a few nights ago at Café DeTra. Weren't invited? Don't worry—neither were we. But word has it Sparks and his new American friend were very, very cozy. They're definitely an item, according to several sources. Sparks was seen with his arm around the friend, even kissing him once or twice. After a little bit of snooping, we found out the American's name is Ian Baines, one of the digirati working at Môti on their archives project. We told you about that project a month or so ago, but don't worry if you forgot about it. We have trouble remembering computer stuff too."

My stomach sank when I read it. The world was beginning to close in around me. I showed Luca the post, and he had sighed deeply and told me to put it away. We stayed in bed for a little while longer, but I needed to get out of that room in that tiny apartment. I had suggested breakfast out, but now I felt as if everyone was looking at me. I took a sip of coffee and tried to force it all out of my head.

"Luca, can I ask you something?"

He nodded slowly. "I don't see why not."

"You mentioned you had a wife?"

"Yes." He put down his coffee and looked at me. "Is that the question?"

"No. Not exactly." I swallowed. "How come you never talk about her?"

He looked at me, his eyes narrowing in on the bridge of my nose, and I could see he was deliberating on what exactly to say next. "She was a photographer with the *Associated Press*. She died in Basra."

"What was she like?"

"What is your wife like?"

I looked away from him out at the street. It was a fair question, but brave for him. For all the strength he routinely showcased for me, he was very careful never to bring up my other life. I think he was scared of my guilt and what it would mean for us.

"She's very strong," I finally said.

"Strong enough for you to leave her?"

I looked back at him, and we were both silent for a moment. "I'm not leaving her, Luca."

He shrugged. "That is not my affair in any case." He reached across the table to put his hand gently on top of mine. "My wife."

He let out a long sigh. "I loved her, but we were not such a good match."

"But you said before you were lucky to have had her."

"Yes," he nodded. "I was lucky. She was a wonderful woman. But she wasn't cut out for the life I brought her into here in Paris. She was a journalist, always so serious about things, always wondering why we had to go to so many parties all the time. She kept going only because I did. But it wore her down. She never liked being in the spotlight, even if it was with me. Her last assignment was in the Middle East, and sometimes I think she took it to get a break from everything that was happening here."

"Were you two on the rocks?"

He shook his head. "No, not on the rocks." He took a sharp breath. "But I think I can be a very hard person to live with, and she just needed her own space. I think about her occasionally now and wonder what I could have done differently."

"So, you do have guilt?"

"Not guilt. I promised myself I would not feel guilty about her death. I was never unfaithful to her. That would have been the only thing I would have felt guilty about." He stopped, suddenly realizing what he'd said. "I'm sorry," he said, rubbing the top of my hand. I hated myself for the excitement that I felt every time he touched me. The feeling of his skin on mine made my heart race, and my jaw tighten. "I didn't mean to imply..."

I met his gaze and let a faint smile play across my lips. "You didn't mean to imply that I should feel guilty?" I looked away from him, out the window. "It's okay, Luca. That's not your affair either. I'll be the master of my own conscience, I'm an adult."

He was silent for a moment, following my stare out to the street. "If I was taking a picture right now, do you know how I would compose it?"

"How?" I said blankly, still staring out the window.

He reached out and gently touched my chin. "I would focus on your eyes. I would try to capture what I feel when I see them, looking out of this window, wishing the sky would clear up so we could go for a long walk in the Tuileries and maybe get some ice cream."

I couldn't stop myself from grinning. "How do you know that's what I'm feeling?"

"Ah, I don't know that for sure, but if I'm taking the picture it's for me to decide."

"Really? That seems kind of unfair that you get to decide. The picture might be inaccurate."

"Ah, but this is not photo journalism, it's just photography. Nooo." He drew out the 'no', smiling at me and shaking his head as if I were a child. "I will tell you a secret about how to be a really good photographer." He waited a second before he continued. The restaurant around us seemed to go quiet, and I could hear the rain outside the window, gently splashing down on the sidewalk and hitting the brass railings on the windowsill.

"Okay." I nodded for him to continue.

"The secret, Ianto, is that you have to decide what you want to see." He looked as if he'd just revealed the secret of life to me. "Lee Miller once said the photographer must make a decision. He must decide what his subject looks like before he takes the picture. We have to decide what we want to see Ianto. What do you want to see? What do you want your world to be?"

I let my focus drift for a few seconds, absorbing what Luca had said. "Is he ever wrong?" I finally asked. "The photographer? Does he ever make the wrong decision about what to see in his subject?"

"Maybe some photographers, but not me." Luca shook his head. "I am never wrong."

This time I laughed. The surety in his face played out in a wicked expression. He took a sip of his coffee and reached out again to touch my cheek. I wanted to back away. I didn't want to feel his calloused fingers on my skin, to be reminded of our intimacy, of the things we'd done the night before and the night before that. I feared I was letting myself become a possession. But I didn't back away. I sat still and closed my eyes and listened to my own laughter against the sound of the rain as he touched my face. I wondered what it must be like to take that approach to the whole world, to decide what to see. "Who was he, anyway?"

"He who?"

"This Lee Miller. Another photographer?"

Luca pulled his hand back and laughed, a gentle roll to his shoulders as he tried to stifle the chuckle. "She. Lee was a famous American photographer during the war. Well, actually you could say she was British. She spent most of her life in England."

I nodded.

"But she's right, you know."

"About what?"

"You have to choose what you want to see." His eyes were so alive, dancing in different shades of blue, all the more potent because they stuck out against the grayness of a morning where the clouds and the sky seemed to match the color of the granite sidewalks.

"I suppose you're right." I tried to maintain my sullenness, reluctant to give up my sulking so quickly. But his charm was infectious. For all the dragons in my mind, he had a way of lifting me up, even when I didn't want to be happy. I couldn't help it. My face started to lighten almost involuntarily. My eyes met his, and I could feel my mouth slowly forming into a grin. His smile deepened as he watched mine grow.

"So, what are we going to see today?" He asked.

Yes, indeed, I thought. What are we going to see today and every day after today? But I pushed that thought to the back of my mind. "How about a walk?"

"In the rain? You're crazy, you know. We'll both catch cold and then have to miss work! You can't let that happen. After all, work is the reason you're over here."

"So true," I said out loud. "What would my world be like today without this job?"

PART FIVE: WORLDS TOGETHER

The photographer Edward Steichen is credited with taking the first collection of fashion photography pictures for a French magazine in 1911. He was the first to try and capture the essence of the garments: what they looked like while they were on, the properties of the fabric, the feeling of them in the room. He did more than just cataloging a collection of garments. He brought them to life.

CHAPTER NINETEEN—PARIS VISIT

When you look at a Luca Sparks photo, you see into his mind. I think that's what makes his portraits so amazing. It's not like you're seeing the subject of the photo at all. People say that Mapplethorpe's photographs were all about friction. Emotion causing controversy. Herb Ritts was all about contrast—bold strokes of black and white, simplified glamour. Annie Leibovitz gave us a new way to look at the landscapes that surround us. But Sparks? What did he give us? The answer is far more personal than his contemporaries. He gave us a look into his own soul. The eyes of his subjects were his eyes. They reflected what he was feeling. They were a pulpit and a proxy at the same time.

Did I know this before I met the man? I'm not sure. I must not have, but I really can't remember. As I began to get to know him, I recognized the passion he had for everything in life. That passion drew me in to him in a way that scared me to death.

Is photography a question of first impressions? Do we take better pictures during new experiences? Do we notice things more acutely or more fully when they pertain to someone we just met or something we are seeing for the first time? Perhaps that's also what makes new love affairs so potent.

The time with Luca existed at an altitude where the air was thin, and my head was continuously foggy. That fog lifted briefly before it got worse when Robin and Gary came to see me in Paris.

Ellie had insisted I take a full week off to show Robin and Gary around the city, and I had reluctantly agreed. Even though I knew it would be difficult not to be on email and phone when we were getting down to crunch time at work, I needed to spend the time with just them. Luca had taken the news easily when I told him I wouldn't be able to see him for a week, but I could tell he thought it was unnecessary.

"I don't know why I have to go," Luca said on the morning of the day they were arriving. We were lying in bed, and I was starting to feel that gnawing sensation in my stomach again. "I think they might like me. Kids usually like me. I'm a fun guy."

"Look, Luca." I rolled over and faced the opposite direction from him, pretending to fiddle with my phone. "I think they might like you too, if we weren't fucking." I meant for the words to sound funny, but that's not how they came out. I heard my own voice, and it sounded crass and cold. I lay in bed with the phone in my hand, facing the wall and thinking about my own words. I felt his hand on my shoulder, gently rubbing my skin as if soothing a bruise.

"Don't make this ugly." He kissed me lightly on the neck. "Please."

"It's not right." I closed my eyes. "You know it's not right."

"I know." He took his hand off my shoulder, and I rolled over to face him. "But let's leave it at that and not make it ugly, huh? Americans, you always want to make everything into an enemy. Let's just leave it for now. I will go, and I will see you after your kids visit."

I nodded and then lay my head back down on the pillow. He propped himself up on an elbow and stared at me. He ran his hand through the front of my hair. "You are not what I expected, Mr. American."

"No kidding. You weren't what I expected either."

We got up, and I made coffee as he got ready for work. I realized, as we circled each other in what had become a morning ritual, I had become accustomed to him in a way I hadn't anticipated. He brushed his teeth while I made the bed, I brushed my teeth as he poured the coffee. The familiarity of our routine was surprisingly intimate when I recognized it.

When it came time for him to leave, he looked at me for a long time and finally said. "Have fun with your kids. I really do wish I could meet them. They must be wonderful people."

I kept looking at him and held my breath. I couldn't think of anything to say, so after a few seconds, I just nodded.

"I'll miss you," he said.

I think he wanted me to say I would miss him too or acknowledge what he had just said. But I didn't. I stood there with my lips pressed together, afraid and angry with myself for knowing I would miss him. Yes, I would miss the nearness of him, the physicality, the adventure of the nights with him, even the smell of him. But no, I wouldn't miss the guilt I felt in every embrace and every breath I took with him.

The imminent arrival of my sons made those emotions of lust and shame, intimacy and regret, all the more vivid. He was right in front of me, and I couldn't even look at him anymore. I stared at the floor. He stood back a few feet from me, then after a second, he stepped closer and put his hand on my chin. We were in the living room of my apartment, and the door was still closed. He lifted my face and kissed me roughly. Even though he had just shaved, I could feel the stubble on his chin and his upper lip, and it sent a chill through me. He tasted like coffee and toothpaste, and all the things of the morning yet to come. I could feel my face go red and the heat of blood rushing downwards.

"Bye Luca," I said, ending the kiss, my hand on his chest. I pushed him gently away from me. He turned around and opened the door to leave, only glancing back and stopping after a few steps, his hand still on the doorknob.

"Ianto." He leaned into the door jamb, a blanket of silence filling the space after my name. He stood very still with his back to the hallway. Somewhere on one of the floors below us, someone shoved a door shut with a loud bang and a group of kids made their way noisily out through the courtyard door. "I know I'm not supposed to love you." The color had drained from his face, along with all the usual liveliness and energy that seemed to emanate from him constantly. "I know that loving you could be a disaster. But I do, you know. I do love you."

"I know you do," I said. I turned my head and looked back towards the tiny kitchen. It was littered with the detritus of our morning routine. Coffee grinds and cups and one of us had even left a tube of toothpaste on the kitchen counter. "And you're right. It will be a disaster."

He sighed, and I could see his face tighten in pain.

"Luca," I said, unsure of what would come next. I walked towards him, lifting a hand to his cheek. He was trembling a little, just barely enough to notice. "I'm scared."

"I know." He bowed his head, touching his forehead to mine. "Me too."

We stood there for what seemed like hours, until finally he kissed me gently on the forehead and stood up straight. "I should go," he said. "You have some work to do this morning. See you in a week or so?"

"Yeah," I said slowly, "in a week or so."

He turned to go, only looking back quickly to wink at me.

Then he was gone, and I stood alone in the silence of the room. I felt like someone had taken my insides out, organ by organ, until nothing was left but my heart beating wildly in a great open space.

I scoured the place after he left, removing any trace of him ahead of my kids' arrival. I stripped the bedclothes and washed his coffee mug. I vacuumed and wiped down the counters. But it didn't matter what I did; I couldn't get rid of the smell of him.

I tried to keep myself busy for the rest of the morning. After I scrubbed the place from wall to wall, I worked out an itinerary for the week. I even ran down to the Mono Prix and shopped for enough food for a month. Still, I had time and I was unable to get out of my own way in the apartment. So, I went early to the airport, and I waited outside the international arrivals hall, a crowded and dank room with black-tiled floors and dirty white walls. Along one side of the room a giant glowing arrivals board listed all the incoming flights. I sat in front of that giant board with a cold latte in my hands, waiting, watching as the list of flights rolled over in updates every few minutes, trying to think of anything but Luca.

Their flight finally arrived after what felt like hours, and I stood up to watch the parade of weary faces, groggy eyes, and stiff limbs come limping out from the Customs door. They emerged, standing out from the crowd of business travelers and tired grown ups, their faces bright with contagious excitement. Gary let out a yelp when he saw me, breaking into a run and crushing me with a giant bear hug. Robin trailed behind him, measuring his steps carefully, mindful of maintaining a sense of coolness. He was, after all, the older brother and now an international traveler.

A few steps closer, though, and he dropped the act and rushed me with his own hug, layered on top of his brother. The three of us stood in a pig pile in the arrivals hall. Seeing them finally there, embracing them, hearing them made me feel like I had spotted land after a long time at sea. I felt a sturdiness return to my soul. There was no ambiguity here. I was their father, and I knew what that role required. I took a deep breath and let the world pass around us in that grey little hall, thankful for the nearness of them and the surety they provided.

The boys had lots of news from home, and the three of us talked nonstop on the subway ride back to my apartment. A good chunk of the summer had passed since the last time we'd all been together, and they filled me in on the sporadic details of life in our neighborhood, catching me up on everything from the San Francisco Giants to the neighbors' cat.

"Then there was a new cat next door." Gary sat on the subway seat, looking around at the graffiti-covered windows and talking at the same time. I marveled at how his brain could process the two activities at once. "Mrs. Walker wanted the cat, but Mr. Walker didn't." Our neighbors were a start up power couple. "He said they didn't have time for a cat, and they got into a big fight one night and everyone on the street could hear them."

"We didn't hear that much of it," Robin added in. "He's being dramatic. They only yelled at each other for a little bit."

"For like ten minutes." Gary was indignant at his older brother's effort to minimize the story. "And the whole street could hear them."

"Wow," I said. "That must have been some fight."

"Mom made us close the windows and put the TV on," said Robin.

"Speaking of television, how is the summer reading going."

Groans emanated from both of the boys. "Ugh, Dad..."

"I'm just curious. I want to hear about all the good stuff you're reading."

"I finished *Portrait of an Artist*," said Robin. He stared out the window as we went through an above ground section of track passing one of the tent cities in the outlying areas of Paris.

"Did you like it?"

"It was okay." Robin obviously didn't want to talk about his summer reading list, and Gary had gone completely silent. "It didn't really make a lot of sense."

I could tell he didn't want to talk about it, so I decided to let it rest. "So, what do you guys want to do first? Do you need a nap before we get started? Did you sleep on the plane?" That jump-started the conversation again. Both boys insisted they'd slept enough on the plane and they didn't need to take a nap.

As the subway car rumbled and jostled us along, I listened to them volleying back and forth about what they wanted to do first. A sense of relief came over me. We'd bounced back to what we had been all along. For them, nothing had changed. I don't know what I expected that day. Perhaps I was afraid they would notice something wrong with me, or a distance would be between us. Sure, I knew they'd missed me that summer, at least as much as I'd missed them. But they were resilient in the way boys are, and they had gotten along and had an action-packed summer without me, full of everything from bike racing to baseball to nights at the movies and the Westfield Mall downtown. But the journey back to the apartment was full of talk, just normal, everyday talk, and it filled me with a deep sense of peace.

We emerged from the Metro station in my neighborhood, and they both grew quiet, their steps getting faster as they made their way from the train, up and out of the subway to the street above. Emerging into the daylight, they both stood silently side by side, eyes cast upwards, taking in everything around them. I tried to imagine myself in their shoes and seeing the neighborhood as they were seeing it now, for the very first time.

How very different everything must look to someone who has only ever known the West Coast of America. What did they think about the café awnings and the BNP bank machines straddling the corner, across from a tabac and the little salon de thé? Did they notice the strange household products in the windows of the little hardware shop across the street, colorfully lined up with sale prices marked in Euros? I thought I saw Robin's eyes fix in on the slow hiss and click of the line of diesel Renault taxicabs. To his ear, they would sound different from the gasoline engines of the cars back home.

"Dad, what's a Salon de thé?" Gary asked, pronouncing "thé" like "the."

"It's a tea shop, and it's pronounced 'thé' like 'hey'," said Robin, quickly before I could answer.

"Wow, that's pretty good, Robin. Have you been brushing up on your Français?" I asked.

He simply shrugged and looked up at the sky. "I read the travel guide on the plane."

Gary had already forgotten the question as he gazed into the window of the little hardware store. The wide-eyed stares on the way back to the apartment that morning were just a taste of what the week was going to be like. The storybook landmarks in real life, the Eiffel Tower coming into view for the first time, the Arc de Triumph, something that only existed in French text books until now, the Mona Lisa, real—tiny and amazing against the crowded sea of shoving flashbulbs. I couldn't wait to see all of these things through the eyes of Robin and Gary.

They were even impressed with the apartment. They trudged up flight after flight of marble stairs, dragging their carry-on bags. They found the little fifth-floor walk up with its small living room, single bedroom and tiny kitchenette "cool" and "awesome." We got in and Gary instantly opened the French doors out onto the balcony.

"Can you see anything from here?" He craned his neck right and then left to see the not-so-sweeping vista of the building's courtyard and the tops of a few buildings beyond that, little more than chimneys and antennae.

"Not really," I said to him as I tucked the two suitcases into a small coat closet.

"Dad," Robin called from the kitchen. "Someone left their wallet here."

I froze. My stomach sank as I thought about how I had rushed Luca out of the apartment that morning. He couldn't have left his wallet. How could I have missed that with all the cleaning and running around I'd done in the apartment before leaving to collect the boys.

"A wallet?" I took two deep breaths and quickly forced myself to relax before stepping back from the closet and over to the kitchen where Robin was.

"Look," he said, pointing to a large light brown leather wallet on the table. I glanced at it and breathed a sigh of relief. Of course it wasn't Luca's wallet, it was my passport. I'd purposely pulled it out of my dresser drawer when I went to pick up the boys. I was going to bring it with me in case I needed another form of identity to prove I was their father. But I realized I'd left it behind.

"Oh, ha," I said almost betraying my relief. "I knew I'd forgotten that somewhere. That's just my passport."

"Can I see it?" Robin asked, not waiting to pick it up and open it.

"Sure," I laughed at his eagerness. "What do you think of the photo?"

"That doesn't even look like you!" he said.

"Look like who?" Gary yelped from the balcony, rushing in to see whatever it was his brother had discovered. "I want to see too."

"Sure, you can see it, but first we have to call your mom and let her know you got in safe." I reached into my pocket for my cell phone.

"Yeah, but won't it be the middle of the night?" Robin asked.

"It will be very early in the morning, you're right." I thought for a moment. "Maybe just text her now, and then we'll call later on when she's awake."

"Okay," said Gary, grabbing the phone out of my hands.

"Careful with that, I've got lots of work stuff on that phone," I said, watching him punch at the numbers on the screen. "You need to dial a plus one before the number," I gently pulled the phone from his hands and entered the number, giving it back to him afterward. "Go ahead and type something to Mom, then give it to Robin so he can too."

"I don't need to," Robin said casually. "I'm cool. I just saw her."

I laughed. "I know you just saw her, but it would probably be a good idea to send her a quick note."

"Whatever Dad," he huffed.

"It will take you thirty seconds. Come on, I'll send one after you."

"Fine," he said, taking the phone from his little brother after Gary had finished his note and pressed the send key.

❖

We spent the week doing everything tourists do in Paris— the Eiffel Tower, the Louvre, Versailles, the river boat tours, all of it. We started early in the mornings and kept going until well after conventional bed times. They were dazzled by it, but more importantly, we got to spend the time with each other, something we hadn't done in a long time.

My worlds finally collided on our trip to the Eiffel Tower. We had decided to try and get to the top of the tower late in the afternoon. The sun was out, and the sky was a brilliant shade of blue you only see in the late days of summer. We were walking up from the opposite side of the river, crossing the Pont Alexandre III, the bridge right in front of the Eiffel Tower, when I heard Robin's voice first. "Whoa," he said, tugging on his little brother's sleeve. "Check that out."

Gary and I both turned to look at the same time. "Wow," Gary said. "What are they doing with the silver shields?"

"It's a photo shoot," I said as casually as I could.

Robin and Gary both stared at a tall blonde model standing idly with a bored look on her face at the center of the bridge. A crew was around her, and two of the assistants were working those large round reflective discs to throw light on the model's face. I'm not sure if the boys would have thought much of the sight if a crowd hadn't already gathered around the shoot. The backdrop was obviously the Eiffel Tower, and what could be more perfect to see in Paris, as a tourist, than the glamour of a high fashion photo shoot?

"Is she a supermodel?" Gary asked, leading us closer to the shoot. He kept walking, and Robin and I kept following him. He stopped a few yards back from the scene, continuing to stare the whole time.

I laughed at my son. "I suppose she is some sort of supermodel. She looks kind of familiar." Then, the model waved at me. At first I thought I was imagining it, so I just looked down at the street. But she kept waving, making a bigger gesture with her hands as if she was trying to get my attention. The boys were looking back and forth between the model and me. Finally, she called out to me. "Ian, eh, Ian—Ça *va? C'est moi, Michelle. Tu n'a pas oublié, non?*"

Then I recognized her. *"Ah, d'accord! Michelle—tu es magnifique. Qu'est-ce que tu fait ici?"*

"Ah, cheri, je travaille!" She blew a kiss at me, her eyes as wide as I felt mine must've been at that moment. "Are these your boys?" I could tell she wanted to walk towards us, but she was surrounded by the crew, and her dress would not allow it.

"Yes," I waved at her and put my hands on my boys' shoulders. "We're out sightseeing today."

The photographer, who had been patiently waiting for her to complete her socializing, suddenly whistled at her and snapped his fingers. She rolled her eyes and shrugged her shoulders.

"Au revoir," I said and steered the boys off in the direction of the tower. They both had stunned looks on their faces. After we had gone a considerable distance and we were almost underneath the base of the tower, Robin looked over at me.

"You know her, Dad?"

I swallowed, a little nervous now about what they might think. I nodded. "Yeah, she's a friend of a friend. I met her at a work event,"

I lied. But it was a small lie. I didn't need the boys going back and telling Ellie I was out partying with models.

"You know French?" Gary asked, more stunned with the conversation than the supermodel.

"Come on, boys," I shepherded them toward the line at the entrance of the tower. "We better get in line now, or we'll never make it before closing."

❖

The three of us were sitting at breakfast at a small riverside café on the Friday of that week. The sun was already hot even though it was only about nine in the morning, but despite the temperature, we sat with hot lattes in our hands. The two boys had started drinking coffee earlier that week. I wasn't sure if it was a display of maturity on their part or if they just liked saying the words café au lait. They'd even started their own ritual of sitting after a meal, holding the cup in both hands and leaning on the table. I caught myself doing the same thing, and I'd wondered if they had picked it up from me or I from them.

"Are things okay between you and Mom?" It was Gary who asked. I knew the subject was going to come up sooner or later, and I wasn't surprised that it did. I was surprised at the depth of concern in his voice, though.

His older brother elbowed him immediately and gave him the look of death that he'd been cultivating on his younger brother for the past decade. I had to admit, he had that look down pretty well.

"Owww. I can ask, Robin."

"No, you can't. Mom said not to."

"Mom told you not to ask what? Exactly?" I kept my voice smooth and tried to sound as if it were just a casual question. It's true, we had stopped talking as much as we had when I'd first left, but we'd had several check-in calls that week.

Both boys sat at the table looking at me, silent. Robin finally said, "She said not to ask you anything about how you two are getting along."

"What?" I blinked, looked back and forth between them, and decided that I couldn't have this conversation with them. I couldn't put them in the middle of whatever was happening between Ellie and me. "We're fine," I said. "It's just hard sometimes because I'm away for so long right now."

"She cries a lot, you know." Robin added. Gary sat still, watching his older brother. He'd folded both hands in his lap, ignoring his coffee now. I sat looking from him to his younger brother and back. I couldn't say anything to them, so I folded my hands on the table and eventually looked out the window. I realized the city I saw out of that window had remade me, changed me into something I didn't know what to do with.

They left that Saturday, and I think I was just as exhausted as they were. As I watched them walk through the security doors at the airport, my heart sank just a little. I didn't know how long it would be before I saw them again, and I was just a little afraid that things would be so different when I did see them, we would never be the same family again. I wandered through the airport on the way back to the trains, watching the people I passed and trying to imagine who they were dropping off or picking up.

CHAPTER TWENTY—THE CHALLENGE OF CHOICE

I went to see Luca again the last Monday in August. I had taken Robin and Gary to the airport the night before and spent the rest of the evening sitting alone on my couch in silence. That Monday after work, I went without even thinking about it, without knowing what I would say or do. I just walked from my office to the construction site, straight up to where Luca was working.

It being just a little past the end of the workday, all of the other carpenters and painters had called it a day already. The room was on the top floor of the house and the fading light of the late afternoon poured in through two sets of elegant French doors, bathing the walls and the wooden floor in an orange glow. The smell of new plaster and paint gave the place a fresh, unused feeling and, at the same time, set my stomach a little on edge. The room was empty, except for the two of us.

"I can't do this." I stood looking up at him. His back was to me, and he was on top of a stepladder. He was using a small paintbrush to delicately trace the edges of a particular piece of molding. Most of the room had been completed, except for this last panel. The walls shined in brilliant golds and blues and greens—all his work, I thought, as I stood there staring up at him.

He silently finished the piece of trim he was working on, then turned around after a few moments and looked down at me. "Your children are gone, I take it?"

I nodded.

"Good, then you are free to see me tonight?"

"Luca." I looked up with him and felt the corners of my eyes burn. I had to keep my resolve on this. "I can't do this anymore. It's tearing me apart. There can't be two of me. There can't be the me that is with you and the me that is with the rest of my family."

"I knew this would happen." He stepped down off the ladder. "I knew you would be confused when they left. I knew it would be like starting all over again."

"I'm not confused Luca. I can't be confused. I'm too old. I've chosen a life already, chosen a path. And Luca, I can't do this. I just can't."

"You just need some time to re-adjust." He looked at me and nodded as if agreeing with himself. But I just stood still and a silence grew between us that stretched out for miles.

"Luca," I said after a few moments. "I need you to tell me something, honestly."

He nodded slowly. "Of course. I tell you everything anyway. What do you want to know?"

"You said you had a wife."

"Yes." He looked straight at me. "For many years."

"Did you ever have a relationship like this before?" I circled a finger in the air between us.

"What does that even matter, Ianto?"

"I want to know."

"Why? You come here to break things off, to tell me you don't want to see me anymore and then you need to dig into my past? For what? To see if you're the only one?"

"To see if you've been honest with me."

"I've never lied to you."

"You said this was new to you, too."

"It is new to me. I've never been in love with someone like I am with you." His eyes were full of rage. "I'll say it again, Ianto. I've never lied to you."

"No, but you've never said anything about being gay either. You let me feel like this was something that just sort of happened. That I've been somehow changed by being here."

"You are so full of shit." He slapped the edge of his stepladder hard with his hand, tipping it over. A loud crash filled the room as it hit the floor. I stood, startled by the sound but still. "You want the truth about my past, then fine. Yes, I've been with other men. When I was a young man, I had several boyfriends. Some of them for money and some of them because I really liked them. But I didn't love any of them. Not one. And you ask your questions, always wanting to find some sort of truth about your heart. But in the process, you just make it feel cheap and dirty because you're uncomfortable with being in love in a way you don't approve of yourself. Your family comes to town and now you feel even worse about yourself and about me. But it's not cheap, Ianto. It's not dirty. It's love, and I'm sorry if it's not packaged up in a pretty little pink and blue bow with a man and a woman, but still it's beautiful."

"I knew it. I knew you were lying."

"What is it with you, Ianto? You thought you were my first man? No."

"You let me think that." I almost spat the words at him. "You wanted me to think that."

"I did not drag you into this." He held his ground. "You felt everything, every bit of this on your own. And you know, down deep inside yourself this isn't a choice, Ianto. It isn't something I talked you into. This is a relationship."

"No, it's not." I brought my hands up to my face, feeling tears of anger starting to well up in my eyes. "This is not right. I have done awful things. I've thrown away everything that I loved in my life, and I don't even know who I really am."

He took a deep breath. "That may be the first honest thing you've said today." His voice was suddenly calm and soft and kind. "Listen, Ianto, I know you're hurting. I know this is hard." I felt him reaching for me, but I stepped back before he could touch me. I couldn't let him reach me. I couldn't feel his skin on my skin, not then. That would do it for me and I would crumble. But stepping back the way I did was one of the cruelest things I could have done. I could see the hurt in his eyes, and I felt my heart break.

"No," I murmured softly. "I can't do this anymore."

"So, that's it." He stared at me, his ice blue eyes piercing my heart and his voice now taut with a pain I didn't recognize. "It's all over? Done?"

I couldn't speak to him. I nodded and then turned around quickly to leave.

"Fine then. Leave." I heard a thunk as he threw the paintbrush to the floor, but I didn't turn around. I couldn't. This had to be over. I had to leave it alone and get on with my life in the right direction. By the time I reached the bottom floor of the house and jogged out the front door, I could feel hot streams of tears on my cheeks. But I kept going and I never looked back. I told myself I had done the right thing, and at the time I believed I had.

Later that evening, I sat in front of my computer screen, trying to catch up on the week's worth of work I had missed while Gary and Robin were in town. I thought about calling Ellie, but I didn't dare. I was miserable, and she would know something was wrong by the sound of my voice. I couldn't let her see that. Not now that I'd put things right. I needed a few days to get myself settled and then I would be fine with her. Until then, I needed some distance.

CHAPTER TWENTY-ONE—LIVE

We finally went live with the new archive at Môti on an early September morning. I woke up that day to a soft warm breeze coming through my window. The mornings in Paris were just starting to get a little later and the heat of the summer had passed, leaving the city cooler and more livable. I lay in bed, my eyes fixed on the ceiling above me, unable to move for the first few moments of being awake. The tiny room floated around me, and I felt as if I wasn't really inside my own body, like I was lying about six inches above my own skin. The feeling stayed with me when I finally sat up, placing one foot gently beside the other as I eventually shuffled into the bathroom. I hadn't seen Luca for almost two weeks.

I ran a shower and as the steam surrounded me, gently coaxing me to life, I thought about Luca again and how I'd be heading home from Paris in the next week or so. I felt a mixture of relief and anxiety. Neither felt dominant; it wasn't so easy as that for me. I thought about Ellie and the boys, I tried to imagine how much simpler my life would be when I was back home.

I had gone to bed early the night before but still my eyes felt heavy and my body was sluggish. I made my way to the tiny coffee machine in my little kitchen and flipped a little caplet of coffee grinds into the slot at the top of the machine. I thought of Luca and the easy routine we'd had in the mornings here. The machine had started to dribble out a hot slick black fluid onto the counter, and I realized I'd forgotten the cup. I searched around only to find that there were no clean coffee cups. I slipped a juice glass into place at the base of the machine. Half a minute later, I grabbed the steaming glass of coffee and finished getting dressed.

I made my way to the office through the hazy light of the Paris morning, down the Boulevard Saint-Germain and then onto the cobblestone streets and back alleys, the short cuts I had learned over the last few months of living here. My path brought me out to the river just above the Île de la Cité, and I stopped to look across at the trees lining the Tuilleries and the massive walls running below them along the bank of the river, the stones a warm yellow in the morning light. Each step I took that morning felt like a step towards the wrong end of a story I didn't want to finish reading.

The project was finally complete. We were presenting the new system to the Museum team at Môti headquarters and to its board and management team that day. If everything went well, we would be able to search for and find any outfit, accessory, handbag, shoe, or piece of jewelry that Môti had ever designed or produced. All of it would be at the fingertips of whoever wanted to see it. When you were looking for an actual piece of clothing in the vast Môti archives, the system would point to the exact storage location of the garment. Even the location could be updated automatically because everything had been tagged with a tiny tracking chip. If you wanted a magazine spread or video of a garment, the system would produce a file full of digital photos and videos, many of which I myself had spent hours scanning and uploading over the summer.

I went early to the large conference room where we would present, only to find everything just right. I had almost hoped for something to go wrong, but it didn't. I wanted the distraction. The chaos would have helped me. When the time finally came for me to show off the system, I stood in front of the room full of designers and executives and explained how it worked, what it would do, and how it could serve as the cornerstone of the Museum Project, helping the team to locate anything they wanted. Then I turned on the laptop and a large screen at the end of the room lit up. The neatly designed interface with the Môti logo came on screen and presented the user with two options—a search box and a button that read "Scan Picture or Textile." I hovered over the search button. "What should we search for first?" I asked the group.

A murmur ran through the room, and one of the designers I'd seen occasionally throughout the summer finally spoke up. I had been presenting up until that point in English. But the designer spoke to me in French. "I would like for you to search for hemlines in the 1990s." I'm not sure if she was trying to get me off my game or if she just hadn't considered language.

When I answered her, I did so in clumsy but adequate French without even stopping to think. "*Alors, on va chercher pour ça.*" Her jaw dropped, and as I looked around the room at the designers who had regarded me as practically deaf for the months that we'd worked together, I saw glazed looks of surprise. Their eyes raised and their cheeks reddened in what I could only assume was embarrassment. Of course the executives and board members had no idea what was going on. I just smiled and typed in the words.

But as the search results came up on screen, I felt the room start to spin a little bit. Môti hemlines in the 1990s had been captured and showcased by one photographer in particular. As the resulting images flashed up on the screen, one or two at first, then five, six, seven images, followed by even more until the entire screen projected a wall of Luca Sparks photos. At the top of the page was the first photo of his that I'd ever seen, the one that Alfonse had shown me back in June.

I caught my breath and managed to continue the demonstration, taking a few more search terms from the audience, then showing them how they could sign up to use the program. The audience asked a few questions, all of them in French. I struggled through the language but ultimately managed to deliver adequate responses without having to revert to English.

And then it was over.

The crowd of designers and executives filed out of the room exactly sixty five minutes after they had entered, having seen the results of the project that had taken me three months to finish. After they left, I sat in the empty conference room and picked up the stray handouts people had left behind. I unplugged my laptop from the projector and then went back to up to my desk on the eighth floor and sat there, alone.

Someone once told me that regardless of how good a shape you're in, running a marathon mimics the effects of a small heart attack. As I sat back at my desk in the attic of the Môti building, exhaling after the months of chaotic preparation, I wondered if the same could be said for such an intense work project.

The buzz of my mobile phone shook me out of my thoughts. I looked down at the screen to see Andrea's name brightly blinking at me. I pressed the button to answer.

"Well, hello there Mr. Software Engineer. How did it go?"

I smiled. "They were suitably mute. Which means they love it, hate it, or don't understand it. But never mind that. How is the baby?"

"Oh, she's wonderful, Ian, just amazing."

"Two weeks, right?"

"That's right. She's pretty much just sleeping, eating, and pooping now."

I laughed. "Well, are you getting some rest?"

"I'm fine," she said. "I'm more concerned about you, honestly. How are you holding up? Are you ready to come back here and catch up on the rest of your life?"

"Yeah, something like that. I think I'm heading back next week. I want to stay here and train the IT guys on the platform and make sure people know how to use it."

"Well," her voice sounded softer. "I got a call from the CEO. She's very happy. She said it went very well today."

"That's great to hear. Nova Vocé now has that big 'everybody knows em' brand under our belt. Just like we said we needed." What I didn't say was it was what Andrea thought we needed, and that getting it all done had almost cost me my sanity and much, much more.

She was silent for a moment, and I could hear her take a deep breath. "Are you sure you're all right, Ian?"

"Me?" I let the word hang in the space between us for a few seconds. "I'm doing okay, I guess."

"It's been hard on you this time, hasn't it?" Andrea said. I could imagine her face, her eyes softening the way they did when she knew she'd pushed someone to the limit. "I can tell, and I'm sorry we—*I*, actually. I'm sorry *I* had to make you do this."

"It's the job."

"Yes." She stopped for a second. "But this time there was a price. I can hear it in your voice. Are things with Ellie all right?"

"We'll be okay." I started to feel like the room was getting smaller. "I won't lie to you, it was tough. But we'll end up okay. We're going away when I get back." I could hear my own voice picking up a false enthusiasm, and I suddenly realized how insincere I sounded. But I clung to the idea that this would help me. If I said this enough times, it would strengthen my conviction, my determination, to get my life back to where it had been when I left for France.

"Where are you going away to?" She sounded uptempo, but over the phone, I couldn't tell if her brightness was for my sake or her own.

"We found a small beach shack in the Pacific. Well, Ellie found it. It's in Hawaii on one of the more remote islands, I can't remember which one—Maui or Kauai or something."

"That will be good. It will give you time to get bored."

"What's that supposed to mean?"

"It's not a bad thing, Ian," her voice was like warm tea. "You need to be bored for a while. You've been working so hard."

I don't know what it was inside of me that wanted to tell her everything at that moment, everything about Luca and my time in Paris and what it had really cost me. I wanted her to understand the price I had paid by being over here. I wanted her to know this wasn't me anymore, but the wreckage of who I had been. But I didn't say anything. Instead, I nodded to the phone. "Now that you put it that way, yes. I could do with some boredom."

In the background, I could hear the baby start to cry. "Well, nap time's over," she said. "I've got to go. You're back in a week or so?"

"Next week," I said. "I have a few ends I need to tie up here."

"Good work today," she said as the baby's crying got louder. "I'll see you when you're back."

As I hung up with her, I noticed a text message from Alfonse on my phone. "Looks like you made headlines again today…BTW, nice job in the presentation." At the end of the message was a link to the latest post on *Runway Confidential*:

"The Spark Dies: Looks like Luca and recent American fling, Ian Baines, are no longer an item. The two haven't been seen together in weeks. What happened is anyone's guess. Did they simply lose the fire? Maybe they're just taking a break. Baines hasn't been seen anywhere except the Môti building. Sparks has been spotted occasionally drinking at the Marigold."

I closed the screen and turned my phone off.

I saw Luca one more time before I left for San Francisco, on the morning before my departure. I had stopped at a newsstand on the Saint Germain to look at a couple of magazines. I felt him first, as if the whole world had gone on mute. I could hear nothing, and the air around me was instantly heavier. I looked up and he was across the street, staring at me from underneath a BNP sign. I stared back for a few seconds and then lifted my hand to wave. But he turned his back at that moment and walked away. I could hear his voice in my head—not specific words, just what it sounded like. All the conversations we'd had, all the evenings we'd spent laughing and talking through the great mysteries of the world. I could hear bits and pieces of it all in that moment.

And then it was gone. He was walking away down the street in the other direction. My hands started to tremble, and I put down the magazine I'd been holding.

CHAPTER TWENTY-TWO—THE RETURN

The Museum Project turned out to be a flop, though none of us could have foreseen it. The technology worked flawlessly, and it was easy to understand and use. But Môti was having a string of unprofitable quarters, and the first thing to get axed was the museum. The stockholders didn't care about their brand's heritage, they cared about its bottom line. The designers didn't really care much about the past, either. They didn't want to repeat anything that had already been done. They were in a race to establish their own name, their own look, and their own cuts of clothing.

I closed the email from Andrea explaining her latest conversation with the Môti CEO. I lay down my tablet on the table next to me and stretched my legs. I could only read so much about it. I couldn't help but feel like it was a reflection of my life in Paris. When I came home to San Francisco, I was satisfied with the work we'd done on the project, but I guess it wasn't going to change the nature of the fashion industry. It was only a software program, and it didn't matter what they did with it. We had still built it, and we could still count it as one of our small company's accomplishments.

I had been home for two months by that point, and Ellie and I had been planning a trip together to that South Pacific island. She had been planning it, really. I didn't do much of anything in those days. I slept. I ate. I wandered in to work when I felt like it and wandered home after hours of sitting at my desk staring at documents that seemed to have less value than they had before I'd left for Paris.

After the months in Paris, the Nova Vocé offices in San Francisco seemed stainless and clinical. I had gotten used to the wooden floors and the forgotten chandeliers of my Paris attic. The designers and techies I'd worked with in Paris seemed to have an accidental grace we lacked in America, even if they were jerks. The familiarity, the casualness I had missed so much was now difficult for me to embrace again. It seemed false and contrived. The friendliness, the hearty invitations to lunch, the *de facto* fraternity of drinks after work, all seemed to be a manufactured effort. These things that had felt native to me before I left felt harsh and irritating upon my return. I told myself this irritation would wear off as I tried to assimilate back into my old life.

I drifted at work, moving from one task to the next, weighing in on projects all around the world, but staying particularly focused on things that were happening in California. As much as my heart was not here, I was trying to focus my head on something concrete and near to where I was. I figured if I could get myself back into the swing of things at work, focused on what was happening in this part of the world, that would somehow transfer into my personal life. I would be able to reconnect with Ellie and be again what I had been before, my San Francisco self.

As the days and weeks passed after my return, I began to notice how people tried to look after me. I watched Andrea as she watched me, and I wondered what she saw. I noticed the worried look on her face as she stopped by my work station at the end of each day. Sometimes she would stay and chat with me about whatever piece of business we had just won or lost. Sometimes we would talk about market trends we saw emerging or the latest thing some eccentric venture capitalist had proclaimed to be the future of our world. But we didn't talk about France.

I tried not to think about my time there. I tried especially hard not to think about Luca. Sometimes it was difficult when I was alone, so I made sure I almost never was. At work, I could at least focus on some project, some paper or some plan, and that would help me get my mind off him. The less I thought about him, the better I was, but I was never able to keep him completely at bay.

For some time after my return, I had maintained the belief I could separate myself from those days in Paris and from Luca. I had to believe I was still the same person I had been before, that the affair had not changed who I was. Years earlier when things had happened with Vince, I had separated myself in the same way. Even though I severed my relationship with Vince much more gradually than I had from Luca, I had employed the same strategy with both men. But both affairs haunted me in ways I couldn't shake.

The funny thing is that in those days, I seldom let myself think of my time with Vince or Luca as affairs—not because I couldn't stomach the infidelity, although I felt guilty beyond belief about that. No, calling it an affair would make me something I wasn't ready to be, or rather, something I wasn't ready to admit. I thought recovering from the time with Luca required me to be exactly the same person I was before I met him, unchanged and unmoved.

Of course, I now recognize that Luca had changed me. It had been an affair that taught me more about myself and about the darker side of love than I ever wanted to know.

A moment at work in those days after my return crystallized things for me in a stunning way. It happened during one of my good days, one of the days when I had been able to focus on work to the exclusion of all other thoughts. It had started early with a minor client crisis and progressed from one urgent project to the next, in an almost unbroken chain of blissful busy-ness until the afternoon.

That afternoon, Andrea and I were interviewing several candidates to build up our team of engineers. The company was chronically understaffed, and we were always looking for new programmers.

The conference room was set up with a table at the back of the room along a row of windows. We were facing a white wall with nothing on it. There was a single chair for the interviewee, and Andrea and I sat facing him. The interviewee's name was Brant Cade, and he was new to San Francisco. He had graduated from a school back East that nobody would know by name, with a degree in nothing particularly interesting. But he had almost a decade of coding experience going back to junior high school when he built his own programs on a Compaq Armada that his mother had brought home from work.

He had chocolate brown hair and deep brown eyes that searched the room as he sat facing us. He kept moving his hands. For a moment, they would stay neatly folded in his lap, then he would place them flat on the surface of the table, then he would put them back in his lap. This continued through most of the interview, even as he spoke. His eyes seemed uneasy too, scanning the room as soon as we said our introductions. Eventually, his gaze stuck on me. He nodded slowly at me as I asked about his experience, letting his mouth slacken so that it was just a little bit open. The effect was a look of desire, at the same time alert and curious, like a child who had just asked a question no one would answer. I found myself unable to hold his stare, so I looked down at his resume on the table in front of me while I finished my questions.

For some reason, Brant Cade wanted the job badly. Most of the people we interview know how tight the talent pool is for qualified engineers, and they walk in with a fabricated cool, I-couldn't-care-less ethos. But Brant spoke quickly throughout the interview, eager to tell us about everything that he had accomplished.

Eventually, I'd asked all of the questions I could think of, and an uncomfortable silence filled the room. I looked up to see Andrea typing something on her phone. She glanced up to meet my eyes and gave me a brief nod, indicating that I should move ahead and finish up with the interview.

"Do you have any questions for us?" I asked, to which he nodded his head.

"I do." He raised his eyebrows and let his mouth rest open for just a split second, elongating his cheeks and giving them a hollow look that instantly reminded me of the conversation Luca and I had had about hunger and discordance. "How is the environment here for gays and lesbians?" He stared at me, his eyes not moving for a second, the look of hunger hanging on his face.

I was caught off guard by the way he had asked this specifically of me. I am sure now, in retrospect, I was putting more weight on the question than he meant there to be. But all I could think about in hearing it was: he knows. I could not respond. I could not think. My throat went dry, and I had to look down at the table. I glanced over at Andrea to find she had put down her phone and was looking back and forth between Brant and me. Her eyes rested on me for a brief couple of seconds before she spoke to Brant. "We have an inclusive environment. We value everyone on our team and we do not discriminate."

After we had finished the interview and Brant had left the room, she turned to me. "I think that's enough for one day, don't you?" She didn't wait for me to respond. She looked down at the table and collected the resumes and scraps of note paper in front of her.

"Yes," I said blankly. "I think that's enough for me."

She stood up and made her way towards the door but I stayed behind, by myself in the room below a bank of windows, staring at a blank white wall.

So I had changed.

The days with Luca had catalyzed something deep inside of me, something others could see. Alone in the room now, I suddenly found myself very thirsty and just a little cold. I swallowed hard and decided it was time to go home.

CHAPTER TWENTY-THREE—NOT HOME

On the weekends during those months, I would sit on my deck overlooking the Marina from high up in Pacific Heights and read the *New York Times* or *Businessweek* or some other business publication, and that would take my mind off of life and Luca for a little while. But the distractions would quickly fade, and I'd end up thinking about him again and again. We had spent so much time together in those summer months, it seemed like almost every hour that I wasn't at work I had been with him. And at the time, it felt like I was adrift in an ocean of the unfamiliar, the bits and pieces of my life and my job floating by me like so much flotsam and jetsam. Everything that I had built and built on was merely driftwood. And all I had wanted was to be back on solid ground, back on shore with my family and my old life and all the stability of that life I had with Ellie in The States. Now, it was the opposite. I would sit for hours alone on the deck, wrapped up in a wool blanket against the fog of the San Francisco fall and wonder who I was.

One morning the sliding glass doors opened and shut behind me as I sat out on the deck. I looked up to see Ellie. She set a hot cup of coffee on the table by the *Businessweek* magazine that I'd just set down. "How are you feeling?" she asked, her voice as warm as the steaming cup.

I nodded to her, meeting her eyes for barely a second before looking away, down the hillside below us and out over the Bay to Alcatraz. "I need to get out of this place." I looked back to her and noticed she had followed my stare out across the Bay. I hadn't thought about what she must be feeling like, watching me all those weeks since I'd been back, quiet and still as winter.

"Soon," she said. "We have a whole month together on that island. Just the two of us." She sat down beside me and put her hand on mine. "Ianto, I wish you'd tell me what's wrong."

I shook my head. "Nothing's wrong. I'm just not myself."

"You haven't been yourself since you've been back from Paris. Even in Paris, something was wrong."

"It's just the stress of work." I slipped my hand out from under hers to reach for the coffee. I took a sip then held the cup in my hands. She sat looking at me for a few minutes without saying a word. Then she stood up and silently walked back into the house.

I'm not sure what our boys thought in those few weeks leading up to our departure for the Pacific. We had left them to fend for themselves a little bit. I don't mean that in an irresponsible way. We were still home in the mornings and after school. We still made all of the games and school events. We never let them go without a meal. But after supper and homework, we would leave them and head out for a quick glass of wine. When we returned a couple of hours later, they were usually in bed. But sometimes we'd come in and Robin would be awake, still in front of the television.

"What are you doing up?" I asked him one night after we had gotten in from a wine bar in the Castro. Ellie had headed for the bedroom without a word. I knew she didn't want the boys to see her with wine on her breath. I, on the other hand, was okay with it. I had come home so many nights from business dinners it wouldn't be a surprise.

"I couldn't sleep," he said. "I never can when you guys are out."

"Oh." I sat down next to him on the couch. He had the remote control in his hands and was staring blankly at an advertisement for Clearasil. "Sports?"

"Music videos."

I nodded. "Anyone good?"

"Dad, don't."

"Don't what?"

"Don't try and make stupid conversation and try to sound cool. You don't like my music. You don't have to pretend like you're interested."

I nodded and began feeling that sense of floating again. I tried to push it away. "Hey, I can be interested." I nudged him gently in the arm. "I know I don't always like your music, but I haven't given up hope yet. Maybe I'll find something I like."

"And then you'll stop listening to Pearl Jam and Nirvana?"

"Well, let's not go crazy."

His face cracked, and he smiled. The commercial ended, and we sat for a few minutes watching the next two videos, each a blend of hip hop and pop music that, I had to admit, was pretty easy to listen to. After a while, Robin got up and handed me the clicker.

"I'm done," he said, turning to go up the stairs. "Good night Dad." He leaned over and gave me a kiss on the cheek.

"Good night," I said as he bounded up the stairs in huge sleepy strides.

I sat there for a few more minutes staring at the television screen but not really watching it.

❖

We finally took the trip Ellie had been planning since the summer. She had scoured the Pacific Ocean to find the perfect island that had absolutely nothing to offer but sand, lush jungle, and plenty of time and space to relax. Her thinking, she'd told me, was that we should focus on escape—separating from what we did every day and how all the stresses of our lives were weighing us down. It was code though for *me* to separate. She was fine, or so she kept telling me. I knew that wasn't the case, though. I could see in her eyes the toll my silence was taking on her. I had tried to wake myself from it. I had tried to forget Luca and all of those nights in Paris together. I had tried to blot out the feeling that I was disconnected from everything in this life. But I knew it wasn't working. She was feeling my absence even more than she had when I was away for all those months at work. She was not fine.

The island was beautiful. Ellie had rented a tiny cottage right on the beach, tucked in off the sand under a grove of papaya and banana trees. A single avocado tree towered above the rest of the greenery, and sometimes in the middle of the night, an over-ripened fruit would drop onto our tin roof with a thud so loud it would wake me up with a start. On the nights I was able to sleep, that is. On the nights when I wasn't able to sleep, I would lie awake anticipating the avocado's thud. But it never happened at the same time. Night after night this went on. I thought at first I would get used to it, but I never did.

We couldn't talk to each other anymore. At least when we went out to cocktail parties and school meetings, we could make small talk with someone else or have something else to look at. It didn't matter what the distraction was. We were looking for some sort of noise in our lives to take our minds off each other and everything that we had created. On the island, we were forced into a different type of silence, a silence that was so open and overt it was nearly impossible to comprehend.

We would sit for hours together on the beach and not a word passed between us. The crashing sound of our silence drowned out the energy of the waves and the sun on the sand. When we did talk, we talked about nothing. We talked about the boys' school work or a new floor for the house. Ellie read fashion magazines and from time to time she would show me a picture of some shirtless movie actor or some bikini-clad model and ask if I could believe what they were doing or wearing or who they were with. I would smile, yanked out of my silent stare, and nod. I would offer a couple of sentences, whatever was minimally appropriate for the story. But mostly I just sat. I did not read, I did not listen to music, I just sat.

In the fog of this stillness, Ellie finally broke through to me late one afternoon on the beach. "Why did your Môti thing fail?" she asked.

"The Môti thing?" I knew she was talking about the museum project and its subsequent crash, but the question was so far out of left field for her it took me off guard.

"The thing you went to Paris for? That thing you worked so hard on for all those months and kept you away from your wife and family?" The edge in her voice betrayed the thread of anger underneath the airy question. I could tell she was trying to be light about it, but it was hard for her.

"I don't know. I guess they just lost the funding for the museum they were building."

"So it wasn't anything that you did? Or the team at Nova Vocé?"

"No." I shook my head. "There was nothing we could have done differently. Nobody knew that Môti would run out of money."

"Did it reflect badly on you?"

I took a deep breath. I had thought vaguely about that in the last few weeks. "I don't know."

She took my answer differently than I had meant it. "Is that's what's wrong?"

"What's wrong?"

"Yes, Ianto. Is that what's been eating away at you since you've been home?"

"No. I'm not all that worried about that. I don't think anyone will judge my career on Môti. The launch went fine, the platform was fine. The training we offered was solid. It didn't fall apart until after we packed up and went home. The computers are still up there in the Môti attic. You could probably still go up there and look up anything on them."

She nodded, silent for a few minutes but still looking at me. Then, with a look on her face like she'd just resolved to jump into a pool of freezing water. "What is it then?"

I didn't respond. I didn't mean to be cruel; I didn't want to be silent, but I couldn't think of anything to say. As the seconds ticked by between us, it was stronger and stronger proof that something was wrong, something had been missing since my return.

"I wish you would tell me what's on your mind." Ellie edged closer to me, her feet dug into the sand.

"Nothing is on my mind. I'll be fine," I finally managed to say. "I just need some time." I laid my hand on top of hers.

"But you've had time, Ianto. You have been like this since you came back from Paris. It's like you're not even here anymore. Not at home, not here. You've been staring out into the ocean all morning. I know something's wrong. I'm more scared that you can't or *won't* talk about it."

The last thing I wanted to do was talk. I wanted to simply sit and let the sun bake my skin, every pore and wrinkle, until it was achingly pink and brown. But she sat looking at me, expecting, hoping for me to say something. Anything. I knew I had to change things. They had to be over between us.

I had made a decision in Paris. I had chosen this life, this family. I had chosen to come back to this and not to venture off into a life with Luca. I had known then I couldn't live both lives, and I had been scared of what was happening with Luca. I had loved him. I still did. He was beautiful, but the prospect of a life with him was too frightening for me to comprehend, and the guilt I felt for that love was a bottomless, black guilt that gnawed at my heart every time I thought about it. That had ultimately driven me to the decision.

But I realized now I had made the wrong choice. My life with Ellie was over. It would be forever over, and even if I stayed, it would always just be this silence between us. I looked at her in that moment and I saw two people. I saw the bright, sparkling, sunny woman I had married all those years ago, and I saw the drained, frail heart she had become over the summer and autumn of this year. I saw what was happening to her, and I knew at that moment that I had to leave.

But I didn't leave.

I waited to make sure I was right. But that never happened, and I knew it never would after a while. I would always be in this limbo here with her. I don't think I would have ever left Ellie on my own. I wouldn't have had the strength to leave her. But as in almost every part of our life together, Ellie was the stronger one. She left me. On the morning three days after our conversation on the beach, I walked down to the little village for coffee. When I came back, she was sitting on the bed next to her packed suitcase.

"This is over," she said, placing a limp hand on top of her bag. With her other hand, she reached out to me. "Here," she said. When I lifted my hand to meet hers, she placed her wedding band and engagement ring in my palm.

I simply nodded. I can't imagine what she saw on my face at that moment, but I've wondered many times over the past few months. Did I look relieved she had come to this decision without me? Did I look scared that I would now have to face myself and the world alone? Did my face show the sadness I felt about the end of something we had built together and I had tried and failed to stay faithful to? I'll never know what she saw in my eyes, and it's either cowardice or vanity that makes me wonder about it. If I had been more resolute about my own feelings one way or another, it wouldn't have fallen to her to end things.

"There is a taxi coming, Ianto. He'll be here soon."

I nodded.

"Let me know when you're coming back to San Francisco. I can leave the house for a weekend so you can get your things."

"I'm not coming back." I said.

"Okay, then…" She paused for a moment. "You're going to Paris?"

I didn't answer her. "Keep what you want, throw out what you don't."

She took a breath. It was the only sign that she let slip to show how difficult this was for her. "We'll talk about it later," she said, "and figure things out with the boys."

I nodded and sat down beside her on the bed. I balled my fist around her rings and I could feel them cutting into my palm. She looked over at me and tried to smile, but all I saw was a vacant, tired stare.

"I'm sorry." I opened my palm and looked down at the rings in my hand. "I really am."

"I know," she said, her eyes starting to well up. "But it doesn't really matter, does it?" She swallowed hard. "Tell me something,

Ian." She lifted a hand and reached across to my face. She stroked the side of my cheek gently; her fingers were soft and warm. "Would you have ever left me on your own?"

I thought for a moment. "Probably not."

"I didn't think so." A horn sounded outside of the thin walls of the shack. The taxi was there. She kept her eyes on me as she started to get up to go. "Whatever is eating you, I hope you figure it out, Ian. I do still love you."

I watched her as she grabbed her suitcase and walked out the door. She turned around as she got into the cab and gave me a small, sad wave. I waved back, trying to absorb the enormity of what had just happened.

I stayed in the shack for a few more days, taking in the silence of the place and trying to decide what I would do next. My days didn't change much, except for the fact that now I was truly alone, not just alone in my own head. There was a rhythm to those days after Ellie left and I was grateful for that. The routine gave me a cadence to life, something to feel.

My days started with a walk alone in the morning for coffee, then a walk back to the shack to sit out under the sun. I would then run or swim in the afternoon and maybe walk down to the little village again and buy something for dinner, usually rice and Spam or something like that. I had no joy for these activities. They were simply tics of a clock, something to mark the passing time. They were automatic, and I barely felt the water on my skin when I swam or tasted the food when I ate. The sun rose and set, and the days passed around me like wind on an open plain. I was empty, a shell devoid even of a soul.

I stayed in this barren pattern for almost a week, until one night I woke up in the middle of the night to the sound of an avocado crashing down onto the tin roof. I realized, with a little bit of a surprise, that I had been dreaming. It was odd because I hadn't dreamt in so long. But that night, the dream was about the Mapplethorpe photo that had moved me so many years ago back in New York City, only this time the faces were twisted and tortured. They were being torn apart by something, and they were angry about it. I felt the *angst* of the whole mangled picture welling up inside of me. And as I lay there for a few minutes in that space between waking and dreaming, I imagined myself as one of the men in that photo. I closed my eyes tightly together and then opened them wide. I knew what I needed to do.

I went to the small table on the side of the room and rummaged around for a few sheets of notebook paper, and I wrote to Ellie. I tried to explain as well as I could what had happened to me in France. I told her about Luca and the nights of Paris. I let her know I would not be back, though I knew that was a moot point. She had left me, and she didn't expect our relationship to continue. But I had held back the only thing I could have given her in the end, the truth. The letter would be a pale comfort, but it was something.

I got dressed in the darkness of the night, brushed my teeth and my hair, and grabbed a small backpack we had intended for day hikes. I stuffed my toiletries and a change of clothes into the pack and started walking away from the shack. It was a two mile walk to the town, and it took me under an hour to get there. From there, I took a cab to the airport and purchased a one-way ticket to Paris via Los Angeles. I posted the letter to Ellie when I reached LA, then I boarded the plane and closed my eyes.

CHAPTER TWENTY-FOUR—PARIS AGAIN

When I returned to Paris after what seemed like days of flying, it was strangely the same city I had left months ago. I staggered through the crowded streets during the morning rush hour, dazed from too many hours in an Air France seat and not enough water. Everything now was frozen and monochromatic. I didn't expect soft spotlights and Rocky-disco music to accompany me as I stepped off the subway and back up onto the streets where I had spent my summer, but I wanted some sign, some sense of acknowledgement that I had made the right decision.

Instead I got a disapprovingly cold Paris. My steps echoed hollow. No one was listening for me, no one was awaiting my arrival home, no one expected me. If there was a truth to what I was feeling and what I was doing, it was concretely mine and mine alone. Making a decision is always hard, but doing so when no one is left to tell you that you made the right decision is devastating. It is perhaps the loneliest feeling I have ever had. All that drove me at this point was momentum and a loss of any other direction.

I had to see Luca. I had to find him and let him know how wrong I had been, and that I'd made the right decision now. I had to tell him I had chosen out of fear before, fear that my life was slipping away from me and I would lose the people I loved and the warm and safe world I had created for myself. I hadn't realized then I was a fraud. I was not who I had built myself to be. I was someone else. Luca had awakened that, and now it would never rest. I would mend paths. I would eventually reach back to Ellie and Andrea and my sons, and I would let them know why I made the choice to leave. When I eventually did do that, it would be from an honest me, a person who recognized myself for who I was inside and took the chance to be something unconfined by a constricted world.

These thoughts ran through my head as I walked the streets to Luca's address, marking each turn with the memories of the first time I'd been to his apartment on that hot summer night so many months ago, my heart beating so hard I thought my ribs would burst, my hands shaking and the heat of anticipation making the back of my neck sweat.

I wanted to see him. I needed to see him. I imagined what his face would look like when he opened the door and saw me standing there. I imagined the irreverent smirk, the "I told you so" glint in his eyes. I imagined, most of all, he would let me into that apartment with the long floor of windowed balconies, high above the skyline of old Paris, and I would have someone to hold me and give me some relief from all the turmoil of indecision that had ripped apart my life for the last few months.

But he wasn't there.

No one answered the buzzer. So I waited outside for the better part of a day, sitting on the sidewalk, the cold of the cement seeping through my thin pants until I was shaking. I waited until a neighbor finally told me he had moved out months ago. I went to the place where he'd worked, the house off the Saint Germain that he had spent so many hours painting. But the work was finished, and in place of the scaffolding were bright lights behind colorful curtains. The workers were gone with no sign anything had ever been under construction.

He wasn't in Paris. The city, overflowing with millions of people, was empty without him.

The sense of purpose that had motivated me to come back to Paris and find him disappeared. That barren feeling down in my soul I'd felt back on that tiny Pacific island returned. But this time it was worse. The emptiness in my heart found new depths.

I had given up everything I was and everything I had to search for someone I loved. But that someone was now a ghost, and I was alone in a city that didn't want me, a city cold with the aching of my heart, a city that offered no warmth. He had gone, and I would never not be alone again.

Because I didn't know what else to do, I rented a room off the Boulevard Saint-Germain, where we had spent so many nights together wandering the sidewalk bars and cafes. I walked around the city every day and drank every night. I didn't know exactly what was happening to my world or what I was going through. I guess I was partly searching for him and partly trying to find myself. The problem was the two searches were intimately linked.

Sometimes late at night, after I got home from the bars, I sat in the dark, hating myself for what I had done and not done in the same breath. I was a coward of the worst kind. I'd run away from everything in my life. Even in the moment when I'd tried to correct for that cowardice, I'd compounded it.

I searched the city for Luca, but it was in vain. I had no way of getting in touch with him. I'd never gotten an email address or a mobile number from him, and the way I left things, I wouldn't be surprised if he never wanted to see me again.

Then one day in Paris, I received a call from my son, Robin. It was early in the afternoon Paris time, and that meant it was morning in California, and he was probably on his way to school. I looked down at the incoming call and wondered what I would say to him. What could I possibly say?

"Dad?" His voice had was just starting to change, and I could hear the crack in it.

"Hi, Robin." I struggled to keep my voice steady as I sat alone on the small bed in my rented room. I stared at the wall and noticed for the first time, the swirling patterns in greens and golds on what must have once been stylish and elegant wall paper.

"How are you holding up?"

"Me?" I was surprised by his question.

"Yeah." He let out a long sigh. "Mom told us a little bit about what happened and I figured you'd be pretty sad."

Silent tears filled my eyes as I listened to his voice. I swallowed hard and tried to clear my throat to speak. "Yeah, I miss you guys."

"Did you go back to Paris?" And it occurred to me that I hadn't told anyone where I had gone. When Ellie left, I just took off. Our vacation was supposed to go for another week or so, and the boys would have been staying with friends for the time. Somehow, when Ellie had gone home early, Robin must have put things together on his own, or perhaps she had read my letter to him.

"Yeah." I nodded blankly to the wall. "I'm back in Paris."

"Because you're happier there?" he asked.

"Not exactly," I said. "But I have to finish some business here."

"Work stuff?"

"No, Robin. Me stuff. I've just got to figure some stuff out about who I am."

I heard him take another breath after a long silence, the sounds of our neighborhood in the background. "I figured it was something like that." Then after a few seconds more. "When are you coming back?"

"I don't know." I continued to stare at the wall, a hollow feeling starting to rip at me from the center of my chest. "But I love you and your brother a lot. Make sure you tell him that, too. Look, Robin, I don't think your mother and I are going to be together anymore. But we both love you guys a lot. You mean the world to me and to your mother. But I have to fix some stuff that's broken in me right now, or I'm not going to be a very good person in the long run."

"Like with the test?"

"The test?"

"Yeah, like when you made me go in and admit I cheated on that biology test last spring? Because I knew that what I'd done was wrong and even if I didn't get caught, I'd always know I had to fix it."

I felt myself smile, despite the tears streaming down my face. "Yeah, something very much like that."

"Are you going to live in France?"

"I don't know yet, but if I do, you and Gary are going to come visit for a long time."

"Okay," he said. "Look, Dad, I've got to go, or I'm going to be late for school."

"Don't let that happen, Robin. Make it a good day. I love you kiddo."

"Kiddo?" He sighed loudly into the handset. "Dad, don't get sappy. I'm not a kiddo. I love you, too."

"I'll call you in a couple of days. Tell your brother I love him."

"Okay Dad. Talk to you later then."

The phone beeped to signal the call had ended, but I held the phone against my cheek for a few minutes. I asked myself again what I was doing, and I could feel nothing except the vast loneliness of my own shadow.

That night I walked alone down the streets Luca and I had roamed together the past summer. Again I asked the bartenders and the waiters about him, but still no one knew anything. The few people that recognized me from my nights with Luca were polite but not very helpful. I began to think it had all been in my imagination. Perhaps I had invented the entire relationship like some nightmare *Fight Club* scenario, and I was completely insane. As each day passed, I began to lose more and more hope and direction.

But as I had learned that summer, Paris has a way with coincidence. She was not going to leave me stranded and wandering forever after all. Things began to take a different course in one of those bars I had visited with Luca early in our time together. I had started out the evening drinking scotch, with the express purpose of getting as drunk as I could as quickly as I could. I expected it to be another night of solitude.

I had chosen a little bar in the 11th arrondissement with nothing special about it. It was full of low lights, dull colors, and hard edges striving to look modern. Late 1990s pop hits played in the background. Nothing in particular attracted me to the place that evening, other than I knew it was a place to drink, and I liked that it was empty. Empty bars always look a little safer to me. But as I sat there, halfway into my second scotch I felt someone brush my shoulder.

"Well hi there." The voice was feminine and vaguely familiar, but hidden in the shadows of the bar. "I don't think I ever expected to see you here again."

I blinked a few times as I looked over trying to make out the face in the low light.

"I'm very disappointed," she said, moving out from the shadows and into the light. "This is the second time you've forgotten me. I don't think of myself as a particularly forgettable person. You're starting to make me wonder."

"Ah, Michelle," I said, finally recognizing her. It had been several months since I had last run into her at the Eiffel Tower with Robin and Gary. "You were in the dark."

She smiled. "Ah, cheri, you remembered after all." She looked at the bartender and then nodded to my drink. "I'll have one of those."

"Are you sure? It's scotch."

"Well, I didn't expect it to be ginger ale, love. I'm a big girl. I can handle a little hard liquor."

I shrugged at her. "I just thought you liked vodka, that's all."

"Wow, thank you for finally remembering something about me," she said. "It is very kind of you."

"It's the least I can do."

"It really is." She pulled out the bar stool and sat down next to me.

I raised my eyebrows, wondering just how much she knew about the way I'd left things with Luca. "What's that supposed to mean?"

"Oh, Ian," she said too sweetly. "Let's not play games? We have no reason to. I've got nothing to gamble, and you've got nothing left to lose, *n'est-ce pas*?"

The bartender placed a scotch in front of her and she lifted it towards me. I raised my glass, and we clinked. "Fair enough."

"So." She took a sip. "It looks like you're a magnet for the blogs here."

"How's that?"

"*Runway Confidential*."

"Oh God." I put my palm up to my forehead.

"Oh yes." She pulled out her phone and read from the screen. "Well Look Who's Back...Ian Baines, the American whose recent fling with famous photog Luca Sparks captured the imagination of the Paris fashion scene last summer, was spotted in the arrivals hall at Charles de Gaulle airport last week. Who is he here to see? I wonder. If it's Sparks, he may have his work cut out for him. The now-elusive photographer hasn't been seen anywhere lately."

"Yeah," I said. "That about sums it up I guess."

She nodded quietly and sipped her drink. "You know, I've wanted to ask you something."

"Shoot." I took a much longer sip than she did.

"Why did you ever leave him?"

I shook my head slowly from side to side. "It's a long story."

"Where are you going?" She looked at her watch. "Because I've got all night."

"Michelle, I have a wife and a family back in the States."

"And?"

"And I thought I had to go back to them."

"So you left Luca to be with them." It was not a question, just a statement. She grimaced and took another sip of her drink.

I nodded. "Yes. I thought I needed to forget him and everything he and I had done."

"And what, exactly, had you done?" She looked down at the bar for a few minutes, drawing little circles in the wet rings of her scotch glass.

"Michelle, I'm not sure how much you know."

"That's not what I mean," she said, pushing aside anything I might say about my relationship with Luca with a wave of her hand. "What had you done except love somebody? Eh? I know it was not who you were supposed to love, but still...love is love, no?"

"That's one way to look at it. It seemed a lot more complicated to me at the time."

She turned so she was facing me directly. Her eyes were glassy, and she looked incredibly sad at that moment. "Why are you back now?"

"Because I was wrong."

She raised a carefully sculpted eyebrow. "Wrong?"

"Yes, wrong." I took a deep breath. "I thought I could just forget about him. I thought I could forget about everything that had passed between us. But I can't. I couldn't. No matter how hard I try to bury it, I just find myself thinking about him all the time."

"So, you were wrong." Her voice suddenly turned sharp, and I sensed an edge of pain. I'd forgotten that she and Luca were so close. If she could have exhaled frost at that moment, I think she might have. "That doesn't answer my question."

I just stared ahead, looking at the bottles stacked behind the bar.

"Why did you come back here?"

"To find him."

"Hmpphh." She held back a laugh. "Well, before you try to find him," she stopped for a few seconds. She seemed unsure of how to say the next thing. "Have you found yourself?"

It was my turn to laugh. I looked around at the dirty, faux chic bar. The sad red and green lights, the grubby paint on the walls, the corners of grease behind the bar. "Oh, yes," I nodded vigorously. "I've found myself, here of all places. I've lost my wife, my kids, my home, probably my job. But I've found myself."

"You know, we were all watching."

"Watching? Who? What?"

"All of us. Alfonse, me, a lot of the designers at Môti. You really have had your head in the sand, Ian. You must have read the blogs this summer." She looked directly at me. "Don't worry. They're big in Paris, but nowhere else and they're in French so your little wife probably has no idea."

"Yes, I read a few of them. So what?" I felt a shortness of breath all of a sudden.

"Paris is a very small city, and nothing goes unnoticed here, especially when the most famous photographer in town has a little romance. Especially when he hasn't been seen with anyone since his wife died almost a decade ago. Especially when that romance is with a handsome, if not altogether charming young American."

"I'm not really that young."

She had that wise smile on her lips again, making me feel like I knew nothing about life. "Were you really so clueless? You never noticed the camera flashes when you were out with Luca? You never saw the people leaning into each other and chatting when you two would walk into a bar? How could you not know what it all meant? You were taking a big risk, Ian."

I shook my head no, and she grimaced.

"Well, everyone thought it was bound to be an epic failure. Even Alfonse, who, believe it or not, really liked you."

"Oh, I believe it." I thought back to the hours in the Môti archives when he would sneak in and just watch me. But I was amazed more people than just Alfonse had been watching me last summer. All those months of thinking that I was a spectator, that I was watching and cataloging the world of photography and fashion. The whole time, I was becoming part of it without even knowing. The camera had turned on me in the end, and I'd unknowingly had an audience as my world fell apart.

"I was a believer, though," she said with that smile. "I hoped it would all somehow magically work out."

"And now? I suppose you're here to tell me you were wrong and I'm an asshole?"

She stared at me, not moving for several moments. She seemed to be deciding something. The frost had cleared from her demeanor. Her face had slackened and she seemed to relax. "You know," she said in a very low voice, "he almost lost it when you left."

I was silent. The sounds of faded pop music filled the air between us.

"It wasn't like when he lost his wife. I think he must have loved you much more than he did her." The ice in her glass clinked as she took another sip of scotch.

"Are you trying to make me feel bad? Because there's really no need."

Then, in a small, silent movement, she slipped a piece of paper across the bar to me. "I don't even know why I'm doing this."

I put my hand on the piece of paper but didn't turn it over. "What is it?"

"You wanted to know where he is, no?" She finished her drink and stood up. "Don't tell him where you got it. I will never work again if he finds out it was me who told you."

"But..." I was confused. "Did you know I was going to be here?"

"Oh, Ian." She took a tube of lipstick out of a small handbag and applied it to her lips in a curt movement. "Remember what I just told you: Paris is a very, very small town. Never forget that."

She pushed her stool back under the bar. "Thanks for the drink, love." She leaned over and kissed me on the cheek, then turned and walked toward the door of the bar. "*Bonne chance,*" she said as she walked away. "I wish you two the best. You deserve each other."

CHAPTER TWENTY-FIVE—AVIGNON

I did not look at the piece of paper Michelle had given me right away. Instead, I took it home that evening and put it in the front pocket of my suitcase. Something in our conversation that evening caused me to stop and think again about where I was going.

I spent most of the next day walking. It was a Sunday, and the streets were empty and cold. I headed down to the Seine, the wind slashing my face as I looked out across the icy water. Every once in a while, a lone jogger would pass, teeth clenched against the cold, the kind of heated determination in their eyes you sometimes see in the eyes of mental patients in the movies.

I walked alone all day, along the streets and sidewalks I used to walk with Luca, thinking about him and what I might say when I saw him. Michelle had been right. Paris was a small city, and here you were forced to live with your past lives in a way that other cities didn't require. I wanted to see his face again, but I was suddenly afraid of how he might look at me.

I decided to cross the river at Notre Dame, wandering along the church gardens and finally stopping in front of the cathedral. I stood looking up at the giant façade, marveling at all the saints and apostles lining the arches of the grand structure and the huge circular window in the center of it. I remembered what Luca had said to me one evening about light—that too much or too little of it blinds us, and the same was true for religious illumination.

I stared up at the church for the better part of an hour before I eventually made up my mind to go in. I'd been inside the church that past summer with Robin and Gary, but this time it was different. I wasn't there as a tourist. I wasn't there to see the statuary and the stained glass or learn how the French had hidden art there during the occupation. I was there with no agenda. And the feeling of the place was very different.

It was getting on in the evening and Mass was well over. I sat down in one of the chairs towards the back of the building and stared up at the enormous vaulted ceilings. I wondered how anyone had ever had the imagination or audacity to build something like this in a time when the rest of the world was full of thatched cottages and wooden barns. It must have been such a drive to escape, to create something beautiful, to establish sanctuary.

I thought about the millions who had wandered the cloisters of the church or knelt and prayed for hope or forgiveness or deliverance. These walls had stood through wars and plagues and famines, and in every era since, people had come here for escape, for sanctuary, for peace. But these walls and soaring arches could only do so much. They were, after all, only stone and glass. Everyone who had ever crossed this threshold seeking deliverance had to eventually leave. And there was no deliverance outside these walls that you didn't set up for yourself. Believe what you want. Whatever religion is right for you, whatever divinity your fathers and mothers pressed into the fabric of who you are, you must participate in your own redemption.

As this realization dawned on me, sitting inside that great frigid cathedral on a fall evening, I felt a resurgence of purpose. I had started this journey for myself. That was why it had been so hard for me. I'd had to leave the people I loved behind to find out who I was, and the feeling of regret tore through my stomach like a hot blade. But I would never be whole until I had made this journey. I would have always been a shell of a person, hiding away in lines of code and the perfect fit of algorithms and numeric sequences.

I thought about Luca and about how much his love had cost me. The price had been my identity, but it had also freed me. It had revealed who I really was. If this was illumination, maybe it was too much. It blinded me, and I felt weary for all the hurt I had caused him and Ellie and my sons.

I sat for a while longer, knowing what I had to do next. When I got up, my back ached and my legs were asleep. I hardly noticed the tears streaming down my cheeks. I thought only about my journey and I'd lost track of the time and of where I was. When I stepped outside the church, the sun had set and the streetlights had come on. As I walked across the stone-paved square in front of the church, I promised myself that was the last time I would think about this. I had taken my decision, and I had tortured myself enough about it. The regretting part of this was over. I had one thing left to do—find Luca and tell him I wanted to be with him and that I needed his love. The next move was out of my hands. Whether he would open his arms to me or close me out of his life, I could not control. I could only hope.

When I got back to my room, I pulled the piece of paper that Michelle had given me out of my suitcase. I unfolded it and looked at the address on it; a rural route outside of Avignon. He had gone to his father's house.

CHAPTER TWENTY-SIX—
INDECISION IN THE FINAL MILE

I arrived in Avignon later that week. The journey down from Paris by train was as smooth as slumber. I sat watching as the landscape changed from the brown winter fields of central France to the dusty greens and golds of the warmer southern countryside. I tried not to think about what was at the other end of the journey, but at the same time I was feeling a certain anticipation about seeing Luca again after all these months. Being so close to the end of the journey intoxicated me.

I rented a car at the train station. I punched the address into the GPS and drove, turn by turn, as the brick and sun-kissed city faded quickly into little vineyards and fields, butterflies filling my stomach the entire way. I watched the blur of bicyclists passing me in the other direction, the movement of sheep in the distance, the clusters of little villages along the way—all the stamps of a careful country life, spread out across miles. It was such a vivid contrast to the cramped cityscape of Paris.

And then I was there.

The drive had taken over an hour east towards the Mediterranean coast, but I hardly noticed the time. Luca's father's place was well off the main highway out of Avignon, off a long, winding single lane road and down a gravel lane that ran through a grove of ancient, gnarly olive trees. Eventually, a large, white stone house emerged out of the distance above the trees. I thought of Luca's description of it as a small country home, and I briefly had to look down at the directions to double check that I was in the right place.

It was not a small dwelling by any modern standards. I pulled the car through a wrought iron gate and up to a small circle in front of the house, stopping next to a little grey Citroen sedan. A pair of huge cedar trees framed the giant oak door, and large floor-length windows ran the rest of the way down the side of the building on either side of the door. Over to the side of the house was a small patio, filled, as far as I could see, with a somewhat dormant potted garden. Opposite the house stood a smaller brick and stone building that must have been a carriage house at one point. I wondered silently if that was what Luca had been referring to when he described the "barn" where he found his first camera.

I pulled the emergency brake and took a deep breath before unfastening my seat belt and swinging the door open. The air outside the car smelt of lavender and earth, and aside from the noise of my feet on the gravel, I didn't hear a sound except the wind blowing through the distant olive trees. I stood outside the car for a moment, facing the house, unsure what to do next.

I watched as the door to the house opened slowly and he stepped out, his eyes drained but still that brilliant blue. The shock of sandy blond hair was tousled and a little haphazardly brushed to one side. It took him a second to realize it was me, and I think I saw him start to back up and close the door. But he didn't. He took a few steps out onto the stone walkway. I could feel my feet moving towards him, but I stopped before I reached him. We stood facing each other in front of the house, about a foot apart.

"What are you doing here?" He stood in a pair of old jeans and a sweater, his hands on his hips and his head cocked to one side.

"I needed to come, Luca. I needed to see you again." I swallowed hard. "I made a mistake before. I don't know how to say it any other way."

"What, exactly, is it you're trying to say?" He stood there motionless.

I looked beyond him, to the house, then up at the sky before staring him straight in the eyes. "I'm trying to say that I'm sorry. I love you."

"Ha." He threw his hands in the air. "Love? I'm sorry Ianto, but I don't think I understand."

"Luca, I'm sorry about before."

"You are? Because I'm not. You were right. I was the foolish one."

"No, Luca, you weren't."

"No, really." He cut me off. "I must have been crazy. What could I have been thinking? What did I really think we could ever have?" He looked directly at me. I stood still, unable to answer. I hadn't thought ahead. In all the time in San Francisco when I had sat alone out on my deck, staring at the bay below, searching my soul for why I was so miserable, I had never thought of this moment. I had only thought I needed to find him again. I needed to be with him. I hadn't bothered to think about the details of how it would happen or what he would say.

"There was something there, yes. But it wasn't love. You said that, not me. But you were right. Can't you see—" He stopped for a moment, his eyes sadder than I had ever seen them, and they were fixed on me. As I stared back at him, it seemed as if that beautiful ice blue color was draining out of them with each passing second, leaving them grey and his whole face lifeless.

"Can't you see that I am broken? There is nothing left in here." He pounded on his chest suddenly. The movement startled me, but I held my ground and fought the urge to take a step back. "There is nothing I can love you with anymore! I don't know what you thought you came all this way to find, but there is nothing here. I have no place I can come from to give you anything."

"No," I said softly, my voice shaking. "I love you. You." I reached out and put my hand on his chest, right on the place that he had just pounded a few seconds earlier. "You are enough for me. Even if you are broken, you're beautiful to me. You make me see light, Luca. Light like I haven't been able to see ever before."

He covered my hand and gently pulled it off of his chest, setting it down in front of me. "And what about your other life, Ianto? What did you leave to be here and how long until you go back again, huh? We're both broken," he said, "and there is only heartache where this is headed."

"Well, then let it come," I said. "Because my heart is already breaking. Can't we at least try for something? I have left everything for this. Can't we try? Or do we have to give up and surrender to always having nothing?"

"We didn't always have nothing. I had my art and you had your family. We threw them away. What does that say about us?" He looked at me with all the sorrow of France in his eyes, and he shook his head gently. "I told you once that this would be a disaster, and it has been, but despite all that, I love you too. But I'm afraid that makes me a king of fools." He closed his eyes and walked back towards the door.

I stood watching, wondering if he was going to leave me standing out there. But he turned back to face me as he got to the door. We stood looking at each other for what seemed like hours. Finally, he nodded towards the house. "You might as well come on in," he sighed. "You can meet my Papa."

❖

Juno, the vibrant 'Papa' from Luca's stories, looked up at me when I followed his son into the small sunroom off the back of the house where he now spent most of his days. At one time, he must have been as I'd pictured him in those stories: lithe and tan and strong, with a grey beard and thick shaggy grey hair. But age and illness had taken its toll as he lay quietly in the warmth of the room. He was frail, with only a few wisps of hair left on his head and a few scraggly barbs where a full beard once was.

He nodded at me when Luca introduced me to him, looking up from the makeshift hospital bed set up for him. The winter light streaked through the dusty windows of the room, illuminating the same fierce blue eyes his son had. He had once been so full of life, I could tell just from the eyes, but his time here was close to being over. Luca had left Paris to spend his last months with him, and I could see it was breaking his heart to watch the decline of the man who had raised and looked after him for so long. But I didn't ask Luca about any of this. Instead, I stood sentinel alongside him, spending the days watching and just silently being with him week in and week out.

Luca had put me up in a bedroom at the end of the hall upstairs, opposite his own room. But there had been nothing between us, no conversation, no frantic lovemaking, no casual brushes of skin on skin, nothing but silence and the occasional few words to let me know where things were or when dinner was ready.

Luca moved about the house like a ghost in those days, cleaning things, cooking, taking care of his father. He occasionally went out to run errands in a nearby village, picking up groceries or medicine or books to read to his father, but he had nothing but a dull stare for me. He wasn't hostile or even rude, he just wasn't there. I told myself I would give him time. He had so much more to deal with right now than me. I was, after all, a pale issue in comparison to his father. Besides, it had taken me months to come back to him. I could at least give him some space on this. But the silence between us was overwhelming.

One day a few weeks after I had arrived, I sat by his father's side while Luca was away. I often sat with Juno when Luca was out running errands. Some of the errands were necessary and others, I knew, were just because Luca needed to be alone. I didn't mind. I liked spending time with Juno. But that day, Luca had gone out to pick up some medication in the next village. It was more morphine. At that point, all the other medications had ceased to do anything.

I sat there watching the labored breathing and deep creases on the man's face. I could feel the familiar blank stare on my face. It was the same blank stare I'd had in San Francisco for all those months after I came back from Paris. But as I sat staring at Juno that day, I spotted a stack of photos on the bedside table and couldn't help but pick them up. They were photos of the sun rising behind the house, the light of the first bit of day folding over the tops of the olive trees.

"Beautiful, *n'est-ce pas?*" Juno had woken up when I wasn't looking. He was groggy with a combination of sleep and drugs. A spotty grey stubble covered the parched, paper-thin skin of his face.

"Yes," I said, "they are. They're magnificent." Then after a few minutes, I realized something funny about the pictures. I flipped back through them. The car in the driveway was the same grey Citroen sedan that was there now. "How old are these?" I asked.

Juno grinned. "Oh no…no, no, no," he gurgled, the edge of laughter in his fatigued voice fighting with the effort of speaking. "I am not supposed to say," he murmured softly.

"Not supposed to say?" I asked. I could feel a sense of urgency in my own voice before I even realized why. "What aren't you supposed to say?"

"He is taking the pictures again." Juno smiled and closed his eyes for a moment, taking in a deep, ragged breath. "He has even set up his old dark room in the barn again."

I thought for a moment, maybe that was where he went when I couldn't find him. And all the errands, maybe those were to get film as well as medicine and food. He never opened all the packages in front of me when he returned home from those trips.

"Why?" I asked, unable for a few seconds to put the pieces together in my head.

"*Vraiment?* You really have to ask, young one?" he said. When I didn't speak, he opened his eyes wide and looked up directly at me. His eyes were so blue at that moment, just like Luca's had been that first night I met him on the side street in Saint Germain. Juno's eyes were so clearly full of life, such a contrast with the rest of his tired face. "You," he said. "You have gotten him to feel again." He shut his eyes. "You make my boy happy. Even if he won't say it, I know."

I tried to look grateful for his words, but, I could feel the tears beginning to form in my eyes. I tried to breathe, but the air only came in sharp gusts that seemed to get stuck in my throat. I looked at this frail man lying in the bed beside me and tried to gauge how much hope he had invested in anything his son and I might ever have.

"No." I shook my head, deciding to be honest with him as the tears broke from my eyes and streamed heavily down my cheeks. I tried to form the sentences I knew I should say to this man, but most of my words failed me. "I don't think so," was all I could choke out.

"Why?" he asked. "You don't love him?"

I tried to keep my voice steady, but it was no use. "No, Juno, I love him completely. I didn't know I did. I didn't know it for a long time, and I didn't say it when I should have. But I know now that he means so much to me. He is so deep in my heart."

"Then why no?" Juno grasped at the air with an open hand.

"He doesn't want to," I said. "He thinks we're both too broken to have anything."

He frowned and turned his head away from me. "Foolish boy," he said, trying to wave his hand. "He's a foolish boy, and he's just scared. But he'll come around, and when he does, you will be there to love him, I know."

I nodded, wiping the tears out from under my eyes. "Yes, Juno. I will love him if he...comes around."

"Not if," Juno raised a finger at me. "Not if. When."

I nodded. *"Bien sûr, Juno. C'est bien."*

"Trust your heart. I know you will take care of his heart, too. I know it."

CHAPTER TWENTY-SEVEN—HOME

I stayed with Luca and his father for the rest of the winter and into the spring. I helped out around the house and Luca and I would take turns sitting with his father, sometimes reading to him or talking with him. When I wasn't sitting with Juno, I busied myself preparing his little garden for spring, or exploring the olive groves, or just feeding the chickens. There were a half-dozen hens and one rooster. Juno had told me their names at one point, but I could never remember them.

Juno lived longer than the doctors expected, but not by much. He went peacefully in his sleep one night not long after the crocuses and forsythia had bloomed and the lavender had just started to come to life. He managed to see the start of one final spring, and I knew that meant something to him. Luca found him in the morning, when he went to give him his morphine. Luca was sitting by the bedside holding his father's hand when I walked in and joined him. I wasn't sure how long he'd been there, but I didn't ask.

Luca and I still didn't speak much in those days, but there was an easy peace between us. I found a place of my own to rent just out past the small village down the road from the Spark's farm, and I moved out a few weeks after the funeral. I had come to the full realization of what I had done with my life, the wreckage it had become. But the person I had uncovered in the process was more truly, honestly me than anything I had been before that last summer.

I felt Luca probably needed space from me then. At any rate, I knew I could do with some time alone to sort everything out in my own head. After all, I still had a lot of loose ends in San Francisco. I was doing some freelance work for Nova Vocé. It turns out I'm very suited to working alone—the summer at Môti taught me that. I was taking care of things with Ellie. As a lawyer, she made more than I did, but we were splitting everything in half, except for the house. She got the house. I spoke with the boys regularly, checking in on homework and sports and all the little things of everyday life. Ellie and I both agreed to keep a friendly and united front with them. They were coming to visit over the summer break in a couple of months and I couldn't wait to see them. But I wasn't going back to San Francisco. Not then, not ever.

My cottage now is bright and airy with a small garden and a beautiful view out onto a hill of olive trees. I bought a bike, and I've gotten in to the habit of riding every morning—more to give myself time to think than to exercise. Some days when I'm feeling particularly energetic, I will ride down along the fields and olive groves and past the little village center with its café, bakery and supply store. I'll peddle up into the hills to the Spark's farm, and Luca will bring me a glass of water and we'll sit and look out over the olive groves together.

The other day just after dawn, I rode by to find him out back by the barn. He was standing over the chickens, with a little black box in his hands. When I got closer, I could see that it was the Kodak Brownie camera that he'd first used as a child.

He looked up as he heard me approach, and he looked happy for the first time since last summer. I came to a stop and he stood there with the camera, his grin beginning to widen. He slowly pointed it at me, looking down into the viewfinder, and snapped.

About the Author

Born in a small town outside of Boston, Ralph Josiah grew up as a Coast Guard brat, wandering around helicopter hangers in New Orleans, Cape Cod, coastal North Carolina, and Sitka, Alaska. He currently resides in San Francisco and Boston with his husband and partner of more than 14 years, Dana Short.

Ralph Josiah holds a bachelor's degree from Greensboro College and a master's in communication from Emerson College. He has a passion for good books, exciting travel, and long runs—where he happens to do most of his thinking. He is inspired by things that are different and believes that grace happens when and where we least expect it. His first novel, *Brothers*, was a finalist for the Lambda Literary Award, the Saints and Sinners Emerging Writer Award, and the IndiFAB Award in 2016.

For more information check out his website at www.ralph josiahbardsley.com

Books Available from Bold Strokes Books

The Photographer's Truth by Ralph Josiah Bardsley. Silicon Valley tech geek Ian Baines gets more than he bargained for on an unexpected journey of self-discovery through the lustrous nightlife of Paris. (987-1-62639-637-1)

The Thassos Confabulation by Sam Sommer. With the inheritance of a great deal of money, David and Chris also inherit a nondescript, brown paper parcel and a strange and perplexing letter that sends David on a quest to understand its meaning. (987-1-62639-665-4)

Funny Bone by Daniel W. Kelly. Sometimes sex feels so good you just gotta giggle! (987-1-62639-683-8)

Crimson Souls by William Holden. A scorned shadow demon brings a centuries-old vendetta to a bloody end as he assembles the last of the descendants of Harvard's Secret Court. (978-1-62639-628-9)

The Long Season by Michael Vance Gurley. When Brett Bennett enters the professional hockey world of 1926 Chicago, will he meet his match in either handsome goalie Jean-Paul or in the man who may destroy everything? (978-1-62639-655-5)

Triad Blood by 'Nathan Burgoine. Cheating tradition, Luc, Anders, and Curtis—vampire, demon, and wizard—form a bond to gain their freedom, but will surviving those they cheated be beyond their combined power? (978-1-62639-587-9)

Death Comes Darkly by David S. Pederson. Can dashing detective Heath Barrington solve the murder of an eccentric millionaire and find love with policeman Alan Keyes, who, despite his lust, harbors feelings of guilt and shame? (978-1-62639-625-8)

Men in Love: M/M Romance, edited by Jerry L. Wheeler. Love stories between men, from first blush to wedding bells and beyond. (978-1-62639-736-1)

Slaves of Greenworld by David Holly. On the planet Greenworld, the amnesiac Dove must cope with intrigues, alien monsters, and a growing slave revolt, while reveling in homoerotic sexual intimacy with his own slave Raret. (978-1-62639-623-4)

Final Departure by Steve Pickens. What do you do when an unexpected body interrupts the worst day of your life? (978-1-62639-536-7)

Love on the Jersey Shore by Richard Natale. Two working-class cousins help one another navigate the choppy waters of sexual chemistry and true love. (978-1-62639-550-3)

Night Sweats by Tom Cardamone. These stories are as gripping as the hand on your throat. (978-1-62639-572-5)

Soul's Blood by Stephen Graham King. After receiving a summons from a love long past, Keene and his associates, Lexa-Blue and the sentient ship Maverick Heart, are plunged into turmoil on a planet poised for war. (978-1-62639-508-4)

Corpus Calvin by David Swatling. Cloverkist Inn may be haunted, but a ghost materializes from Jason Dekker's past, and Calvin's canine instinct kicks in to protect a young boy from mortal danger. (978-1-62639-428-5)

Brothers by Ralph Josiah Bardsley. Blood is thicker than water, but you can drown in either. Jamus Cork and Sean Malloy struggle against tradition to find love in the Irish enclave of South Boston. (978-1-62639-538-1)

Every Unworthy Thing by Jon Wilson. Gang wars, racial tensions, a kidnapped girl, and a lone PI! What could go wrong? (978-1-62639-514-5)

Puppet Boy by Christian Baines. Budding filmmaker Eric can't stop thinking about the handsome young actor that's transferred to his class. Could Julien be his muse? Even his first boyfriend? Or something far more sinister? (978-1-62639-510-7)

The Prophecy by Jerry Rabushka. Religion and revolution threaten to bring an ancient civilization to its knees…unless love does it first. (978-1-62639-440-7)

Lethal Elements by Joel Gomez-Dossi. When geologist Tom Burrell is hired to perform mineral studies in the Adirondack Mountains, he finds himself lost in the wilderness and being chased by a hired gun. (978-1-62639-368-4)

The Heart's Eternal Desire by David Holly. Sinister conspiracies threaten Seaton French and his lover, Dusty Marley, and only by tracking the source of the conspiracy can Seaton and Dusty hold true to the heart's eternal desire. (978-1-62639-412-4)

The Orion Mask by Greg Herren. After his father's death, Heath comes to Louisiana to meet his mother's family and learn the truth about her death—but some secrets can prove deadly. (978-1-62639-355-4)

CPSIA information can be obtained at www.ICGtesting.com
Printed in the USA
BVOW08s0503200716

456173BV00001B/4/P